A MAN WANDERS
s o m e t i m e s

KENT BAKER

Stoddart

First published in 1989 by
Stoddart Publishing Co. Limited
34 Lesmill Road
Toronto, Canada
M3B 2T6

CANADIAN CATALOGUING IN PUBLICATION DATA

Baker, Kent, 1938-
    A man wanders sometimes

ISBN 0-7737-2296-3

I. Title.

PS8553.A43M36 1989	C813'.54	C89-094481-4
PR9199.3.B33M36 1989		

Typesetting: Tony Gordon Ltd.

Printed and bound in the United States of America

For my father, Raymond Baker,
and to the memory of my mother,
Hazel Baker,
1912-1987

One

S he has been there I don't
know how long, sitting in
that classic rocker, her hallowed form tall and flower-filled,
colored cloth rising and falling though there is no breeze to
stir it, or her. Perhaps there are feet busy pushing beneath that
skirt, rocking her sweetly, secretly. Her face, from where I
stand, is almost masklike: graying skin stretched around thin
dark slits, shallow pits eternal against the sun. I watch waves
squirming in uneven curves, shattering toward her, toward
that rocker, far from me, across the bay.

I watch with binoculars. Naked on the roof, I search the sea.
Hours, days, years seen and unseen, her face there and her
depths predictably unpredictable, mysterious, foreign and
familiar. Old words in new mouths. Common words in foreign tongues. But you could learn, couldn't you. Fishermen
read the surfaces of this face, know it with a parent's eye,
detect in its flux the way things will be that day, or at least for
the moment.

Behind me, inside, back where I am not looking, I hear Joan
before she even reaches the window leading to the roof, and
I recall her saying to me, "Try this for diversion," handing me
these binoculars, black tubes like gigantic insect feelers, a
new sense to bring it all closer than it will ever really be.

So I watch the whitecaps, the distant pine trees tearing across a distant bluff, point these antennae straight at the farthest edge —- you know, the line we made in school, the teacher (Miss or Mrs. then) dividing the paper between earth and sky, guiding us into the manila reality of four edges with straight, clean corners all so simple and so very plane. Beyond that, if we look, is the unwhite farther than we can see, light and crisp and sharp, deep to its own depth, penetrating. No blackness at the edges here, no shadow, no rim; only a desert of expanse without even a cloud's puff to stop the eye. Yes, the perimeters — if there are any — are cleverly concealed.

"See anything?" Joan asks.

My buttocks feel the rasp of asphalt shingles' grit as I turn. Her face is unclear and close in the lesser light near me, but I remember her features, the galaxy of miniature mass, the soft rise and fall of flesh living and moving with human grace. She is looking past me. No ships. No craft whatever. Nothing there. Magnified sameness. Her eyes, too, are big with nothing.

"It's beautiful," I say. "You can almost get lost in it, it's so clear."

Joan pauses for a moment more, smiling, one hand on the window ledge. The lace curtains over her shoulders are like visual props, artistic markers of some kind, a painter's comment, an accent in contained space.

"I'll get lunch," she says.

It is only whim, or maybe no more than a need to shift my weight, that makes me look in toward the bay. I spy her almost immediately. She is alone, rocking in her rocking chair. I trace the landscape to either side expecting family or friend, car or trailer, something to make this merely eccentric, not mysterious, not captivating, not bewildering, not what it is, or might come to be. But then it's all a matter of established perspective, isn't it? Add two children playing nearby in the sand or water, put this old woman — if she be a woman — in a bathing suit, or at the very least get rid of that kind of chair, and the whole thing is something quite different, something perhaps to remark in passing, or more likely ignore, but this scene as it is with her there like that and no other person anywhere in sight . . . Well, I admit it puzzles me. I watch the water creep closer. It seems to stop just short of her feet. Now she is hues of black and white and gray against a canvas of finely crystalled sand. All around and in everything the sea-fresh shocking purity of noontime sun.

Joan calls me for lunch.

"No. No," I shout back. "Come here, Joan! Hurry. Look at this."

She doesn't come. Nor does she answer. When she finally appears it is with sandwich, with pickle, with milk. I am waiting for her at the window.

"Look!" I say. "Didn't you hear me? I want you to see this."

"You got tar on your ass," she says.

"Look. See her?"

"Where? Who?" she asks, pressing the glasses tightly to her eyes.

"Over there. Across the bay."

"I don't see anything. What am I supposed to see?"

"The old lady in the rocking chair. On the beach."

"What?" I see the laughter vibrate in her throat. "I don't see any old lady. Come on!"

I take the glasses back. I scan the low, rocky shore. She isn't there. The elephant grass blowing brown-green and yellow seems to lift and drop the dunes, the whole image one of soft release. Then, "There she is. My God! Look! They've got her up on the back of a pickup. And she's still in the chair. Quick!" I hand the glasses to her at eye level; I feel the urgency in the tips of my fingers.

"A pickup," she says. "Where? I don't see anything."

"There," I say, directing her, turning her by the shoulders. "There. There."

"I give up," she says.

I look again. Once more she is gone. Shells, sticks, plastic refuse, polished pebbles' sheen, and larger stones, and too the ubiquitous seaweed in snaky fingers, berry-choked and long as hose. But no old woman.

I explain the whole thing to her in detail.

"Oh, Harry," she says. "Really."

"It's true," I say. "I'm serious. I saw her."

"What was she doing out there?"

"What was she doing! She wasn't *doing* anything. She was just there. She was sitting in a rocking chair, rocking."

"On the beach." She says it almost derisively and half smiles.

"She was just there," I repeat. And I'm listening now to my voice, vacant and even, registering these words with finality, as if they are the last lines of a tragedy when I know in fact there is much more yet to be played out. But I don't elaborate; there is no need. Nothing disappears forever; all things come and go, following their own mysterious rhythm.

"There's your lunch," Joan says, climbing back through the bedroom window. "And you do have tar on your ass. I can guarantee you that."

Three days later she is back.

"Quick!" I shout. "Quick. Quick." As if it has something to do with speed.

Joan looks again, and again she is too late. The figure is gone. This time I missed the end of the charade, or it was changed, for the truck carrying her away was nowhere in sight. She simply vanished.

"Come on," I say, climbing through the window. "She'll leave signs. There'll be tracks in the sand."

"Harry." Standing barefoot on the black shingles, she whines my name, stretching it like a child's song.

"Come on!" I command. "You get the car, I'll get my pants."

Almost in one motion and quite undeliberately, I trip over the windowsill, whack my knee and get a sliver in my hand. "You move as if children hang from your knees." Who said that? And was it to me or to someone else?

Joan glides by me and out the bedroom door. I hear her on the stairs. I pull on some jeans, a shirt. The back door slams. The dogs are barking. The tarry creosote on the bottoms of my feet sucks at the floor. I put on old clogs. As I clomp through the kitchen, the car puffs like a tin pterodactyl struggling on long after its time. The fan belt is old and loose and tiny tears sing steadily in breathless little pings.

"Hurry. And watch for a pickup. They may be on the way out."

Joan backs the car around toward the barn, scattering ducks and dogs and whatever lies hidden in the unmowed grass.

"Stop!" I say. "Wait!" I open the back door and Boss and Tongue, the farm's two mongrels, climb into the back seat and sit there sweating off the ends of their tongues. I won't turn them loose on her, but they might show the way.

We drive along the shore road. I study the few cars that pass, the wide windows wearing heads and shoulders. I peer down the logging roads, dusty brown pock-marked rips into the bush, but I see nothing unusual.

"You never believed me, did you," I say.

"Of course," she says.

She is masterful; like that. Such beautiful strokes. And so quick, so accurate. "Of course," I repeat. "Neutral. Squatting on the line. Don't get a rope burn."

She lets it drop, a handful of down in a soundless wind. Lately we live in the strain closeness can bring. Human rust or corrosion, something disturbing spilling from the tight,

5

thin, eye-defying space between us, space we once felt only as connection, a clean, pure spark. Something happens. There is no blame. *Corrosion.* That's it exactly.

Fifteen minutes later, on the far side of the bay, I leap out and race to where a pink plastic bottle lies. It is my marker . . . I'd seen it, or one quite like it, from the roof. Inside it muddy salt water or rain water, or both, gurgle around. I return it carefully to its print in the damp sand.

"See. Look here." I point to two creases, curious uniform tracks. The water rolls over them, then back. The tide is coming in. The cold stings my legs, innumerable tiny bites, each particle of salt tasting my flesh.

"If anyone were sitting there, their feet would be wet," Joan says. Then she pouts, pressing her lips in an anal pucker like a warthog's snout in full sniff. "Besides, I don't see any tire tracks. And I don't see any footprints either. Unless you want to count yours."

I drop to my knees, and wait for the wave to roll away. The tracks are almost level, or if not level, pitched to the slope of the beach. One track is a bit deeper than the first joint of my forefinger, the other is nearly to the third joint. Perhaps she sits to one side. Hemorrhoids. Or habit. Maybe the clothes she wears bunch to one side. Or is it just that the sand is softer here than it is there?

I stare back at the house through the binoculars. The cat is on the roof, licking milk from a glass. She stops, glances at me, wets her lips, then begins to lick herself, head and neck a heavy, taut comma moving across her breast.

"This must be the spot," I mutter. "This has to be the spot."

"Maybe she's a ghost," Joan says. "A spirit." She gives her left breast three knuckled taps. "Through my fault. Through my fault. Through my most grievous fault."

I bend near the tracks and stare at them with the field

glasses. The enlarged tide covers them, then bubbles away in noiseless puffs.

"Get me that tape," I say. "Hurry."

"Hurry," she says. "Hurry. Hurry."

I measure the distance between the two marks. "Twenty-two inches," I say, turning around.

Joan is sitting in the sand. She has her top off. She puts them out there, decorations brought home from school. The blood-brown of nipple falling away to areola, and areola to the tan of her breast, shelter for resting shadows where beads of sweat collect.

"Let's stay," she says. "This is a nice spot. I can see why she likes it." She smiles again.

I leave her and walk along the beach. Clam shells, sticks, fossilated board, smashed sea urchin bodies pecked by gulls, strands of seaweed rubbery clusters with tangles of dark berries. No prints. No tracks of any kind. I gaze out at the water. A boat? Water whirls, swirls and bursts in uneven runs over a hidden ledge. No boat could navigate that. But a hovercraft, perhaps.

"Why not a seaplane, or better yet, underground, underwater tunnels?" Joan asks when I mention it. "Or a time machine. Zap." She swings her arms and her boobs bounce, leap up then back, shimmying and quivering like jellyfish dropped on the shore.

I laugh. They are large and lovable. Silly. Like me, like us, like all of it. I kiss her. I suck at her breast.

"These are beautiful," I say.

"Finally," she declares. "Finally."

"Finally?" I ask, spitting out word and tit in garbled union.

She stares at me. Her breasts are wet with my mouth and slightly red and I believe I see the place of my hand.

"I didn't mean anything. I only meant . . . well, *this is* real, isn't it? That's all I meant."

"I can't stand that," I say. "I told you."

I told her at breakfast a week ago. I cultivated words. I selected, sampled, testing all against where she was, partially masticated but not swallowed. I'd been seeking the right moment until I accepted that for her, too, there was only the one, eternally unfolding. And so before breakfast as she leaned over the woodstove, her back turned, the twin bulbs of her ass pressed pleasantly toward me, I began. She listened. Sat. Ensnaring, desperate eyes like plungers about to seize. I asked nothing of her. For me it was no more serious finally than telling someone to sleep on their own side of the bed. I just wanted to jar her certainty, her sense of Absolute, that desperate crutch that hobbles the mind and sets it to creeping where it would run. Some people believe in truth and that's not the same as life. When I finished, she said, "Well, cook your own fucking eggs, then." But she had remained calm.

This time there is quizzical memory in her face. "I'm sorry. I was just relieved. I didn't mean to upset you."

She leans past me toward her top, a sleeveless bit of cloth, thin, red and nearly transparent. She will put her toys away. She will forbid my eyes now, deny my tongue and touch. The twin gourmet globes, these two delectable, done-to-a-T tastees will be withdrawn as of 12:21 p.m. Atlantic Daylight Time. I don't break into tears as they disappear beneath the red, but I feel the fissure between us widen and I want to press it all together again, make it solid beneath our feet.

"Please don't be hurt," I say. "It's just that certainty thing."

She stands up. Between her legs I can see the ocean, an inch of sand, then a four- or five-inch triangle of white-capped sea.

"You're always so certain," she says, "that I'm too certain."

Not looking at me, she slaps the sand from her ass, gazing, ostensibly, at her feet, or at the strands of stiff life lying in the fragile sand, brittle-soft shattered stone on which we stand.

But she is registering none of that now; it's something else that concerns her, something remembered or forgotten, or something that never was, not really.

"I just tell you what it seems to me," I say.

"And what do you think I'm doing?" she asks. "Lying?"

Her bare feet scatter sand as she stomps toward the car. She glances back over her shoulder, hesitates, then says, "You know what, Professor Fleet, sir! I think you're losing your fucking grip."

I stay sitting. I feel her alternately not watching, then watching. Things don't *begin* to change. Suddenly they *are* changed. One day it is this way. The next day, that. Like a landscape in fog, snow, sunshine or rain. Things don't change; it's essence, aura, energy that changes. When I met Joan she had on that same red blouse. She was the same woman. Tartly beautiful, pulsating a wholesome exoticism. Before I talked with her, I sat on the rocks that fringed Dagley Beach, watching her backdropped by her friends, all of them young, tightly strung in flesh and pose: but Joan rose to the eye like a curiously special detail in an otherwise pleasant but uninspiring canvas. It was the way she moved, that intriguing soft gallop through the sand. And it was the comic way she swung at the volleyball, boloing her arm and thrusting it forward like an outsized tan banana. Yet her charm lay most in her stillness, where I read evocation of something fraught and ready, something strong and undetermined. "Plug into energy," Nebula told me that first awful spring when I clung to the drain shield of my life by my fingertips, sure I'd no choice but to go down. "Go where life is," she said, "or bring life to you. Don't sit around here like a soggy Dixie cup. You're negative, boy! A bit of that don't hurt, but you better learn to balance the poles."

Now Joan too is thick, sludgy and slow, all that playful energy degenerated. Was it me? I have a flash of that self-elevating guilt that puffs its chest to the world, proclaiming,

"Yes, I am the source of this person's suffering. I hold in tip of finger and tongue the fate of another; I have such power. Punish me if you will, but admire me." No, it's not that easy. There is no blame, be it egotistic or otherwise.

The car engine struggles to life. Metal anemia. Fender disease. Tongue licks my hand anxiously, an act of almost desperate love. That right-here, right-now love. Trying to smarten me up. Then he runs for it. Boss is already there. His is a more practical love. The motor signals the ride. Going or returning doesn't matter. Or who drives. It is the ride itself that's important. They have no problem with "balancing poles." Poles are something to piss on.

I walk through the grass, hip-high, sword-thick antennae in the sand. Grasshoppers leap on and off the car hood. I break away a green stalk and press it to my lips, make some shrill squeaks and squawks that bring the dogs electrically to the windows, ears pointed up, half frantic at this sound that means nothing to me. Boss and Tongue lick my hand, happy that the noise has stopped — or happy that it has happened.

"I'm going to check around a bit more," I say. "You go ahead. I'll hitch back."

She glares at me.

About a half mile down the beach I come upon an old man. Full white beard. Patrician. Woodsman. Disparate worlds locked in close dance. Bare feet. Wide shoulders rounding. Posture: stooped from the low back as if some invisible sprite tugs at his beard. And his eyes are blue beams like lacquered robin eggs.

I sit near him.

He nods. I nod.

We sit that way till two Cape Islands boats vanish around the point and another is on her way toward us.

"Did you see her, then?" I ask.

He shakes his head.

"Nor the pickup?"

He shakes his head.

We sit for another long spell. Then I rise, brush the sand from my pants, pull at a spot where they cling, all the while listening to myself as I tell him where I live and how I enjoy his company. I thank him and prepare to leave, but the words keep coming till finally he tips his head back, his grizzled, red larger-than-life face magnificent against the sky. "It doesn't matter," he says.

"I know," I say, like a child attempting certainty.

I want to pull him close, hug our knowledge, but I don't. I walk to the point, and when I return he is dead asleep in the sand. Two huge gulls stagger about only inches from his face.

Everett gives me a ride as far as the village. We don't talk. His tractor roars and lurches like a wounded animal along the shoulder of the narrow road. The smell of henshit bites into the salt air. I take deep breaths. Before he pulls away, he takes the plug from his ear and hangs it next to his Walkman.

"There's Irish moss at Chapel Beach," he says. "Free fertilizer for them that wants it."

A trinkle of sound drains from the plug, a thin wire of words.

The village is deserted. Dust motes of half light and shadow play in quiet bursts through Bones' store. Boxes and cartons of local fruit and vegetables, canned goods, drygoods, cheese, vinegar, patent medicines, hardware, clothes, nails, pots, pans, and Maud Bone's soft moon face rising from behind the counter with a smile.

"Some hot, what?" she says.

"I was just on the beach. It's cooler there."

"It would be," she admits.

"The breeze," I say.

"Some days it'll be hot here and the bay will be right cool."

She accents *cool* almost critically, holding it up for ridicule or praise. "Ten degrees difference," she continues. "Yes, days when you'd be burning up it'd be so hot here and over the way there it'd be as nice as you could want. Now ain't that somethin', what?"

"Yes," I say. "Listen, I'm looking for a present."

"Oh yes," she says.

"For someone older."

"Yes, I see. All we have now is chicken. Once in a while we get the odd turkey or duck. More like at Thanksgiving and holidays, you know."

"Well, that's not what I had in mind, exactly."

"I see."

"Have you some stationery?"

She stares.

"A present!" she says, putting her porky finger to her lips. "Why, I thought you was sayin' *pheasant*! Oh, we got plenty of those." She disappears behind the counter.

As she unearths her dusty specials, she talks on about the old man.

"Strange one he is. No one knows where he come from. Not around here for certain. Ever turnin' up on the beaches drivin' that old tow-truck. And them some dear, what? Why, the men say he's apt to be most anywhere anytime. Like a ghost. Mental, do you suppose? He seems. A tow-truck and no home at all. Some strange, what?"

"I can make suggestions," the old man says. "But I don't see that it matters. You can put the thing anywhere along the whole bay, but if she doesn't want to find it, she won't. At least I don't think she will. That's the way it seems to me. And if you're only interested to prove she's been here, well . . . " He shakes his head sadly.

The sand strolls between my toes, a close and dark experience. I hold the package between my fingers, twisting it about absently, straightening the tiny bow. The twin portholes of past and present, then and now, spiral in.

Tom has great horny feet with long, jagged toenails, which he sets about cracking and peeling with his fingers, tossing the small yellow strips into the tide.

"If she were my lady," he says — I wonder for a moment if she is indeed his lady — "I . . . " He continues stripping his toenails.

"You — " I say expectantly.

"I would respect her," he says. "But she's not mine. She appears to be yours." He stares at me and his eyes freeze for a moment, his mouth half open, hanging whiskers and wind-red skin.

"She is mine, all right," I say. "No question about it."

"I don't think gifts work," he says. "At least they never worked for me. Maybe they will. Maybe they do. I can only say what I've seen."

"So you see, Joan," I say, "you missed meeting this fantastic old man. Tom. He said it was a . . . what do you call it when you take the first letters of a series of words and make a new word?"

"Pretentious."

"No. Be serious."

"Why do I have to be serious?"

"Never mind." I feel myself slipping into a yawning cavern of pout.

"I'm sorry," Joan says. "It's called an acronym, professor. Now tell me all about this acronymious Tom character."

"He said they were initials. Tired Old Man. T-O-M. He was, too. Tired and old. There was something about him." I laugh. She doesn't. I feel a bit offended when she's indifferent. Still, I go on to tell her all that I remember, all that it seemed to me.

"What does he do with a tow-truck?"

"The tow-truck!" I say. "Everybody's so concerned about

the old bugger's tow-truck. Tow-truck, Good Humor truck, milk truck, dump truck, roller skates. Who cares about that? Do you really care about *that*?"

"Well." I know that pitch. She is approaching the whine. "I don't think every old beachcomber has — "

"Stop!" The word firm like a sign, and to accompany it, my hand trafficking up. I press on her shoulders, force her gently down into the rocker.

"He uses it to dig clams."

She stares at me.

"It all started when he was ten. His father made him dig three buckets of clams each day. It took hours. The other boys were bigger and faster and better clam diggers. They had systems. And they knew exactly what the clams were after and exactly where they'd go to find it. But Tom! Tom had only the vaguest notion of what was going on. He never felt free enough to have a private thought, never mind a publicly useful one. So he spent his days mimicking and pretending. He joined the rest of the boys — and one determined girl. He stomped the smelly, wet, clayrot, shit-yellow-brown flats. He watched the holes from which the vulgar devils might, hopefully, spit at him. He stared with much interest at the other boys' — and even the tomboy girl's — curious rituals. Even so, he never got to know more than the razor-edged lips of the clam. You see, it never occurred to Tom to decipher their cross-tunneling complexes, their secret ways, their motions and movement and propulsion patterns. He couldn't *think*. He was never allowed, never encouraged *to think*. So always the other boys finished first and with more. Now he's got a tow-truck."

I look at Joan; she looks at me. We sit in a crush of silence till Joan gets up and goes back to stuffing the fish. Haddock. All white and gray and blue and black and charcoal. Colors shading, dotting, stroking, brushing, diminishing one into the other, all so close and yet distinct. I gaze down with her at the cold fish eye that will crunch as cold fish eyes crunch when and if the cat or dogs get their way. Joan doesn't worry about sounding stupid. She couldn't care less about making profound observations. She just never likes to be suckered. She pokes the mix of brown bread, onion, green pepper, egg and spices into the splayed belly and thinks.

"So he's first now?" she says. "First on the block to have a tow-truck?"

"Joan . . . why don't you . . . " I don't know how to put it. I watch her not watching me. Finally I pull close to her, press up against her length and reach around, filling my hands with her breasts.

She pokes a large paper clip through first one then the other side of the fish's belly and draws it shut.

"Clams," she says. "Tow-trucks." She laughs, and I laugh. The haddock slides belly-up into the oven where it will cook away its old salt-sea smell.

Later Joan sits in the rocker, and as I watch her I flash through myriad associations, none of which fit, for it is *this* rocker, *this* woman, *this* kitchen. Here all is quite simple and definite, everything in its place. I shudder when I think of the long, unavoidable leap I must make, the risks I must take if I am ever to reach her in all her drab, gray majesty as she rocks and rocks and rocks away.

The next day Joan is back into it, the whole thing now explainable, more pieces for life's necklace. "I've got the lowdown on old Tommy Tow-truck," she says. "Billy told me."

Billy is a fourteen-year-old who helps when we need extra hands. One day I walked into the barn looking for something or other. There was Billy, eyes out the window, watching Joan sunbathing nude on the roof, a fistful of busy burlap bag down around his fly. Ouch! I crept away.

"What did old Burlap Billy have to say?" I ask.

"Burlap Billy?" She makes a wry face.

I haven't told her about it. She'd think the whole thing was fully understandable, merely funny, or somehow had something to do with her. It's curious how quick the ego is to embrace.

"He's a squatter," she says firmly. "That old fart takes over private property. He tells everyone who asks that if no one is on a piece of land, then he has a right to it, and on he goes." Her eyes are livid with anger.

"What do you think?"

"What do I think. Well, he's on private property. He's going on people's land and calling it his right whether the owner is there or not. He — "

"What do *you* think?"

"People own that property," she says. "Like you own this. You worked for years so — "

"Bullshit, Joan! If there's no one on the land he *does* have a right to it. You know that. You must know that. Sometimes I think the only difference between a Canadian and an American is the spelling."

The dogs and ducks begin their noisy welcome. I look out. A car is turning around by the barn. An old Chevy. Its blue-black hood is a crust of impacted dust, salt, and highway exhaust.

"Good day, sir. Any Rawleigh products today? Liniment? Ointments, cough syrup, pie mix, toiletries, syrups, seed, spice? Any soap or dust? We've got a dust for the dogs; kills ticks, mites, fleas. Maybe the missus would like some yard goods. Thread, pins, needles? We have a nice assortment of syrups for soft drinks. Just add water. They're quite popular with young and old alike."

"Thank you very much," I say, "but we're all set today. Maybe next time. Thank you."

"Thank *you*," he says, and he waves and drives away. After this I'll see him often along the shore, and I'm sure I've seen him before, too, but didn't recognize him because until today we had said nothing to each other.

"Who was that?" Joan asks.

"The Rawleigh man. Incense, spearmint, blackjack gum? Common sense, ten cents."

"A peddler?"

"Yes."

"Even way out here." It's caught between question and reprimand.

"The world is a found object," I say.

"I admit I was wrong about Tom," Joan says.

"You could find a thread and pick it up and the whole thing could unravel," I say. "Or break. Or drag you along. Or pull you over, or leave you behind holding the slack."

"I must have sounded like a damn capitalist."

"There's a view, a twin porthole there for the seeing," I say. "Now if you — "

"*Goddamn you*, Harry!" she screams. "If you have something to say to me, why don't you just come out and say it?"

"I can't," I say. "I really can't." And I take the binoculars and go up to the roof. The whitecaps glint like cats' teeth as they move effortlessly, relentlessly, pointlessly across the bay.

Two

I use a pillowcase. It holds everything, yet leaves room for slinging over the shoulder. Inside: two bars of chocolate, a thin blanket, some Kleenex, three tuna sandwiches, binoculars, sourdough biscuits, a flashlight, matches, a thin strand of rope.

"In case you need to tie her up?" Joan kids. "Or for tricks?"

I'm not laughing.

"Do you really expect to find her?" she asks as we pull up at the beach entrance.

I study her tone, inflection for me like waves rolling the meaning of words in my ear and mind.

"I don't expect anything," I say.

"I forgot," she says.

She doesn't believe me. She won't. She can't. She takes my hand and kisses it. "I'm sorry."

I know she is.

"You shouldn't be," I say.

She thinks, then says, "Well, I am."

"Do Tongue's rash with that stuff," I remind her. Then she is gone.

That afternoon she asked me what I wanted from life. The question was suddenly there, as inevitable it seems as sunshine, or rain, or thought itself.

I could feel the wheels begin to grind. "What do I want? I want world peace. An end to violence and distrust. A safe environment. Letting Third World countries off the greedy bankers' hook. Controls on banks, the consummate pricks of society. Let's see. Concern. Yeah! Real human concern — that's what I want. That would take care of the rest."

"Not for the world. Not for anyone else. What do you want for you?"

"For me . . . I don't know. Nothing special. To be happy? What do you want?"

She said, "I want to go out of this world at least as good a person as I was when I came into it."

It is dark. The moon lurks behind a smear of cloud. The sound of the sea night is mainly one: the threshold sound of a world waiting. Even the dark is waiting. If that sound stops even for an instant, I know it will be a sign.

My sandals press into the damp sand. It is cool. I zip my jacket. There is where she sat. Of course I don't expect to see her, not tonight.

In the shelter of the dunes, almost equidistant from where I'd first spied her and where I'd last seen Tom, I drop the pillowcase and sit. Not many stars tonight. Sometimes they're so revealed, so numerous, that it's dizzying to behold. Out there before me the dark, pulsing pull-suck-gurgle-and-dash. The sensuality of water and rock mating. Night air, ocean breath cold and damp, licks over my face. I stare again at the curtain of misshaped masses, tiny dots of blinding, hurtling light.

"The earth," I say, "rotates like a spit cooking us on all sides."

A bell buoy clangs softly in the uneven pitch of the waves. I eat two sandwiches and three biscuits. Lazily I raise the binoculars and turn them to the water. I see black, like the black behind the eyes. Black that moves, is felt as soft pressure or escaping silence. When two darknesses meet, they give off a light much like that that engulfs the bust I see burst by.

I come to my knees and look again. Left to right, on a bike pedaling along the beach is a nude woman. She is pedaling toward me. I see my choice: stay put or confront her.

"Don't be scared," I say to her.

She almost falls from her bike, but comes to rest one foot on the ground, the other on a pedal.

I shine my light on my face. She can see my broad forehead, my eyes clear as glass and blue like reflectors. She can see my gaunt, long-boned face, my sure mouth and chin. It is a face to love, I know. I love it.

Even though I hold the light beneath my chin, I can see her, too. Together we are a chiaroscuro of flesh, a cubist circus poster of light to dark shadows in indescribable patterns. She is cautious, but not scared. Like a rabbit: alert but vulnerable. I recall fall and winter. Hunters. Jackers driving back in the woods with lights and guns. She is beautiful.

"I won't hurt you. I'm staying there." I shine the light toward the dunes then switch it off. Our eyes dilate, expand within their shelters, everything growing more clear. Her flesh seems a dusky gray powder, but is clearly flesh and clearly hers. I cannot distinguish the color of the bike she now climbs from. She leans over to pull down the kickstand and as she does I am captivated by the curve of her bum and hips, the fine line of her delicate back. I step closer. The moon squeezes from between the clouds. We stare at one another. Animal apprehension still there. I put out my hand. She takes it and a shiver runs through our bodies. I wrap my arm around her shoulders. "Come," I say. "Come." The words surface automatically, wrapping themselves tenderly in moonlight

and mist. I think of slaughter, eating Hebb's lamb. I had patted
the beast's head. "Lamb's for eating," he said. "Real life's no
fairy tale, eh?"

I spread the thin blanket for her. She sits serene and ageless.
I guess fifteen, forty, fifty. I don't want to cover her, but she
is shivering. I place my jacket over her shoulders. She gathers
it at the throat with one hand.

We sit like that, nibbling biscuits and chocolate. The cloud
is gone completely now. There are two moons. One in the sea.
With my thumb, I brush some crumbs from the corner of her
mouth.

"I am love," she says.

I nod and glance down the beach where the bike stands
above its shadow.

"Love," she repeats, and her eyes like the stars are quivering distant masses.

"Love," she says, and she lies back on the blanket and raises
her knees.

"Do you own a rocking chair?" I ask. "Do you come here
often?"

She places her hands along the soft inside flesh of her
thighs. Her eyes are closed.

"Love," she says. "I am love."

I sit, arms locked around my knees. Shadow purrs over the
grass and sand, and the smell and sound of the sea whisper.

"I've been here for almost two years," I say. "I didn't flee
the States. I haven't divorced myself from anything or anyone. I'm not a romantic. I don't believe this life is innately
better than any other."

She reaches over and grasps my arm. I release myself and
she pulls me toward her.

"Love," she says, her voice soft but distinct like the sound
of that lone buoy, that soft bell. Her body is so very warm.
Her nipples tiny peaks and soft like chewy candy sweetly lift

to my tongue and lips, and the flesh of her breasts is thigh-soft and luxurious.

It leads nowhere. There is nothing ahead, no rush, no down-hurrying dash, no prelude, thus no ultimate, thus no end. I think only of this sweetness, the feel and taste and moment. I feel myself burning inside. Candle. Container. Eternal flameless, painless, explosive energy. It is universal flushing, flash after flash of insupportable pleasure akin to suffering, my body contracting in awe-inspiring, awful spasms of effortless strain.

A gull wakes me. He calls while gliding against the sun in soft streaks. When he nears where I lie gazing up, he cocks his head, looking before an outstretched wing. I watch his eye roll to look down at me. Behind him a sky, beautiful with brush-thick strokes of red, rests over the water. Red sky in morning, sailor take warning. Red sky at night, sailor's delight. The bike, also red, is partially under water. I survey the beach with my binoculars. Nothing unusual. If I step from my shelter I may be seen, and if not the bike will be.

I slip into my pants, survey the beach once again, then crawl, creep and tumble down the dunes onto the flat. On my belly at the water's edge, I realize my predicament intensely. The gulls call in stiffly feathered voices. I am confused. There were no tracks from the night, but now my wormlike scrawl splits the sand, an accent of intense stupidity. I inch into the cold salt water. Soft spits of foam bubble bits of seaweed past my face. My hands press into the silty sand as I move over pebbles, shells, rocks, hunks and bits of tossing life. It is a Red Flyer. I pull it over on its side while keeping myself up with one arm. Light is full now. The low waves balloon my pants as I crawl, pulling the bike toward shore and then up the dunes to shelter. I grab the binoculars. Still no one in sight. Lucky.

The sun is a yellow-red crush of color inches above the sheet of water. I take off my wet, sandy clothes and wrap myself in the blanket.

The biscuits last for hours. I eat them while watching for boats far across the bay. Perhaps they don't leave by this side. Perhaps they head out another way.

A vaporish apron of mist eases in from the east. Suddenly I am in it. I can see nothing. I pack my goods and adjust the blanket along my length and walk Indian-like away. The temperature is falling. When I see her, she sees me. So when I can't see her, she can't see me. Perhaps. I stop when by some quick calculations I judge myself to be within twenty-five yards of where I first saw her rocking on the sand. I hear women's voices. Clearly. Moving. Voices coming toward me across the fog-shrouded beach.

And so they went forth and multiplied.

I freeze.

Their forms develop and they stop when they see my long legs hanging from the blanket. A portrait: Abe Lincoln with Sack in Sand. But he didn't have a beard, Esther. But he *was* tall and sort of dark, Estelle. They regain their composure and walk past.

"Did you — " I say. They turn.

"Good morning," I begin again.

They stop, still smiling, and greet me.

"I wonder if you saw urbasee." I slur the word, hoping that anyone they have seen will fit.

"Who?" the fatter one asks. "Herby?"

"I've been looking everywhere."

"We haven't seen anyone," the other says.

"Ever?"

That gives them a start. They look at each other. I am being unfair.

"Mrs. Ever," I add. "She walks here in the morning. Or so I understand."

The are relieved not to be made fun of. They are, I know, Americans. I'd recognize them anywhere.

"We're from Illinois," the fat one says, obviously irritated. There is heft to her voice. "We don't know anyone here. We're camping over there." She points across the bay.

"Then you didn't see her? A beautiful gray-haired, ageless woman. Stunning. She sometimes goes swimming along here." I place my hand alongside my mouth. "There's those that claim she's got" — I whisper it — "skinny-dip-itis." They stare at me nervously. "Or her mother. You'd remember her. All black and white like a Bogart movie? She sits here on the beach rocking. Sort of a curious duo. You haven't seen either of them? I guess you'd recall, what?"

They start to edge away.

"No one here but us fish." I smile kindly. "Well, it's been a pleasure talking with you ladies. Enjoy your visit. I hope it clears up for you."

When I return from the beach, Joan has the woodstove fired up. I walk the long drive toward the house, watching the smoke blowing white to gray as it curls away from the red brick chimney. Exhalations billowing to some hidden place in the dome. The mystery of diminish. A magic trick from where I stand, but in the scheme of things it's routine sleight of hand. There once was a man named Space, who exclaimed, "For me, there's no place!" Silence was his answer. So he contracted cancer. And vanished from disgrace.

"Well," Joan says.

"No," I say.

She spoons instant coffee into a cup. The hot water bubbles and steams. I sit in the overstuffed chair near the stove; its heat presses like a hot rag against the right side of my face.

"There's a couple of biscuits left," I say.

She shakes her head, then sits looking at her coffee.

"She wasn't there, then?"

"I didn't see her."

We sit quietly for some time. The wood snaps and spits and blackens in the belly of the stove.

"You got wet," she says.

"Yes."

"Not the rain."

"No."

We sit listening to it all.

"Did anything of interest happen?" she asks.

"Of interest?" I say.

She sighs and gets up from the table.

"That depends on what you mean by interest," I say.

"Forget it," she says, slamming new chunks of wood into the stove.

"No. I mean for me, being alone, getting away from routine, always jogs the mind. I always learn something. It's not a . . ."

She turns and her eyes fix me, freeze me, and my words lump to a stop heavy as stones in my mouth.

"I love you, you jerk. Can you learn that? We live together. We make this life ours. We share. We are here right now in this place, in this moment, in all of time and in all of space. In all of everything. Can you be here? Can you drop in for a visit, Professor Fleet, just for a while?"

She comes to where I sit nervously cupping my coffee. She throws a leg over me and straddles me, almost spilling my drink. The smell of the wood smoke on her is fresh as the outdoors. She says nothing and leans back a bit as if examining me. I'm not sure what she expects. I notice a pair of small pimples on her chin. She will be having her period soon. When she is premenstrual she can become emotional over just about anything. Last month she cried when . . .

Joan shakes her head and unhooks herself from me. She

returns to the stove and lifts the lid. I watch her poke at the fire.

"I'm sorry," I say. "I'm just . . . tired, I guess."

"Sure," she says. "Me too."

Late that afternoon the sky opens like a great, gray cup and the rain streams down. All night I listen. I lie next to Joan, her fingers closed in mine, the hot flesh of her stretched along my side. Rain. Rain. Slant slivers cool my brain. Rain. Rain. Rains past. Rains present. Rains to be. I can't sleep. I should say I am not asleep. *Can't* implies futility, exasperation, unsuccessful attempts. I am asleep or I am awake. The states are equal in my mind.

Black-white. Darkness-light.

If darkness is the natural state, then seeing is the falsest sense. It is only the sun that alters darkness. Conscious-unconscious. Everything has its opposite, has its opposite, has its opposite. I think I must go all the way back to the beginning to find the purity of self, the me untainted, my birth. A fragment of moment in the midst of all moments and all other fragments, yet mine for all that.

A feckless rescue by the bung-lipped doctor. He gets right down there, leans so close I can smell the garlic wafting through my sweet mother's cloves. He's so close that his bifocals are steaming. He cleans them on his gown, says, "Forceps and more light." There is a weariness in his voice, for I am the second this day and the twenty-third of the year, the four hundred and ninety-second of his career.

Mother is concerned. She has her fists clenched tight. As long as I know her she will have her hands clenched like that. In the one hand a tissue, in the other fear of everything from water, to change, to absence of change, to strangers, to the multitude of dangers in life, the threatening and heaven-denying evil whose special mission it is to devour her children.

For two days Mother has wanted me out. For two days I have wanted out. But we're both scared. So she's still there straining and moaning and generally putting the squeeze on me. And I can't say I've been the epitome of graciousness either. Maybe it all began right there; maybe it's just that hard to love someone you've carried within your body for nine months, only to have him repay you by lurching around in your private parts like a boxed-in truck. Of course it's no picnic for the truck either.

Shimmying through tiny holes takes courage, even if you know what's on the other side. Why else would a generation of adults continue to rise to the challenge of fitting through coat-hangers, visiting Japan or squeezing into foreign cars? It is not nonsense, or non sequitur, that we strain at buckles and belts, wriggle into clothes so tight a fart couldn't escape, jam our feet into shoes, inch and ease and struggle to recapture that old feeling. Believe me, I understand the magnitude of the task. The squeeze is particularly poignant when it's your cranium, your almost pure, almost untraumatized little dome that's in the vise.

Now he's got my fucking ear caught. The disdain! You'd think he was pulling a tooth, gutting a fish. Get it all out, Doc. Don't leave a trace. Actually I think that, not say it. My mouth is shut and packed full. Besides there is not room enough in this orifice for anything extra. Not a word. Not a sound. When my bubble burst, I almost choked in the rush. Talk about chaos. There I was comfortable, if a bit cramped, calmly toking on the mainline listening to the soothing roar of Mom's plumbing, when the . . .

Jesus. Now he's twisting my head around. Oh, you're a subtle persuader. Hippocrates be damned. *Owww!* Why not take an ax to her. Rip her up the middle. *OOOO!* My poor fontanel, my tender little blow hole.

"It won't hurt baby," he says confidently. "Their heads are soft."

27

So are your balls, Fatso! Thank God we're not lobsters or soft-shelled clams. Mother's lost in some strange rift, bleating like a lamb, musical accompaniment for the quivering in the fat of the doctor's face. Frozen at the helm of decision, he says, "She's fully dilated."

He peeks again. Again I smell the linguini and sausage, the red wine and garlic. His words are a little garbled because now the tongs have me by the ears. Wait till someone designs a stainless steel baby-hook. Dr. Troll-and-Jerk-It. Hold on, boys, it's a whopper!

"I don't," he says thoughtfully. He don't what? Wear jockey shorts because they ride up his ass? Know what the fuck he's doing? But whatever it is that he don't, he's not giving it away yet.

Hey, out there. Yoo hoo! It's me, little Harry Fleet. I belong here. I'm not some forecastle stowaway, not some mysterious and unexpected miracle. I'm doing the best I can. If I could shoot out there and pee on top of Dr. Lasagna's black, pointy-toed shoes, that's what I'd do. But it just so happens that I'm all twisted up in here.

"More light," he decides.

Looks like they're going to burn this little mole out. Bake him down like fatty hamburger.

Oh, those damnable muscles. Gentle as hammock ropes for so long, now they're going crazy, whipping and strumming me half to death. There's an awful rhythm to it. The fat conductor presses one finger next to my jammed-at-the-junction dome. She moans in pain as he reams her with his rubber pinkie. My head feels like a grapefruit being stuffed inside an orange. Then, suddenly, one of those spasmic lashes uncorks my knees and my head pops out. The light drives like acid through my lids. It's a cold mother, too. And strange. I mean, it may be comparatively quiet, free of rumble and roar, but when you leave that tepid little way station, are flushed into this antiseptic den of measured efficiency, of course you

28

scream. You scream your bloody ass off. And you keep your eyes closed, too.

I'm screaming so hard my eyes are crossed and I'm turning blue. But nothing is coming out. Talk about panic. Then Tubby sticks a red rubber finger into my mouth and flicks a stopper of mung out. I could kiss him. All is forgiven. I want to embrace all of them, these others, white-breasted birds all feathery and in flight attending to this and that, yet losing nothing of a curiously feminine aura unique to each of them. All my days I would carry with me that same impression or, if you will, infatuation. I would love them each and every one. For the very thing that made them the same made them different — and I'm a fool for paradoxes no matter the state of dress or undress.

The sheets are wet with gunk and sweat. It is one of the few times I will see my mother perspire, for she avoids both hot and cold, always preferring the artificial, be it in the temperature of a room or in its decor.

The liquids they prepare for me are anything but natural. They want to get the salt water off me. And the blood. I could . . . whoops! I'm all here now. It's me. Little Harry Fleet. Hail, hail, cruel world.

For days every moment either Mom or I will contain the memory of this mutual resistance. The water running down her leg like common piss. Hell! Flushing, gushing down splat like a water balloon tossed from a tenement window. Don't get me wrong. I'm not complaining. Back when I was born, trauma was something some of us experienced, but it was no big deal. A traumatic birth got about as much acknowledgment as two weeks at summer camp. At least camp provided you with some skills, or at worst, a tan.

Even in the telling am I trapped, hooked, the line going back through a tangle of years and experience without even emotional continuity. This chronology of people and places I swim through, ever seeking the wave, the one that will pick me up and carry me clear. Why do I always believe it will one day make sense — coffee and toast sense, right here on planet earth sense? Wake up, Harry. You're in bed, Harry. With a loving, gorgeous creature. Harry. Harry! Harry!

My toes make little tents of the sheet. Joan's feet follow the twist of her body to one side and point like fallen parapets toward the open window beyond which the air is washed with rain. I hear it and feel it, and the ocean, away, separated from us now by the rain, makes a different, more hushed and throaty response.

A cool breeze comes over the terrain of bed sheet, tracing our geography, unaware of the hot layered life below, a fabric of mind and matter.

Once we walked far from the farm following the fish shacks and thinly wooded sand toward the open sea. Joan pissed a damp circle in the sand. She wanted me to explain to her where I am. I told her I couldn't.

"I can give you images," I said, "bits and pieces, old and new. That's all I can do. And anyway, where I am for you depends on you, doesn't it, your sense of what I say or do."

She thought about that. Bounced once or twice, then drew her pants over her thighs and buckled her belt.

"I'll make a quilt of them," she said, "a crazy quilt of all your little tales and stories, your words. Even your evasions. And then I'll sew them all together and . . . " She reached out for my hand.

"And what?"

"Crawl under it."

The morning rain behind the screen lands softly. I think of concrete walks, roads and windshields where these same tossing drops spray and stab, become water jets bursting in anger. Here the birds search the green grass. Here the ducks trumpet and honk. Here the dogs lie beneath the verandah, staring sleepily between its peeling bars. Here I stand gathering the rains. The droning *zzz-zzz chuck-chuck* of windshield wipers comes to mind.

"Why don't you go sit in the car," Joan suggests.

I do. But I leave the wipers off, for I'm caught now in this water cave; memory floods my mind with vague suggestions of other days still alive in mind. Hours of restrained kissing, balls in biological despair, losing the struggle against smaller and so much weaker hands, desperately dreaming of no more than to just touch it not even caress not even move my fingers I swear if I can only just feel it, that most strange and fascinating of things, that paramount, priceless, inviolable godhead of their making, that seedbed of life, mystery, and fear.

Joan leaps into the car beside me. Her hair and face drip water, her wet shirt clings wonderfully to her; her large dark nipples poke out like little dicks above alternating patches of rayon and skin.

"Let's go parking," she says.

"First," I say, "a shower."

I slip out of my pants. She pulls her shirt off. There is something powerful about a woman topless. Maybe it's the comedy. Humor is a mighty weapon. She wiggles and squirms and her bum cheeks like soft rubber baubles pop from her jeans.

"Now!" I shout, and I leap from the car into the cold rain. I look up at the dark sky. A seagull tilts past the barn roof in fine-line arcs.

"Whee!" Joan calls. "Wheee!"

She is racing across the grass. The look is right. Gorgeous white flesh on the move. But it isn't her noise. It doesn't suit her. Whee. Whee. The greening grass, mud and earth squish as I pounce after her. I wish she had a bigger lead. I wish she could run faster than me, or at least as fast so these naked lunging leaps, the kicking thrusts, this hurtling wet charge and chase, so precious and precarious, could last. But it's doomed, like orgasm. Doomed like all things of the body, all things human. It's what gives a sense of loss or nostalgia to the moment.

I tackle her and she laughs and gargles, grunts and groans. "That's you," I say. "That's you. Here you are." Boss's cold nose sniffs against my ass. Joan laughs as Tongue licks her face. "Go away," I say. "Go." I sit on her wet breasts, my rod pulsing over her chin. She takes it, and I watch her closed eyes, her hair in strands and clusters matted against her face. I drag my fingers along her cheeks and throat. Time stands still. When I finally pull away, she stirs as if coming up for air or rising from sleep, pond or prayer. I kiss her deeply and enjoy the taste of the salty slick on our lips while she guides us toward detonation, the silent explosion that will come at the center of us in the soft, centerless rain.

The barrel at the corner of the barn overflows. She hands me the soap and turns. I lather her back, her bum, between her legs, her thighs, I kneel and soap her feet, working my fingers gently between her toes. She presses my head against her soft wet patch of hair, nature's yield sign in smothered curls.

Three

Anyone attempting to tell takes only a piece, puts a frame around part of it. All of me, if I could tell it, is only part. Pictures within pictures. Not to tell is only that. Honesty chews my leg like a mad dog. When the bitch is brought to heel, will it stop?

Below and beyond I hear the sea. Rock ledge. Stone roots beneath undulating waves. I think of Andrew's thick hands and fingers, flesh never far from itself. Andrew is his own clock. He moves slowly, but it's not the slowness of years, though he owns many; it's his dance, that's all. Right enough for the occasion. So I am surprised, Maud Bone saying it before I am fully in the store:

"Andrew Hayward is in hospital. It's his heart."

"His heart."

"It's somethin' to do with circulation. He took to faintin'. Now ain't that the strangest, what? Andrew was never sick a day I know of. That the way? A man like Andrew."

"You never know," I say.

"No, you never do know," she says.

The stove hasn't been on, so the water is cool. I hack the

bristles from my face, then drive to town in the Beast. Nice town. Piles above the river on a steep bank. Storefronts like a poster design, all manner of color and shape, a two-dimensional spread of old-time personal commerce dead or dying, a beautiful footstool for the sterile shopping center poised efficiently above it on the hill.

The blue-haired lady returns from the freezer with one yellow rose. I reach out to touch it.

"Would you like it wrapped?"

It is soft, unlike anything I have ever touched. The cold stem and petals put it somewhere beyond natural, lend it the false feel of life preserved beyond its time. The feel of the wake.

"I could wrap it for you."

She seems to mellow as she watches me run my fingers over it.

"Thank you. Please."

She grows loquacious. "I love flowers myself. I think everyone does. They're such a pleasure. You never tire of them. I noticed how you touch them. So many people today never notice a flower, never mind touch one. And yet flowers are so. . . " She searches the fluorescent-lighted ceiling for the word. "I don't know," she says, "real, I guess. Natural. I think we need more of the natural today, don't you? You take those plastic flowers there. I don't like them myself, but people want them today. They ask for little else. They're insulted if your flower shop has only real flowers. 'Oh, you don't have any artificial flowers,' they say, getting right snuffety. 'Well, I was more interested in the synthetic,' they say. Synthetic!" She wriggles her nose disapprovingly beneath her glasses. "And so there they are. All colors. And kinds, too. I guess you could call them kinds. Cloth, plastic, wood. Is this lovely rose for your wife?"

"I'm not married," I say. "It's for my friend Andrew."

And once again I recall Andrew discovering me by the sea at a time when I was sure of my death (as sure as we all should be, each and every day), yet unsure of life. Then I was a man acting as if a sentence's meaning was entirely in its end, its period. That view allowed me to construct what was for me, under the conditions, a reasonably acceptable stance. Others had been there before and left markers. I was well lectured, well read. But the responsibility of writing my own life, of constructing my own sentence! What had I to go on? Where was the first word?

"Harold Fleet."

The voice simply came one day, appeared at the side of the bed cutting through the clouds of depression. My eyes opened to the dark mass of a figure in Inquisition black, the image clarifying until I saw even the nicotine-stained teeth in its grin, the putty-colored lips squirming around my name.

"Harold Fleet," he repeated.

I saw the surface of the dream and I struggled, as I recall doing as a youngster, trying to break water: struggling to rise from the deep lung-bursting pressures down under. But, as then, I couldn't move, couldn't possibly make it, till suddenly, at the last most desperate instant, I awoke.

"I am Dr. Daun. That's with a *u*, not a *w*. Dr. Launder asked me to speak with you."

As he sat, the chain of his pocket watch snaked thin and golden down his lap.

"How's the pain, Harold?"

"The drugs help. Help the pain . . . "

"But?"

I too had noted the tip of the thought unspoken. Almost at the same instant, I too had silently wondered "but," had felt something lay untouched behind my words. I moved like a mother hen to protect it. I flapped my verbal wings and nestled belly-down over it.

"But I'm still here," I said. "So . . . none of the tests or X-rays tell why I hurt."

"Why do you hurt?" he asked.

The detached passivity of his presence frightened me. He leaned forward, placing one hand on my heart. With the other he took from his vest pocket a gold watch so large that it virtually filled his hand. As I stared it grew larger, until its numberless face pulsed around two central lips.

"What are you going to do?"

"Merely take a look, ask you some questions. Lights," he said, and the room grew dark, all transparency gone except for our flesh, and the face of the clock.

"Why do you hurt?" His voice changed in the dark. It became the voice of an old lady I once knew. A neighborhood eccentric. I stole tomatoes from her garden till she caught me one day and shook me with febrile vehemence telling me God God God would make me pay pay pay.

"Who are you?" I asked.

"I told you, I'm Dr. Daun. Who do you think I am?"

I watched my fingers move across the black above my belly. His hand, white as white, still rested on my heart. The clock face glowed nearby, off to my left, but it seemed suspended in midair. Where was his other hand?

My heart fluttered in a rush of steps, climbing, seeking a way out. The lips on the face of the numberless clock asked How — tick, Why — tick, If — tick, So — tick, Then — tick, and I noticed the hair, a faint mustache around his lips, and I stared at this dark hole, stared until I realized the mustache grew around the lips, all the way around!

"A man," I said quickly, "an old man rickety as old cane, so old he crinkles like newspaper when he moves, well, this special old man, at least I find him special, because we've taken all these tests together, you see. Why, we've gone through so much together that our toilets even flush at the same time. I sit next to him on benches, in wheelchairs, here, there, everywhere, and all the while he never talks, never says a word to anyone. And then suddenly one day as we wait for the elevator he begins weeping heavily, calling 'Mama Mama' over and over. 'Mama! Mama. Mama.' He didn't stop till I held his hand."

"I understand. Now why do you hurt?"

I adjust myself.

"You're the doctor."

"It is your pain."

I heard that egg cracking within.

The clock's lips grew hairy and, as if pregnant, pursed and pressed out.

"I didn't learn to tell time till I was ten," I said. "My mother couldn't believe it. I can't believe it now!"

"It is your pain, Harold Fleet."

The lips grew large and moved as if to engulf me. I pressed the buzzer and the fart of feet in rubber soles reached my door and then light shot open the room. The matronly night-nurse stood still as a sentinel by the switch. "How's your pain?" she asked.

"I can't sleep," I said. "I think I'm imagining things."

The next day Dr. Launder, kindly, gray-haired, smelling of lotion and soap, sat in the chair to one side of my hospital bed. His tone was bedside cool, his words soft and deliberate seemed to strangulate in sweetness. I felt the dentist's lie in all that he said. Just a bit more, now, almost done. In fact, what he said made little difference to me, for beneath his thirty-odd years of medicine-man manner is the truth, what he does not say. And what doctors do not say radiates like a beacon. The choice was mine: select the reassurance and comfort of the words, or the chaos of doubt and concern that hid just behind them.

"I've arranged for a CAT scan."

"I've heard of it a million times. What is it?"

"Computerized axial tomography."

"Of course. For a minute it slipped my mind."

"It's like an X-ray shot from multiple levels and directions. We end up with a 3-D effect."

"I'm going stir crazy," I said.

"But think of the rest you're getting. And some of the scenery here is good, if not the food. Or haven't you noticed?" He grinned and held his glasses up on his nose with his middle finger before allowing them to fall back, covering the soft rut pinched there by years of wear. "Try to be positive, Harry."

"There's an old man," I said. "He calls for his mother. At all hours of the night. They can't seem to help him. I sat next to him down at X-ray. He sat there crying 'Mama Mama' until a young nurse came and held his hand." I felt the tension and strain in my voice.

"I know it's hard, Harold," he said.

"What do you think it is?" I asked. "What do you think I've got?"

He started to glance away, then fastened his eyes on mine. His face softened like a bubble of gum losing air.

"Oh, it's difficult to say," he said evenly.

"Not even a hunch?"

He patted my leg beneath the sheet. "Let's just wait and see. Why bother yourself with idle speculation?"

"Let me tell you the truth," I said. "I've been concerned about cancer."

I studied his face as hard as I have ever studied a face. I saw breath move his nostril hairs, spittle strands thin as fairy twine stretched between his lips, eyes blown wet with sweat and cosmic wind.

"Well," he said, lifting the glasses from that tiny crevice once again, "that's always a possibility. Even with a tooth-ache. Let's just wait and see. It could be nothing. Or a simple infection. Your white blood cells show a mild shift." He patted my leg again. "Let's just wait and see, all right? Trust me. Trust yourself. You're not ready to go, are you?"

"No. I've hardly been here yet."

"That seems to me to be well worth knowing. See, some good comes from everything."

"You're not keeping anything from me, are you?"

"I don't think you're a man it's possible to keep secrets from. At least not for long. Anyway, why would I?"

I felt the trust bursting forth, rising as if from my lungs. "Because you know how scared I am."

"Fear is natural," he said. "Who wouldn't be scared? It'll pass. Just wait. You'll see."

I recall, foggily, a beautiful child, faceless to me, banging temperately a tambourine. Each measured clap of canvas to skin is a check to his fear, a thumb pressing it back.

All around are others like me, with blackened spoons and pans rippled with years' cadence, red and white plastic flutes with holes to be covered, large wooden blocks to clap, and one curiously soprano drum.

There are more details. More instruments, more children, but I rush now to the tall, gray-maned woman with hands like a boxer. She is standing at the center of us, her arms lashing about, her axis tighter, her turns smaller, freer, more pronounced. She rotates faster than the circle so we are all in her sight as we stomp around her, banging, piping, singing.

"March," she says. "March *and* sing *and* Yankee Doodle went to town. . . "

Her laced black tennis sneakers lift and fall and lift and fall. Her jowls swell with music. "Sing, John. Kathy, cat got your tongue? Went to town. Went to town."

I bang faster so that each time the beam of her eyes searches across me I am doing. My leg grows sore. My fingers are white with gripping.

"Row, row, row your boat, Green Pants," she says, her eyes holding me like a hand.

And they are now, I hear, singing merrily merrily merrily and I bang harder, trying to catch up or join in before she swivels by me once again, her head pumping up and down seesawing with song. Row. Row. Row.

Then it stops.

I hear myself jingling tin. I stop.

The slick hardwood floors slap back light all the way to the doll house across the large room. I'd like to be there, crawl inside and move deep into that corner farthest from the paned, airy window. It's safe there, at least till her gray stare comes suddenly against the sill so close you can see her teeth hanging from her lips, see each color in the circles of her eyes, her face four patches broken by window frame.

"Join hands," she says.

We play ring-around-the-rosy. It is a large ring. There are many of us.

"*Fall down!* girl with red roses. Fall down. That's it. Now again. *Ring* around." Windows open two walls to sun-lit winter air that quivers and steams before the glass where our coiled paper bracelets of red and green hang dry and bright.

"Naps!" She claps her hands with a crack that silences all voices. She watches us scramble for the mats piled along one wall.

I lie with my cheek down, my eyes guardedly open. A stir of bodies everywhere.

"We don't nap with our eyes open, do we, Green Pants."

Light comes against my lids in bars and dim golden blurs. I hear heavy shoes. She is talking to someone. Up high, I hear her whisper, and then there is the sound of her sneakers.

I experience a moment of panic before she leaves the room. Heavy shoes move near the door. Father's shoes. Man shoes. Finally the squeak of her sneakers again and then her hands clap once more.

"Line up for the unmentionable, boys and girls."

We move single file through the hardness of tunnels, caves of faceless noise behind closed doors. One bulletin board, two rows of snowmen with different colored hats, scarves and buttons. Her soft largeness, severe and gray, shuttles past one way then the other. "No talking," she says time and again. "No talking."

No one is.

We go in by threes. Boys left, girls right. Johnny's buttons have to be redone when he returns. She suggests he get a zipper. The floor is sidewalk stone painted gray. We step up to the white urinals as close as we dare. A large ball of yellow-white soap froths above the mesh drain cover. Water trickles from a thin mouth of holes, then flows in rusty stains toward the shallow bowl.

"Flush," she says, directly behind me.

I tip my head back to see her and almost lose my balance.

"Pull the handle. Flush it, Green Pants. Don't you understand English?"

I stretch awkwardly, rising on my toes.

"Don't get your hand in there," she snaps.

The handle is cold and wet. A sneeze of water rushes down, bubbling the soap. It smells of mouthwash and ammonia, like the hot candy from the store.

The line is quiet.

She goes in to check on the last few. One snowman at the far bottom corner has designs on his scarf. The rest are all solids or stripes.

"You get your hand pee?"

I stare wide-eyed at the incautious boy behind me. He is the drummer. This solitary voice in the silence is taking a risk so great that I cannot begin to imagine such. . . is it ignorance, or courage?

"I *said*, you get your hand pee?" he repeats in exasperation.

She appears from nowhere, grabs each of us by an arm and

spins us about. "What is the rule?" she demands. She is talking through her teeth.

I stare up at her, see the words explode from the creases and crevices around her clenched mouth.

She shakes our arms then jerks them down. "What is the *rule*?" she demands again, still cranking our limbs in hopes of pumping the answer from our depths. The tunnel is filled with her.

I feel myself suffocating in the starched gray of her dress that grows out of the walls, unfolds over us in gigantic plaits, the cloth ballooning and hissing till. . .

"No talking," the drummer says, his voice fraught with humility, common sense and surrender. She drops his arm.

"You," she says, giving my arm another yank.

I swallow. The words are easy. The rule is easy.

"Well?"

"No talking," I say. It comes out in a throaty gasp.

"You think it's funny!"

I shake my head quickly.

I hear the heavy shoes.

"Okay, back to class," she says, letting my arm fall.

Baggy pants move by at eye level. Above, I see a portly display of vest, tie, white skin and smile.

"Good day, children," he sings.

The two windows on the far wall are open. Casements at the base of each trap the cold, forcing it up. Even standing close there is no draft, just the radiator's warmth washing dry across the face. All around boys and girls play in suppressed excitement. They plead in whispered earnest. A pile of blocks falls and it is quiet. We all look at her sitting behind the large oak desk that separates her gray bust from the black sneakers and hose in the cubicle below.

"Now then," she says, growing whole and large once again,

looming above and then to one side of her desk. "Nursery rhymes."

We sit crosslegged with our shoes off. She moves about correcting our posture. She jokes about the hole in the drummer's sock. An electric reserve of tittering sits in the air. "If I stick in my thumb, will I pull out a plum?" she asks, pinching his toe. A grimace smile hangs like a hole on his red face. She goes on straightening backs and folding hands, then she rumps down across the circle from me, her vast, gray presence a ship's anchor. Her legs, flat on the floor, open toward me, an ever-narrowing channel walled by ocher hose that runs up one leg, curves, then runs down the other. The bottoms of her sneakers are yellow-white and speckled with bites as if she's run across nails.

We are each to recite a nursery rhyme. One after the other around the circle.

"Who would like to begin?"

Our hands explode upward.

She laughs and stares from one anxious face to the next, slowly and deliberately.

I take courage when she seems to pause longer on me. I remember one. Perhaps two.

She examines me, running her tongue over teeth. All her flesh is reminiscent of that: a tongue behind flesh accenting a puttyish, soft looseness, a not quite fluid mass, like overdone oatmeal. She surveys the group once more and quickly says, "Pamela." Our hands drop. We all measure the distance between ourselves and Pamela, who is removing Twinkle Twinkle, Little Star from possibility.

"Next boy, there. Come on."

Hey Diddle Diddle.

Jack and Jill.

Humpty Dumpty.

Hickory, Dickory, Dock.

I can't know what's coming. I'm no longer sure what's been recited. Tiny voices as if underwater move wordless through my consciousness. The room falls away. The stiff chain of children falls away. It is warm on my face. I feel a shaking. I see green and red checks shaking. I see her hand on the green and red checks. She has my arm. A stiff silence has frozen everything, even the gray mass kneeling before me like a wall.

"Well, a dillar a dollar my ten o'clock scholar."

"A dillar a dollar," I begin.

"*That* has been recited," she says, "to those of us listening."

I hear the glass rattling in the window. She is trapping me in the quiet, weaving the silence around me, lacing me up. Just as I am about to die she says, "There are *hundreds* of nursery rhymes."

I can make out only her face, a whirlpool of larded strips racing in concentrically to a dim black center. I press my free hand to the floor.

"Can't you," she says, jerking my arm, "tell . . . us . . . one . . . little . . . nursery . . . rhyme."

I try desperately to wring the tears from my words.

"They said mine."

"They said yours! All eleven of these nasty, mean little children said *yours*. What nerve!"

"Twinkle Twinkle," I say. "Hey Diddle Diddle."

"Okay," she says. She takes her hand from my arm.

I feel I'm falling. One foot is asleep. I feel the tickle, a snow of trapped blood storming there.

She sprawls back on the floor before me. "Go ahead, then. Recite."

I begin to sob.

Then we are in the girls' cloak room.

"When you are ready, Whiney Pants, you can rejoin us," she says. The door closes.

I wipe at my face with the backs of my hands. It is quiet

now. Safe. Then I hear the heavy shoes coming toward the doorless opening to the main corridor. I push into the hanging snowpants and jackets. He does not see me.

He enters the room.

I run.

I am in the wind of certainty. No one is in the corridor. I run past the snowmen and doors, past grades one, two, three, then down two broad steps. The crossbar of the large double door releases under pressure and both doors spring wide, opening onto a shoveled patch of black. I run across the road wet with slush, feel the cold water seeping through my socks. Steam rushes from my nostrils and mouth. Snowbanks give beneath my weight. Kindergarten. Children's garden. Snow cakes in white balls on my socks. What did you learn today? The closed back door ahead looks stark. But I'm home. Home. Home. I stumble going over the low wall and puncture the cold, white wetness, take it into me like a shot from head to toe, then I am in that door where it is warm, and Mother is there, but it's in her eyes already, the frozen disbelief, surprise and amazement, and before she says a single word I know I shall be returned to learn their rhymes, to keep their step, I shall be returned to join them in that tight circle on that glistening floor. I go back, for I have no choice, but there's not a chance they'll teach me there. Because I've taken that long holiday: obedience, acquiescence, surrender.

Four

Years later, I was ready to run again. Though I doubted I'd get far with the pain in my hip.

The doctor returned that same day, wiped his teeth with his tongue, studied his shoes firmly planted on the floor, said finally, as if starting a new chapter, "Do you have a particular problem? Is anything bothering you?"

I blushed as if caught in some disgraceful act, felt the "anything that was bothering me" lurch sharply to one side as if derailed by the question.

"Nothing special. I'm worried about this pain. Why do you ask?"

He patted my leg again. I wondered how many miles of sheet he'd imprinted with this reflexive concern.

"It's just that we like to check every possibility."

"It's not my head, Dr. Launder. My hip hurts," I insisted. "I *know* it. It hurts so I can hardly move. Christ, I can hardly walk! It keeps me up at night . . . "

"I know. I know," he said with benign, priestly sympathy, a benediction from the eyes.

"But — better crazy than cancer," I said hopefully. "Is that the new diagnosis? Crazy?"

Instead of consolation, I got a series of mental tests, a booklet of questions designed to catch, among other things,

contradictions. They were introduced after my morning bath.
"The tests say you are extremely unhappy," the doctor said.
"Also they tell us you're an hysteric."

"An hysteric! Are you kidding! I *never* fold under pressure.
I'm the first one into the breach. Last to leave the ship. I'm
so cool under stress that my friends find it scary."

"Hysteria isn't just the lay perception of it, Harold. You're
no doubt thinking of the frantic woman in a 1950s movie, the
one we're so relieved to see the hero slap. No. Hysteria is
fixation. The hysteric gets an idea and can become obsessed
with it. It takes over. Nothing else seems to matter. Does that
sound like you?"

"I have to think about it. And you think that's the reason
for my pain?"

"I don't know. We're examining every possibility."

"So it's not cancer."

"We don't know. The CAT scan should give us a lot better
idea."

"What do you do about hysteria?"

"Oh, I don't think that's anything to concern yourself
about. It may be useful information if you find yourself being
a little obsessive or overly concerned about things."

"Am I overreacting now? To this cancer thing?"

"Maybe a bit. I mean, we don't know very much at this
point, do we? Can I say something to you?"

"Sure."

"It's not uncommon for people your age to undergo personal crises."

"The famous mid-life crisis? Oh, please, Doc. Please don't
tell me that's what I'm having. I'll never live it down. Give
me something less fashionable than that."

"Maybe instead of thinking in terms of living things down,
you should start thinking in terms of just *living*."

"What do you mean?"

"You know better than I the answer to that. I'll just say that

I think there's a message in it when a man of your age and intelligence has to wait for a test to tell him that he's unhappy."

Having decided to run again, this time I had the advantage of age. And real independence. I applied for Landed Immigrant status in Canada, quit my job, gathered together all my retirement money and savings, said goodbye to my friends. I felt exhilarated and free.

For weeks I prepared. I scoured Nova Scotia on maps. Coastal fringe, ridges, the edges of this place attracted me. It was old and ocean. I wasn't sure at the time why I was so drawn, but it's all so accurate in retrospect, a matching of geographies.

By the time I reached the twenty-two thousand miles of Nova Scotia coast, my pain was less intense, but even more visceral. I had relinquished tentative control, or more accurately, I had taken primary control by flushing my pain pills down a motel room toilet, so my primary misery had become a faint nausea that could not be fed, and a fear of some awful impendingness, as of doom, or imminent evaporation. I wiped cold sweat from my brow. I talked to myself. I looked at the farms, the hills' sensuous expanse, the brilliant light dancing in and around things. It was truly magical. This was a very special part of the earth.

Relax, I'd say. Relax, I'd think. Sink into it. Don't be afraid. Something will happen. Accept. Accept. The fog moved across the yellowed grass, Burnished browns and blacks hung with mist. All was properly obscure for a frightened man mortally afraid.

But I still trembled.

The sun was most uncooperative that spring; it blared like a warm note from a trumpet, and the robust springtime scene, fish shacks above coarse rock, lobster traps stacked on weathered docks, people even-faced on boats, cleaning fish and hanging clothes — all this insisted on spoiling my final page. When you look around, death is a spare-time thing.

In a matter of hours after crossing the border, I left all cities, and finally highways, behind. I put away my map and drove aimlessly — or so it seemed — but always I stayed appropriately buried in back country.

Chewed by frost, boggled, swallowed, spit-up chunks of asphalt lay atop the holey black mass, a suitably desiccated tongue above the green water. I parked at midday next to a tall, scarred old spruce whose blue-green needles and gnarled branches twisted above a mass of petrified skin. There were other less imposing trees. Pine. Fir. Oak. Ash. Alders and bushes. Rock. Grass. And a beach running in sand tones and pebble shades of white, brown, gray.

I spread a blanket on the rocks and watched the waves. Because the Reaper is grim is no reason we need be. As I lay there listening to the gulls, cool sea breezes and sun sharing my face, I heard a tractor. I imagined Death in its seat, his skull-shrunken face poking from farm clothes, that familiar scythe strapped to his back.

Harold Fleet.

Do you, should you answer?

You are called, Harold Fleet.

I know. I know.

Get aboard, Harold Fleet. We've a piece to go before dark.

Death?

Yes, Harold Fleet.

Why the tractor?

Why not? Death said, and we chugged away.

It was an old man, his belt drawn half again around his tiny waist, the slack end hanging loose like a tie. His white shirt showed through a jacket I'd expect more at place in town or at church. I'll always remember Andrew that way, dressed day to day the way most dressed for Friday shopping trips to town. A tartan tam sat humorously above his blotchy red face. Both hands held the wheel; his pipe poked cockeyed past one cheek. He stopped the tractor. A scythe was tied behind the seat by a leather thong. Later that year I would watch him swing that scythe through the grass, felling the tall blades in effortless sweeps, a soft maw of sound cutting the summer silence.

"Hi," he called, but it was not a city "hi" with its familiar lashing energy. The word drifted, unfolded toward me as if swimming upstream through the air. It was a new sound.

"Hi," I said.

"Better watch the tide," he said.

I smiled. I *was* watching it.

"She'll back in behind you there and you'll be stuck with no place to go. 'Less, course, that's what you want." He laughed around the words. Not quite a snort. I followed his eyes to my left where the water was creeping in behind a low scrawl of rocks, isolating me from the beach and road.

"Thanks," I said, grabbing up the blanket. "Thanks very much. It'd be a cold swim back."

"She creeps up on you," he said. The tractor was quiet. He folded one leg across the other, then, planting his elbow on one knee, he drew contentedly on his pipe and stared past me out to sea. The road behind him was studded with mud chunks spat from the deep rubber treads of the tractor wheels.

"Been in the woods?" I asked.

"Yes," he drawled. "It's still pretty wet, though."

"A lot of rain," I said.

"Yes," he said. "And snow. That's your car?"

"Yes."

"Are you stopping here?"

"Just passing through. This is a great spot."

"Yes."

He told me of seals here on these rocks and, with the quiet intensity of soft reflection I came to associate with him, he also spoke of deer swimming from a distant island, climbing the ledge, resting, taking the sun.

"Winters ago that was." His eyes stayed on the water as he spoke, and we watched the deer approach, their hooves clicking and slipping as they scrambled across the frozen stone.

"Must be cold," I said, shucking down to essentials, discarding words, seeking that terse essence I heard in his speech.

"Yes," he said, smiling, "for you or me." And he chuckled lightly, shaking his head and shoulders.

"You'll be staying handy here?"

"What's that?"

"Have you a place to stay the night?

"Is there a place?"

Before I bought Lester Pheeps' farm complete with a cow that I traded for an old tractor, my life gravitated around Andrew and Della Hayward. Surrogate parents? Perhaps in part, witnesses that they were to the labors of my being reborn. But they hadn't the responsibility of kinship, so they more easily tolerated my occasional relapses and irrationality, and the stigma, the accusation and the public humiliation that must have been some part of harboring an outsider like me.

That first day as I pulled my car behind Andrew's tractor and we crept slowly toward the camp, I felt satisfied and relieved. It was like going home, not to the home of my dead parents (killed strangely enough in an automobile accident just as Lester Pheeps' parents had been) but to a home free of contest, proving, and the pressure to keep up or save face. No sooner did the cabin appear from behind a spread of pine and alder than I knew this was more than a stopping-off point.

The cabin was of planks, not logs, and its most prominent feature was a fireplace of brick and stone. It had three kerosene lamps, one that hung neatly from a beam over the kitchen table. Nearby on the wall was a rag rug. Thick old towels. A wood-burning stove. Outside was a shallow well where spring-cool water bubbled over wet rock. There I would wake into mornings so cold ice lay in the bucket. Those mornings, I'd grab clothes, dance and hop and churn about, stack kindling. I wouldn't have believed April in North America could be so cold. But once the fire crackled and the heat pressed against my face and hands, anxiety thawed, melting away old problems and postponing new. Then I sat for hours, rocking before the flames.

"You have all a man wants here," Andrew said. "Though I guess we get used to more."

I split wood. I carried water. Raccoons ate my garbage. Birds ate my crumbs. Della Hayward made molasses cookies for me. I was supplied with vegetables from the Haywoods' winter store. Despite the chimney's awesome tunes, I had greater courage to poke at the stiffened carcass of my past life.

Water dripped around the flattened soup can I hammered over a hole in the roof. The sound of rain on the shingles was close and familiar. I thought of tents. A week at camp. I saw that little boy sitting alone on the dock, his feet inches into the cool water, everywhere in everything tumult and noise louder than the sun. To be, to have been that small, that innocent, that vulnerable. Then, the only sounds were the rain and the fire mixing and mating in my ears.

"Should be patched from the other side," Andrew said, head back, eyes lifting away from his clenched jaw. Same pipe in his mouth. Pitted, charred, chewed. "I'll patch her after a while. Did you see your deer yet?"

"No. But I haven't gone far."

"Well, it's wet," he said. "And cold."

"If I go too far, I'm afraid I'll get lost. It all starts to look the same. Not really the same. I mean the order gets mixed up. Or I do. I can never remember what I passed when."

Andrew chuckled and his eyes leaped as if tickled by the surrounding crow's-feet. "It takes time," he said. "It is all new to you, what?"

"Yes. I guess you're right. Say, would you like tea?"

Andrew didn't shake his head, instead he waved his pipe from side to side. "No thank you," he said. "I'm full now. Just stood up from lunch."

Two days later he pried up the shingles and patched the leak. I listened as he moved about on the roof, the hammer beating irregular judgment, driving points of nails toward me through the roof.

"That should hold her," Andrew said, bending the final nail back from inside the cabin. "That last one almost spiked the cable. That'd make a man sing." He laughed, his face red with wind and age, the soft lump of tam on his head. "You know you can always stay with Della and me for a bit if you get lonely."

I stared at him.

"We got room enough," he said, his head and shoulders dancing up and down, laughter aforethought, "if you don't mind woman clutter."

ANDREW HAYWARD. The house marked plainly by these words on a smoky tin box alongside the road, the letters black going gray, tiny cracks in the name probably never seen since those early days when first the pole was set and the mailman's tires began to press an arc along the gravel shoulder. The house is a spacious giant unfolding through the years, added rooms twisting this way then that. Della soars in it. Sewing.

Knitting. Mending. Making rugs. Making clothes. And candy. Making, making, making. She moves like a whirlwind. The wide plank floors tremble in her wake.

She wanted to paint the room, just hadn't the time. "It's fine," I said. "Lovely." She'd have new curtains for it by summer. There was no heat duct in that room so she could give me their electric blanket if it was too cold.

"Really, thank you. No. The quilt is all I need," I said. "It's beautiful. It's a history, isn't it?"

She was pleased. "It's my family's. Our children are gone so it's going to stop with me."

"It's very beautiful. How far back does it go?"

"One hundred and ninety-three years. Guests sleep under it one night and then it goes back in storage. Tomorrow night I'll give you another."

She fetched the Family Quilt, sat near me on the couch, then spread it across our knees. Andrew sat nearby in the rocker.

I listened as they traveled the years, stopping to taste their time, others' time: wood-cutting parties, Saturday nights, Sundays, evenings, births, occasions, events and people spread in color for me to see. Barns alive with steaming life, kitchen smells, cold cellars, canning, the staggered schedules of slaughter, neighborly sharing, snow shoveling, smoked fish, barrels of apples, friends dropping in, fresh milk and cream, cheese, butter, bread hot from the oven, and old Aunt Lucy shelling dried beans in the outhouse, "because she always *had* done."

"What about you?" Della asked. "Here we are chattering away like a couple of I-don't-know-whats."

Andrew raised his face.

"Oh. I don't have a history like this," I said, smoothing my hands over the quilt.

She smiled appreciatively, her eyes expanding as she accepted whatever I'd say. "But you do have a history. Everyone has a history."

"I used to teach."

"School?" she said.

"Yes. University."

She nodded. "That's very nice." Andrew puffed on his pipe.

"You're a professor, then," she said with a kind of finality, spreading her large hands over her lap, smiling a close-lipped smile. "Yes," I said. "I was."

"We don't have even one single one of those," she said thoughtfully. "At least not far back as I know."

Five

That night I drifted through my pieces, moments frozen and forgotten till suddenly they are there once again, fresh. I went to the hall, where I could hear Andrew and Della breathing easily in their sleep. The future shortened after so many years. I heard it in their voices that night. Not much ahead anymore. Just the press of passage, new lines for old faces, and space diminishing, narrowing until a catalogue, an album of each moment that had ever been, became not only a way back but a way to go on.

I had seen as a child strangers' faces in charcoal grays and browns, paper memories, other life on the walls of other homes. In our house we had no pictures, real or remembered. Whatever had happened before me was a family secret.

There is something special and true here but only as there is something special and true about any place. The magic of Hayward house is that it is Hayward house. This countryside is filled with four-poster beds and hand-carved bureaus, fancy plaster moldings.

I furrowed my brow, squeezing my eyes half shut, and once more the doctor sat at the side of my bed, drew pictures in pencil of parts of my body, thin lines that he traced and retraced, pointing, labeling, even writing words in syllables with diacritical marks. Brucellosis.

"But you couldn't have that," he mused. "People who work around cattle — mainly sheep — are the ones who get that. And even with them it's rare today."

"I guess I should confess about Sally."

"Sally?"

"The sheep I keep. For those long, lonely nights? Sorry. I'm being foolish."

"Good. We should all be a lot more foolish."

"It's just bravado, Dr. Daun. I'm really scared. I have myself talked into something horrible," I laughed.

He looked down at his pad. "Well. . . I don't think. So there's nothing about your history, your past, family, mother, father, that can help us?"

We were a close family, a pre-war American, post-war family, and the fact is we encompass befores and afters; we believe in Getting Ahead, Heavenly Reward, Good Guys, Bad Guys, Right Winning Out (at least ultimately, somewhere, sooner or later). All this easing us into a construct simply expressed but beyond our imaginings, American, *Life* magazine.

Yes, we purchased the surface. Time payments. They wrapped it up pretty and doled it out in installments. Surface like ice sending us sliding where it suited them, putting us here, there, like dime-store dummies, draping us in platitudes and painting smiles on our faces, filling our frozen existence with the vacuousness that protects their dreams.

Fuzzy Wuzzy was a bear,
Fuzzy Wuzzy had no hair,
Fuzzy Wuzzy wasn't fuzzy,
Was he?

And our eyes wide open, looking ahead as they planned, seeing their plan as they planned, loving laughing trusting, sure it was all right, as they planned.

Didn't they give us heroes and history?
Didn't they let us have jobs?
Didn't they let us have fun?
Didn't they give us schools, hospitals, churches and parks?
Didn't they give us the dream?
Well, didn't they?

Father: Truly Good, two jobs, biceps bursting, body hard like the foundation of his belief and as durable; sweat filling his eyes, he stokes their furnaces with divine gratitude, then walks home whistling, Christianizing, greeting, thinking about family and stew and bread with real butter, and four more hours yet to come squeezing out quarts, pints, cones, hand-packing their ice cream.

And Mother: Always Faithful, assured, loving, tender, kisses and concern, eight hours on the line sorting bearings for their wheels; thinking of the kids in school and the stove they'd probably forget to light for supper; thinking too of the layoffs starting and she with no seniority, and his job, was it any more safe, really? She said a little prayer, promised more later, when she had time.

So after years of steam and hiss and rattle, years of more and more fire, more acceptance, more things, minds aching, and bones, muscles in eternal knots like apples waiting to rot, smiles slower but still sure, the top blows off the material pressure cooker. Recession.

Still there is acceptance. Nodding resignation. It is natural enough in the scheme of things. Not wholly expected, of course, but natural enough. And merely temporary. Not a reflection on anyone or anything, just the way it goes. It isn't the taint that shows when dreams are soured, just the way it is, and how can anyone be blamed for that? Not how can I harvest, not having planted; not how can I sow, all sown before. Not anger, not frustration, but well-drilled submission, a sadness always ready for more.

The other scene: a scene within a scene. Clothes hide a truth that flesh never feels. Next door, back there in that past that never ends but is always beginning, there was a woman. She had hair under her arms, big breasts, and she smelled of sweat and cheap perfume. Men came to see her, and at night, her bed against the wall, my bed against the same wall, I heard her groan, moan, moan, mooooaaannnning. I heard the straining of bedsprings, the calling of names, and I moved closer to my brother Fred who slept breathing through his nose.

But what was all this to me, wide-eyed rope skipper?

My name is Harold
And I come from Hartford
And I sell Houses.

What are they to me, the whistles and winks? What's it to me, the youngest, so always It, the others hiding together, already feeling each other up? Then one day they show me. I'm a patient. They are doctors. They check me over and laugh. I laugh. Don't tell anybody, they say, or you'll be in real trouble. They'll kill you if you tell. I don't tell and I go on living.

Hidden on the shelf I find paperback books. I search for words out of context, words masturbated into print, tickling titillating words, tugging words like *breast* and *passion* and *lay*. I dream of the day I can get hard like Fred and Jim and Bobby, like all of them who stand around our bedroom, laughing serious, pulling at themselves. Bobby, showing a special interest in me, gives me private lessons.

I know the evil of what I do, what I dream, what I hope to do. I've heard it in church. I know the good boys and girls from the bad. I know the hidden genitals from the exposed. Still, I skim the passages, pausing, marveling at these "things" right there for me to read. And there are the You're-Too-Young-For-This-Ha-Ha magazines I watch my father and his friends pore over, leering, gaping, judging and estimating. I find these "art magazines" one day, hidden away in his tool box, and I spread them out in all their glory and with two fingers I practice being adult, dreaming of the day I get big, and hard, and I come.

It was about then, while waiting, expecting, anticipating, that I learned loss.

Wilma and Wiley, nubile neighbors, took me for a walk-talk. Each held one of my hands. At times I'd race ahead, showing how fast I was in my new sneakers. Mostly, though, I walked along, liking the sun on my face and my body, and liking the attention and the smell of their perfume.

I'll always remember there in the bush, the dim cave of honeysuckle hanging down enclosing us, cradling us in its sweetness. But mostly I remember the taste, smell and feel of Wiley's tit, that young tit larger and more beautiful than any other I'll ever see, more full, more lush, more "titty" in every way. It appeared suddenly, flopping from her bra. She smiled and leaned over me, thrusting it against my face, moving it all around, then inching that wonderful nipple into my mouth. "Stop!" I gargled. I was in Heaven. "Cut it out!"

How from the paramount decency of the happy life this twisted monster, this sex-crazed maniac lurking behind his fly, festering like an open sore beneath a sheet? Why not the rapture and delight of orgasm? Because it's bad. Why not the function of shared orgasm? Because it's bad. Bad? Well, okay, it *is* for sharing, but later.

And so the screens filled with tit. The streets filled with tit. The schools filled with tit. The stores and churches, the cars, fields and skies filled with tit. My mind filled with tit until I felt nipples like tiny peters pressing from my ears. I drew tits. Beanies, bald heads, even beach balls sprouted curious protrusions under my guidance. I traced almost revealed breasts under onion paper, and with careful touches stripped women bare. I traced away dresses and powdered my transparencies with muffs like Mother's, like Mrs. Jodrey's, like Mrs. Cabish's: those hairy patches all seen after hours of stealth, then masturbated to in anxious idolatry, in flesh-tearing frenzy, seed spilt and handled, tasted, taut eyes imagining. Oh, Mrs. Cabish, I love, I love, I love your aging cunt that first called forth my pubescent sperm.

Then, staring at my wet hand and sad, raw, hamburger-red rod, I repented. I thought of my happy family that I loved, that loved me, and I clutched at my guilt. How *can* I? How *could* I? And if they knew what I did, if they caught me sitting here in bare-assed disgrace, making my shiny puddle on the bathroom floor!

I mean the guilt was unreal. Mom and Dad kissing me and treating me as if I were any normal child, as if I were clean and decent, even wholesome! Their goodness ate at me like acid. I mourned. There was only one answer, only one way: stop or die. I will, dear God, my Savior my Love, dear Mother, dear Father, dear world, I will stop this sin or I will kill myself by diving from Mrs. Cabish's roof.

And still tit everywhere. The ads dripping curves I long to race, shading crotches I long to trace. I wanted to go back and erase the sin, but I also wanted to go back to Wiley's tit. Everything propelled me backwards. Whatever I sought was behind me. If God appeared right then saying to me "My son, ask and it shall be yours," I'd have looked Him straight in the eye and told Him, "I want Wiley's tit."

So I ended up sitting on Mrs. Cabish's roof, thinking of Mrs. Cabish's magnificent muff and my imminent death. I got an erection. I started to cry. It was a nice day and the shade of the nearby elm cast cool shadows across the street. I was afraid of what God would say when I saw Him. I'd tell Him I was sorry, but somehow that would be so weak in the face of everything, and although I took a bath there was still that raw spot on my penis where it rubbed against the zipper that very noon, when I was shut away in the cellar with *National Geographic* and *Life* magazine.

"Babies," I said indignantly the next day, "don't come from *that*, because I've seen in war movies where the guy goes off to war and his wife still has a baby while he's gone."

"Oh yeah, Smart Ass? Well, suppose you tell us how they have one then."

"Because he loves her, Stupid. He loves her so much she has it no matter where he is."

And those who love me so much lug their worry and discomfort from room to room, watching my dark difference threatening like a distant cloud.

A strange child. Maybe he's seeing too many movies.

That night, late, my final worthlessness is confirmed. I am caught. Exposed. Poor old Mrs. Cabish and I are wrapped around each other huffing and puffing. Wiley, whom I've just finished ravishing, hangs her tits in my face, forcing one then the other into my mouth. Wilma is organizing hordes of other beauties eager to have me have my way with them, when my brother Fred, we shared a bed, reached over and took my arm.

"What are you doing?" he asked.

"Nothing."

"Cut it out and go to sleep," he said.

I waited till he got back to sleep, then I finished, for I was a perfectionist then. I retied shoes, refolded newspapers, bent back dog-eared pages; I even leveled off my jam and butter insatiably, apportioned my food, planning each bite; I couldn't tolerate rust, dirt, grease or stain; I recopied rather than erase. You see, I knew there was right. I felt it. I had always felt it. Ideally there is an America; I felt that as well. It was the context of my struggle, my striving. It was the home of Wiley's tit too, and to say that one or the other — tits or

America — did not matter, that they are finally only of the mind, only dreams — and someone else's at that — and to say that no one is perfect, is perhaps to escape the eternal main feature, the undulating slip and swell of ultimate orgasm that fills the lifetime sky. But if you believe in perfection *and* you believe in Wiley's tit, there's no escape, and you sit forever trapped on Mrs. Cabish's roof asking, "What's a grown man like you doing in a place like this?"

Six

One fall day after shopping in town, I left the main highway and snaked down the uneven shore. The sun and air were acting like a calmative. I wasn't thinking. I was idling and it felt good. The urge I had to find my own place and settle — at least for a while — wasn't deperate or obsessive. It seemed rather just a part of the natural flow of things. I couldn't stay with Andrew and Della forever, so I searched.

I noticed the sign for Gorm Island. Gorm Island is a peninsula. Once isolated during high tides, now it attaches to the mainland by a black road, a tongue of tar with gravel cheeks, shoulders falling away to each side. The view along my right was heavily gulled havoc, splintered wood, rusted nails, and fish heads with sunken eyes, bare bone tails like handles eerily clean above the low ooze of steaming sewage pumped from the shacks and small houses across the road. The sun licked at everything, penetrating and lifting all parts in defined smear. I thought of rural America, the South of the twenties and thirties, I thought of Faulkner.

I stopped the car at a fish shack with a heavily shadowed but open front door. When I shut off the engine, I heard the wonderful soft gargled call of gulls, and waves breaking. I stepped on the first weathered step and the board sank and heads of rusty nails poked up. Ahead in the dark, someone's retching, gurgling, lung-clearing clatter. Sun at my back. Smell of oil and brine and sweat. I stood, feeling my eyes adjusting, calibrating to measure. It was a store of sorts. Suddenly I saw him. He rose like a walrus shoving up from the table, grabbing almost desperately at a wood support that dangled smoked fish in a bunch. Devil's bananas. I saw his hat first. An old white fedora spotted, I would later see, with oil of fingers, flesh, and fish. Beneath that hat his face sat like a sheet of white plastic caked with chopped meat.

"Hi," I said.

He grunted. As my eyes focused more clearly I detected the exertion, the effort it took him to breathe, to move. Milk-gray shirt. Red suspenders. A squash of piss-yellow T-shirt in a fist beneath the fat of his chins.

"I have seventy-three years," he said, and he looked at me severely.

"That's a long time."

"Not so long." He lumbered out from behind the makeshift counter, a cane beneath each fat hand. His belly was an enormous button-popper, a Shakespearean tub, but there was not that humor in it. He was a hard, sad man, all the spirit leaked out perhaps from his open fly.

"I'm looking for Jacob Gorm," I said. He was close to me now. He smelled like the shore but stronger and with the added unmistakable odor of stale urine. He continued to stare.

"I understand he has a house for sale," I said. "Do you know where I can find him? Jacob Gorm?"

"I can't stay long," he said. "Bein's the old woman keeps falling down."

"Oh?" I said.

"It's not far. Have a car, have you?"

I turned toward the door. The brightness hurt my eyes. Sun on the water in warm layers. I turned back to him. It was getting more difficult to see.

"You're Jacob Gorm?" I asked.

"Once she falls," he said, "she has to stay till I fetch her up. Can't fetch herself up. No. She can't do that."

"That must be hard."

"I'm not so fine myself. Was it the old folks' house you was wantin' to see?"

"It's for sale?"

"We can take your car. I don't have no car. Never did." When I slid the seat back, he poured himself in like a hunk of gelatin. And there he sat planted, his two canes beneath clenched hands, his eyes on the road, breathing at the windshield from his open mouth and nose. As we drove toward the far end of Gorm Island, old houses in failing health, massive and noble memories of what probably never was, towered along the landscape. They stood in the tall grass, paint blistered, sore colors dripping down graying sides. Leprosy. The old folks' house was a high affair with turrets and fretwork, a hand-hewn gingerbread Gothic dream, bits and pieces of houses seen and remembered. His grandfather had built it. Seven boys they had. All dead now. His father one of the seven.

"I'm the last of the lot," he said.

I watched him struggling to climb the high step to the sloping lawn. I hesitated. He was breathing in rushes like an asthmatic dog. I moved past him onto the lawn and he reached for my hand even before I offered it. His wet, cold fingers locked on mine and I hauled him up.

The house was in despair. Its was a hair-tearing, deep insanity that throbbed against the sun. I was fighting to keep control again. I thought of a startled animal trapped in a sudden beam of light. Monster's mouth yawning wide . . . No . . . Della's stew, molasses cookies, Andrew caning chairs.

I heard Gorm heaving behind me, waddling along on his canes, poking through the tangle of bush, grass, pots, pans, chunks and bits of debris. I turned back to say I wasn't interested. A large swollen vein throbbed at the edge of his brow.

"This is the well," he said, kicking awkwardly at the rotten cover. Chunks of it separated. I heard them clump as they struck the water. Stench wafted up our nostrils.

"Animal," he said. "Wants to be dipped. Wentzel and Mervin." He looked around. "That." He pointed at a piece of cardboard. Beneath it in the square of dead grass tiny orange roachlike insects squirmed away. He wanted to cover the rotting hole with it. Shutting out. Shutting in.

"I'm really not interested," I said. I handed him the cardboard and then looked out to the clean, crisp fresh sea. The air above it laughed like a maiden's smile in a fairy tale.

"I'll show you inside," he said, thumbing through a tangle of keys.

"I don't think I'm interested."

But he was already fumbling with a huge rusted chain and padlock. Beyond that was a double lock on the door.

"Can't be long," he said. "She's hours once she falls."

"Don't close the door," I said. "Air it out, don't you think?"

He closed the door.

"The old people lived on this side," he said. "We lived there." He nodded toward a wall. "A lot of value in her still," he said, lifting an old scrub board. "Worth something, these days. Yes, value here yet."

The place was devastated. Not chewed by silence, not the ravages of disuse and detachment, but an active malice. I could smell the pettiness, the lack of concern. Plaster dust, oil, mud, muck, clump and clutter of every kind of waste; torn, spattered shades, crayon marks in insane dance along the walls. I felt it all washing around me like water swirling in a drain. There was nothing solid anywhere. I had to hold something, silence the eye. I squatted down and the sand and dirt moved in rasping slivers beneath my shoes. An old doll with no head. A branch. A stick carved into a spoon. Yes. Smooth to the touch. I closed my eyes.

"Eat. Eat," Della said. "There's plenty. You're not dieting, what?"

"No. I'm just not hungry. It's good. I'm full. All filled up."
Filled right to here. Filled all the way up.

"Upstairs," he mumbled, and I heard him struggling, breathing, heaving his way along the dark passage. Step. Heave. Step.
The old chimney was open. The dark hole leered where a stovepipe had been, a black, sooty eye hung with webs. The eye spoke. From it came the soft gurgle of a resting gull.

Deep breaths. Take deep breaths to the stomach. Breathe.
The muscles in the back of my neck seemed strung over jagged rock. I heard him collapse in a heap. I recalled his patched and tattered pants, the rope belt. This is the man all tattered and torn. I had to follow him upstairs. This is the priest all shaven and shorn. I couldn't move. No matter, I never had any doubt. I knew he was dead. It seemed as if hours passed.
Still I could not move. It had all stopped. It was no use. I sat there crosslegged, gnawing on the end of the spoon.

The day Dr. Launder and Dr. Daun showed up together, I was expecting a reprieve, a pat on the bum — good game! I'd promise to keep away from sheep and fixation, and they'd send me on my way. I knew enough about mind and body to believe I might very well have "defensed" and repressed myself into this pain. In fact I was convinced of it. So I was really caught off guard when they told me the last X-ray had found it.

"There's some thickening in the cortex of the bone," Dr. Launder said.

"What's that mean? Bone cancer?"

"It could be nothing at all," Dr. Daun said. "Or it could be an early infection. There's only that mild shift in your white cell count, but we'll watch that."

"We can't rule out anything at this point — even an early tumor," Dr. Launder added. "The hip is terribly difficult to diagnose."

"What if it is a tumor?"

"That depends on whether it's in the bone itself, if it's in the marrow or not. It would be premature to worry about that at this point, Harold," Dr. Launder said.

"And any one of these things could cause this pain!"

"That's what makes diagnosis such an imperfect science," Dr. Daun said.

"So what do we do?"

"Unfortunately, all we can do at this point is wait. We'll monitor it. In two or three months we should know for sure."

"I'm beginning to wonder if we ever know anything for sure."

"Some things. And those are the things we should act on," Dr. Daun said.

"Are you trying to tell me something?"

"I think maybe this whole business is trying to tell you something."

My head was storming. "What?" I asked.

"What do you think?" Dr. Launder said.

"I may or may not have cancer. I'm obsessive, an hysteric. I'm very unhappy, and I haven't even bothered to notice. I'd say I had some thinking to do."

"And some living," Dr. Daun said. "Why don't you get away for a while. Is there any place you want to go?"

"I've been thinking about Mexico."

"This time of year it starts getting unbearably hot there," Dr. Launder said.

"How about Canada?" Dr. Daun said. "Canada's beautiful in the spring. Or any time actually. I'm from Nova Scotia. One of the prettiest places on earth. A great place to rest and reflect."

When I could move again and hear and see, when I felt things pulsing all around, freed like dirt-clogged gears dipped in kerosene, I got to my feet. The sun was still coming through the front windows. Still Gorm Island. But what day? I forced myself up the stairs. Plaster powder, chunks and bits of wall, showed the squirm of cane marks and feet all the way to the top. My stomach quivered. Gigantic gull inside me now, a crazy frantic rush of wings. I didn't want to find his body. I backed down the stairs. Would they accuse me of murder?

The door was locked. I pulled at it. It was locked from the outside. I threw my shoulder against it and kicked.

"Don't panic," I said, "don't panic. Don't panic, Harry."

I crept cautiously toward the back of the house. Something moving there. I froze. I heard it again. The window. The shade raced up then fell on my head. I began to whimper. I didn't want to turn my back. I listened to myself as I fumbled with the paint-hardened lock. The animal sounds continued. Footsteps on the stairs. I couldn't turn around. This is the maiden all forlorn. This is. . . This is. . . That great massive body stinking of piss and shit smothering me, crushing me in fatty filth. I smashed at the window latch with my fist. The latch moved. I banged and pulled and pleaded, but the window was still jammed. I could hear them now, and her too, cackling, all of them there, all of them! And then it gave and I dove into the brown grass, scrambled, crawled, stumbled, running on my knees, almost on my feet when I saw them looming, him pointing his cane, their arms cradling rifles.

"Don't shoot," I stammered. "Don't shoot. Dondondon shsh." And I was flat on my face at their feet.

I paid Gorm for his trouble and for damages and I, "my kind," promised the hunters, local people, I wouldn't return. Then in a rush of controlled sanity, I drove back to the cabin and sat waiting in the car. On the seat next to me sat a copy of the *Weekly Breeze* neatly folded with houses for sale marked in pen. I may have sat there for hours. I never heard Andrew, never saw him until, almost in my ear, he said words I didn't understand, and I wrenched my neck toward the voice.

"Give you a start, did I?"

"I was . . . "

I was disembodied. This body I had not controlled. These thoughts were not my thoughts. These pleasures not my pleasures. My life a reaction to other lives. I was everyone's Harry Fleet and I dared not even dream in any world of my own. Dared not and died a catatonic's frozen death in the healthy body of a happy boy. Happy am I, from care am I free. Am I. Am I free. And happy. Happy. Happy.

"I was dozing," I said, rubbing the knot of muscles in my neck.

"Pull a muscle."

He placed a thickened hand on my neck and kneaded the locked flesh and everything began to diminish, soft sun over the edge leaving the light behind. Heal me. Please. I wanted to snuggle up to his shoulder, bring the green-and-black plaid of his shirt close and be protected in his warmth. I wanted to cry.

"Hurt a lot, does it?"

The tears streamed down my cheeks. "Yes," I said. "Yes." I leaned into the steering wheel.

"Are you fit, boy?" he asked.

"It's just the way I feel," I said into my folded arms. "It's just the way I feel."

Andrew stared and waited.

I was locked to that wheel. I heard the fall night drawing. The car had grown cool. I still couldn't turn to him. In the hospital that frightened old man sat weeping in a wheelchair. "Mother," he said. "Mother." And I and three nurses looked on.

"Are you well enough to spend the night alone?"

Am I well enough. The words scrambled in my mind.

"No shame in being ill," he said.

After he left, the air grew cooler and cooler. The windshield was all steamed. Through the open window near my head came night sounds in firm pieces. A voice deep at the center screamed. Harry! I squeezed my eyes tight and gritted my teeth. Harry! I bit the steering wheel. Harry! It was a silent scream sharply terrifying like a viper's strike and it was at the core of me. Harry! There was no other sound but that vacuum silence and the scream in alternating sway. My head was flooded, rushed, swarming. Harry!

Then I was in the woods. The moon. I had no idea where I stood. My feet oozed with water and muck, my hands, my face, my hair caked with cow dung, mud and decaying life. "Harry!" I shouted. "Harry!" I listened to my name out there beneath the moon charging through the timber and brush. "Harry!" I watched it spread in spirals and columns dancing cold and alone across the sky.

That night the cold woke me. Like damp hands clutching my socks. I shivered. My covers lay on the floor. "Be some weather yet," Andrew had said. I got up. The ice-like floors smacked my feet. I hurried to the kitchen and reached in the bag. The potato skins were dusty to the touch; dirt and wart and pitted eyes and tubes, tiny feelers pouring from their sides. I carried one back to bed. That night there was light snow.

Seven

Once there were oxen in this barn. Two teams. Their musky animal smell lingers surer than memory. Piss-sweet hay. Star and Bright. Left and right. They named oxen like that. Haw, Star. Haw, Bright. Two, two hundred, two hundred thousand Stars and Brights. Rough music. Heavy, wood-thumping dance.

But now as I stand quietly next to the wheelbarrow piled high with the torn outer skins and surface flesh of logs stripped for plank board, these remains brought from the mill to burn in our woodstove, this load ready for transporting to the kitchen woodbox, I am listening to a power saw *crawk*ing back in the woods. Summer. So all sound is a separate thing distinct and alive, and each alteration rends a seam in the neutrality. Is Carleton cutting? Pulpwood for the mill? Firewood? But he has propane — furnace and stove. And Carleton doesn't own a saw.

"Wouldn't have one," he said.

I nodded, imagining that old man a boy back in the brush with his father and brothers, oxen and wagon standing by as the forest accepted the fleshy, incisive sounds: the soft chawing of Swedish or two-man saw, the *thuck* of axes biting into pulpy wood. Carleton talked of then. They all did.

"No, I wouldn't have one," Carleton repeated. "Anyways,

wood's a waste of time today. Man hardly live on what the mills pay. No money into her. No, wouldn't own one. Jesus things cost more'n two hundred dollars!"

I listen to the motor revving free then dulling as it grabs the bark, slices through the trunk, then screams loudly again in the open air.

"Who do you suppose it is?" Joan asks.

I drop an armful of wood into the woodbox. "I don't know."

"Carleton?"

"He doesn't have a saw."

The wheelbarrow is outside the back door. The cat is on the screen. When I open the door to get another armful of wood from the wheelbarrow, she jumps away.

"Do you think he sold that land to someone?" Joan asks.

"I don't know."

"Can you see from the roof?"

"Not that way."

"Well," she says in a tone that indicates there is an answer if someone really wants to find it.

I park the wheelbarrow by the barn and begin walking back through the woods. I wonder if it's Tom. I haven't seen him on the beach lately. Maybe he's given up on waterfront land and is moving inland. Spiritually, metaphorically, what would that mean? I laugh. One thing for sure, it would mean abandoning his tow-truck.

The dogs crash recklessly through the brush, ensuring that I won't see anything move, won't hear anything except their rushing and that distant sputtering roar. Everything else is frozen, waiting and watching.

I near Council Grove. It is not really a grove but a cleared section of charred logs and stumps where saplings sprout like twisted fingers from the brown-black undergrowth of rotting wood, twigs and leaves. At the periphery of this blackened spot, large wood, alive and green, forms arches beneath the clouds and sky. It was here I last pleaded with my family. Council in Rotting Grove: a short history of the family.

When I first saw them in the darkness I mistook them for bats in flight, for they seemed quick and unfocused, more felt than formed. Then a jerk in my gut like wringing a sock, and everything softened, settling more clearly to sight. Mother. Father. Sister. Brother. All of them neatly arranged and staged from stump to log to stump. Family. Ghostly crew. The wings were behind my eyes now, nothing moving out there.

I rose to one knee. "Mother," I said. "Mom."

"When he was young," she said, "he sat alone beneath the steps. I suppose it was cool there. His shirt was clean. I took it from the line smelling sweet from the sun. But his pants were stained with bicycle grease and oil. That wasn't my fault."

"I was tearing strips of rubber from my sneakers," I pleaded. "We must weep for that child sitting there in the cool shadows tearing strips of rubber from his sneakers. We all left him sitting there. He's still sitting there as that shadow stretches wide toward a gulp. He's there just sitting. I was just sitting there, Mom!"

"I told him," Father said. "I told him about dirt. I told him about colds. But no, he wouldn't listen. A smarty pants. You all know that. He was the little smarty pants. He never listened. Always sitting. Always sulking. He just wasn't like us somehow. But we loved him."

"See the undersides of the steps stained with web thick as smudge; torn, slivered wood, dirty yellow-brown-blackened underbelly trampled times; pockets of dirt in cracks, cement prisons of moist soil. Can't you see! Don't you know that's where children grow," I said. "I know."

"In the dark," Sister whined. "Is *that* supposed to have some secret meaning? Anyway, you were *scared* of the dark. Anyone would think you were a *sissy*."

"I went into the cellar. You know, that ledge behind the furnace in the corner. Dirt and ash and . . . and . . . "

"And *what*?" Sister mocked.

"I don't know."

"You're no worse off for not knowing," Brother said. "Imagine if you knew and still couldn't remember. Imagine that!"

Mother looked up.

"It just doesn't seem that big a thing to me," she said.

"Yes, he always made everything sound like it was such a big thing," Father said, "and we don't think it's a big thing. No one else thinks it's such a big thing."

"Nothing is a big thing," I said. "That's not the point. He was sitting alone under the steps. A child is alone under the steps. Don't you see?"

"See what? What *is* it, dear?" Mother said, and she slipped back. I felt her soft flesh spreading against the lip of the high stump. "What's bothering you, sweetheart? Why are you always under these steps?"

I rested the tips of my fingers beneath my belt on stiff curls of pubic hair.

"Everything is always bad," Sister said. "Why do you look on the dark side of things? Are we all *monsters*? Why can't you be happy like everyone else?"

I kept my eyes on the cement. Millions of bubbles and pits tough like a man's beard. I heard footsteps on the stairs.

"The laces on his sneakers are stained with Coke, ice cream, rain water and mud. Look! Look! The black sides are stiff, rough canvas. Where the round rubber patches are removed, see? The neat clean circles, one on each side. The plastic tips of the laces are gone. See how he uses the last bit of it to dig pieces of orange from his teeth. See. See. See."

"Don't ask me," Father said. "There's nothing I can do."

"Some people are just like that," Sister said. "You have to realize. You read a lot about that now. It's not our fault."

"It's not even his fault," Brother said.

"It's not anyone's fault," Mother said. "We did our very best."

"So that's that," Father said.

"But I still don't see why he won't move," Mother said, leaning over and staring at me, her fists tight with concern, knuckles white against the fear. "Why does he just sit?"

"When it grows dark," I said, "the lights come on and the radios squawk and stutter and hum in fits of electrical despair . . . "

"It isn't like he thinks," Brother said. "Not like he tells it at all. I was there. I know it isn't like that. We all know it isn't like that. Family."

"That's right, son," Father said effortlessly. "He's got it all confused."

"Well," Mother said.

"Well," Sister said, "not confused exactly, just wrong."

"That's it," Father said. "Like him. Like *he* is. Not right, not quite correct."

And inside all the smiles, the acknowledgment and laughter.

"If only he'd move," Mother said. "If only he'd sit somewhere else."

"The steps keep him dry," Brother said, chortling. "He knows enough to come in from the rain."

"Yeh, it doesn't rain on him," Father laughed.

"He'll never drown, anyway," Sister sniggered.

Mother laughed with a closed, tight face, little notes trickled from her nose.

I picked up a large branch and smashed the stumps and logs, the trees; I whipped and dashed the emptiness, the eternal black void until, helpless, hopeless, I collapsed.

The saw stops. I imagine a man in heavy boots stooping to a gas can. Now there is only the crashing, snapping rush of dogs to hear.

That first Council Grove day everything was alive. My boots, soggy with mud, squished. Bird calls thundered. All things screamed. Animistic fury all around me. I struggled and stumbled, hunched like an ape. My clothes torn, my head ringing.

I heard Andrew's dogs first. They were on my trail. All night I had plunged ahead, winding my way through the last bowel. Sun-fresh morning mist of sky, steaming leaves, brush brown and black to darkening greens. I lay there twisted raw with pain, weary of looking at all their faces watching, waiting; but I couldn't go on, couldn't climb anymore, so I just lay there wrapped in the crumpled gauze of then, blood lumping like hemp through my veins.

The hounds licked my hands and face. Time-honored tongues. I closed my eyes to notions of myself. I locked away tears. Andrew had a shotgun cradled over one arm. He looked warm and big-breakfast fresh. Accurate in his boots, tam and pipe. Happy wool colors from head to toe. As he stepped into the open he registered surprise. We both knew he didn't hunt anymore.

"Well," he said. "You're out early."

I stared. He leaned the rifle carefully against a tree, then sat near me on a stump.

"We call this Council Grove," he said. "Indians had a name for it I don't just recall. Forbidden somethin'. Micmacs. They were all through the valley and along the river. They did something hereabouts. Though what no one knows. Not likely we'll find out either." He smiled.

We sat petting the dogs.

"The Micmacs dead?" I asked.

He puffed at his pipe.

"Around here? I guess. I haven't seen one, if that's what you mean." And where he would normally have chuckled, now he drew his jaw back and wrinkled his brow. "We're all gonna die, what?" he said.

"Council Grove," I said. "Indians."

"You ask Mildred Patch and she'll tell you about the Indians. Tall, half naked. Singing and playing flutes. She sees'm."

"Mildred?"

"Mildred Patch. Mildred and Morris Patch. You haven't heard tell of them?"

I recovered odds and ends of comments.

Don't smell so good, you know what I mean. Different ones say she's not just right, you know what I mean. Ain't any of them Patches too swift, you know what I mean.

I shook my head. "Not really."

"The Indians give her powers." He snorted smoke from his nose as he laughed. "Love potions and the like. So you want to watch out she don't catch you up here alone. No, really she means no harm. But some say she's a witch. And then some says she's just not right in the head. Yes," he said, "different ones see her different ways. You know your way back?"

I stared at my feet. "I can find it," I said.

"It's not far. If you follow the logging road. Right past those alders there?"

I had vague thoughts of the twisted miles, the circles, loops and arcs, the broken edges of my travel.

"She'll bring you out by the swamp."

"Okay."

He stood and the dogs began to whimper and cry at his feet. Halfway across the clearing he stopped and turned to me. "Oh," he said. "You might wear this." Walking back toward me, he unfolded a brilliant orange hunting vest he'd taken from his pocket.

"You know how it goes?"

I stared at it. A flag of concern. His concern. For me.

"It just snaps along here."

I felt tears in my eyes. I tried to stop my Adam's apple from vaulting in my throat.

"It's okay, boy. It's okay."
I couldn't move. The vest sat crumpled, a silent scream in my lap.

"I'm Burr," he says. It startles me. The dogs sniff at his feet. The saw hangs from one powerful arm. His green jersey is black with patches of sweat. I have never seen him before.
"I'm Harry," I say, my voice a pale echo of his. I recall Andrew saying, "If Burr comes, let him be. He never hurt anyone but he's odd, so you better let him be. He only wants to help, but. . . " and he stared at his boots.
Burr nods and kicks softly at the dogs. I call them away. Behind him stretches a snarled sea of felled wood, fir, pine. He is thinning out. It will revitalize the land. Carleton's land. He starts the saw and goes back to work. I watch. He is squat and large-muscled. A soft wool seaman's cap is shaped to his head. His eyes are dark like coals, dark like his hair, striking. I wonder if such energy is a burden, if there is a place it might soften and slacken pace, or does it just one day pop, go from this state to that.
"He comes," Andrew said, "without warning. You might not see him for months, no one will, and then he's peerin' in the door with an idea for you. He's a mind to firm up your barn, or make some hay. Or maybe he wants to dig you a well. He slaughters cattle. Smokes fish. Dips out cesspools. Mends fence or nets, makes lobster traps. He built a workshop for Rinehardt. All for nothing."
"And he just pops up all of a sudden," I said.
"Yes. Like a holiday at haytime." When Andrew laughs it is never mocking. It is shared humor, sense of himself in everyone and everything.
"And if you don't want him to help?" I asked.
"I don't know a man doesn't need some help now and then."

Eight

S he's an original, all right,"
Joan says.

She has just met Mildred Patch. Mildred was hitchhiking to the valley to see the vegetable farms when we happened by. We gave her a ride to the 103.

"I can't decide which she overwhelms more, the ears or the nose," Joan says.

I don't answer or smile.

"Come on," she says, touching my arm, "I think she's marvelous too, but she does stink."

"Just a bit of extra-old cheese here and there," I say, laughing.

It gets us both silly for minutes. Finally Joan, wiping tears from her eyes, says, "Oh God. She's worth every minute of it. Every minute. Why didn't you ever tell me about her?"

I shrug.

"When did you meet her?"

Winter skies tore in great stretches, canvas of gray-blue whites behind trembling wind, cloud, grass and sea. I walked along out of the near pasture and through the faintly wooded ridge. A crush of alder and birch-hard plants, flower-stiff and naked above the half-frozen ground. January thaw. Mate to Indian summer. High low and low high. I had my watercolors with me and a small canvas stool, *Lester Pheeps* in awkward black letters thick as fingers tilting in and out along its fabric. I found a spot on the hill from which distant bellies of island ran green-black against the sea. Edges. Thick difference. Clouds white as May. Shades of stark in spring-winter light. The paper puckered with fleshy knobs. Not what age does to the skin, sucking it from within, leaving pinched pits, tiny cavities and hollows the cold settles into. The brush made its choice. There. Here. Me sitting between two realities monitoring and directing, but what comes is what's already been. Maybe that is why as the pain in my hip diminished and finally disappeared altogether, these bouts of intense melancholia and vertigo, these sudden rushes of protracted nothingness, became more frequent.

The clouds, the sky, the earth disappeared. It was taking me. I stood and stretched and talked loudly, saying things like "What a day" and "Look at that tree" and "Here I am on the hill," then I grabbed up my things and began walking along the far side of the pasture, a roundabout looping route that would eventually lead me home. I chose that way because of the few houses I would pass. A solid winter of isolation sitting inside the cold, falling inside the cold, contemplating the ice-thick reality smothering the windows, layer upon layer of cold life pressing me further and further in, me resisting, holding a candle against that frozen white life. Now, when I sensed the pit, I changed course, navigated out and away.

"Was she hitchhiking when you met her?"
"No."

When I passed the Patches' I noticed Mildred hanging clothes from the weather-worn rope that droops from the broken porch to the corner of the barn. When she saw me, she began cranking her arm, twirling it not at all like an appendage, but rather like a sword or a broom, something detached. I wondered if she needed help. I stopped and pointed at myself, and she went on waving and started nodding her head up and down and bending from the waist. I started off the road and rushed the fifty or so yards over scattered lumber, old tires, scrap iron from cars and stoves, rotting stumps, puddles, all shape and form of mechanical and natural debris.

"Hi, stranger," she said. She was a wall of woman. Massive but totally feminine. Beneath her ragged sweater, running over at the edges with flesh, more flesh, and fat arms, and below them a butt like a tabletop large enough to balance a water can; a huge person fed by vast appetites and desires that couldn't be hers alone. I smiled at her and the words began escaping from her in rushes like steam from a valve.

"You must be Mr. Fleet. Mr. Harry Fleet what's taken Lester's place."

"Yes, I am."

"I know. I don't get out much anymore," she said, "but I know something what's going on. The dogs chase you, do they?"

"No," I said. "This is — "

"They chase me somethin' awful, and I'm not a well person," she said. "I'm so fat like a house, not at all like what I was before I moved here when I was a Miller, that was before I married Morris, you know. Bet you didn't hear tell that I was a Miller, eh? No, they wouldn't tell you *that*."

"No, I didn't know," I said.

"Oh yes. I was John Miller's daughter! I was something before I married. I sang and danced. All the men was to looking at me so's you'd think I was a movie star or some such, and maybe I was except for not having no chance to be, seeing as I was used as I was when I was young, and who'd look at me now I wouldn't know, 'less of course someone happens by what's in need of a good bearer, cause I know fifty isn't too old. No. My Lord, why some native women where missionaries been, say sixty and seventy years old, have children every day and just go right on mentrating till they die, and so you never know, do you? But I'm not well 'cause as I say I've been used badly for what I am, a Miller and all, but then I was something to see. Oh yes, I was somethin' *then*, for sure."

Beatific expression, distant. I would see that look again. Wilderness queen. Mammoth mother, dancing, the top of her dress drawn down revealing her head-thick breasts, soft as cheese, blue veins running; unsuckled breasts, bursting yet with life, blood-warm breasts beneath the soft shine, dancing.

"She wasn't hitchhiking?"

"No."

Joan's expression is the one she wears when she feels left out. I can imagine her a child wearing that same long face but framed in pigtails. "Beneath all that talk there's something tormenting her, isn't there? Do you feel guilty about laughing at her? Is that why you got so quiet?"

"One day I saw Mildred in the thick brush," I tell her. "She had branches and leaves all over her naked body. Leaves hanging off her, dripping everywhere, hundreds of bits of greenery. Her face was radiant with a happy fear; everything else around seemed frozen. To me it was like watching someone else's dream. I could feel the sunbeams in the branches, feel my breath moving through the sparsity of space. My eyes were drawn to the inner-tube immensity of her bare breasts; their brown badges of areola waiting there in silent psalm. She couldn't see me. She touched the leaves and branches as if they were more than familiar things, and she smiled.

"'Natooma,' she said, and she spread her arms wide and turned and the shake of branches whisked across her body in raspy accompaniment. 'Natooma. Natooma.' I can remember the bones of her broad shoulders poking like wings from her back, and I can still see her flesh in uneven layers like pancakes stacked from the waist. 'Natooma.' She said it over and over, and she implored the skies, or the sun, or the trees, the space above, the ground below. 'Na . . . tooom . . . a . . . Na . . . toooo . . . ma. Na . . . tooom . . . a. Na . . . tooooooooooma.'

"And she held her arms over her head and shuffled from one foot to the other in an awkward private dance. Then, finally, her eyes closed and she fell into a heavy squat; her blubbery breasts, only a moment ago rolling, flopping and heaving, disappeared altogether behind her knees. Flesh pyramids. Maternal sphinx."

Joan sits quietly, her eyes open, her mouth tight and almost motionless except for that pulse, the one an artist can carve into the hardness of even stone or bone.

"Of course," I say, "she's just as you see her, too."

There we sat in one room. Tables, boxes, the floor all platforms for soft tons of household goods sprawled, squeezed, shoved, pressed and stacked from wall to wall. The chair from which I stared was wrapped in rags. Everything it seems was wrapped in or hanging rags. The fired-up woodstove crackled, adding even more heat to what was always a hot room. She may have been boiling some towels she found on the beach. It's hard to tell. In any case the room smelled of ammonia and she stirred and poked about in the coal-black, steaming calabash. Her stirring stick was a skinned green branch. Sweat tumbled from her face. Her eyes shone through the perspiration. Beneath her arms, huge half-moon gray smears of sweat. Mainly the smell was not of ammonia, it was of her. The smell of her large closeness, doored-in life oozing from her, demanding at least essential form. She talked for an hour. Hours. Without pause. She lassoed me with words, and I didn't struggle against them because she knew no knots — neither of us did — and when I really wanted to, or had to, I could slip away.

"Forgotten Seasons," Mildred said. "Got its name from an old magic man, Micmac Indian medicine man named Two

Tongue on accounta he spoke Micmac and he spoke God-talk
is what I call it, but Two Tongue he never gave it no name and
no one else but him and me ever talked the talk as we was so
close you could not believe. Why, from the very first the man
laid eyes on me he fell in love with my fatal beauty and could
not keep his hands off my charms, if you know what I mean.
We was so strongly attracted that we had no choice 'cept to
marry right away as I'm so fer-tile and we expected the babies
would be flowin' like the seed.

"Well, I invited Morris so it wouldn't be just me and the
band, but Morris was some upset. Right angry he was and so
he said to me, 'Now why do ya have t'be goin' and screwin'
Indians now?' I told him there was no need for upset and
animal jealousy, but he's a stubborn one is Morris, so he never
came and I had to be the only one from the white side all on
my own. I think Morris was most concerned about having
children around again is all because they need things and cost
money and such, but that was no problem cause Two Tongue
said all along that he would take the children of our union to
a better place and not leave them in a place where need and
hurtin' blackness filled the soul to overflowin'.

"So anyhow me and Two Tongue bedded in the pines where
he made me a safe nest in which I brought forth our children
one by one. Like miracles they was, each one with diamond-
blue eyes and souls so golden they shone right through their
little leather vests. And Two Tongue was right pleased with
me, boys! He was gay as could be and named them all after
his love goddess. There was Mildred's First Flower, Mildred's
Fishbunny, Mildred's Laughter in the Trees, Mildred's Bark
of the Sow, Mildred's Shadowmagic, and Mildred's Nebula —
who you met and you can tell the real live Indian in her and she
ain't no kin to Morris that's sure. Am I forgettin' any? Snow-
light? No. She ran down my leg one bitter March day.

"Anyway, comes a day when we've been breedin' like we
do and Two Tongue is slippin' back into his leathers when of

a sudden I'm reminded that I don't know how this place we live in got its real name which is not Beach Gate at all but Forgotten Seasons, and so I say, 'Two Tongue, how is it this place came to be called Bay of Forgotten Seasons?' Well, didn't Two Tongue look at me with them coal-black eyes a his and say that in this life are many hard ways, many sharp twists and turns so sometimes the spirit saddens and tears so deep all the good runs out in a gush like water from a stone? And he tells me too that other times the spirit's made heavy with fear and sags to the earth like a bag heavy with bear fat and it can't barely move. That's when the twin demons of Death and Despair decide what evil it is they might play on the already hurtin' because the already hurtin' is ripe for pain like open sores in a hot rain.

"So one day, according to Two Tongue, Natooma and her man Tokeminni was mournin' the loss of their first son Jacumseh, who was strangled while still in Natooma's womb, killed most likely by them same twin demons, but what's to be done about it? So Tokeminni piles high the funeral brush, high as he can reach, even higher by throwin' pieces on top. But when he went to get little Jacumseh's body to toss it on the flames weren't it gone and in its place a handful of red berries made into one a them smiling faces? Well t'hear Two Tongue tell it, that Tokeminni was some black. He was so black that even Natooma her very self was afeared. She suspicioned he might kill even herself in blind rage not bein' responsible and all as he wasn't. Anyway, Natooma got him calmed enough because she is of a loving heart and like that there. She's not one to see fault in even such evil suckers as Death and Despair, because she was adopted and used badly when she was young and knows better than to blame.

"That night they sat and smoked the pipe and thought. And thought. And thought some more. Nothin' came. The next morning as the ravens dig through the ashes expectin' bits of blackened flesh and bone but comin' with nothin' more than peckers full of ash, Tokeminni says he will trade himself for the return of his son, cause his spirit is further advanced in the next world than Jacumseh's. Well, Natooma ain't sayin' much, she's just sort of munchin' some mushrooms and actin' dreamy. Finally she looks at Tokeminni and says nothin' doin' 'cause she don't want to be left with maybe a handful of berries and a memory. That's when she tells *her* plan. Tokeminni listened and finally agreed, but not because he loved it but because he didn't know what all else to do.

"That night when the moon was right Natooma went to Council Grove to meet with Death and Despair. They were some surprised to see her, her bein' a woman and all. What they was expectin' was to see Tokeminni all rigged in his war gear painted to howl and make demands. So they was taken aback to see Natooma, and disappointed too, 'cause they enjoy havin' human mortals on. 'What's this,' they said, 'a woman!' Well, that were plain enough t'see, for she didn't have not a stitch a clothes on her anywhere and bein' as she were just pregnant she had breasts full t'burstin' with milk which was trailin' all down her everywhere for the memory of her dead son was right central of her mind.

"'Let's make a deal,' she said. Well, they laughed their knickers off at that one, but Natooma paid them no mind. 'Come on,' she coaxed, 'tell me. What is your greatest grief with people; what makes you maddest at them?' Didn't that shock the royal shit right outta them, for no one had ever asked *them* what *their* problem was before. Well, boys, without hardly a thought Death said, 'Earth-People can't see the forest for the trees. Why, some Earth-People'd whine like stuck pigs everytime I'd come around. They give me a bad name. And for what? God's truth in the beginnin' I weren't no twin, but all the belly-achin' and snivelin' made me grow so fierce at the lack of manners I was seein' that I grew this here twin named Despair. I was content just workin' the Gate passin' Earth-People out and in, but I took so much abuse from

Earth-People that Despair became part a my name.'

"'Okay,' Natooma said. 'I get your point. And I can help. If you return our son Jacumseh to his father in the Earth Plane, I will join the Spirit World not in Jacumseh's place, but it must be in the place of Despair. I will feed the milk of love and light to each newborn. Instead of Despair people will be free to choose Natooma. Death will again be a friend and not a foe.'

"Well, Natooma was screwed down tight all right, 'cause she also said, 'One last thing I want you to promise is that when three times three seasons is up, my absence from Tokeminni and Jacumseh will be forgotten and all will be as it should be again.'

"So Death and Despair got to waggin' a bit and then they said it were a deal 'cause they was tired of silly pranks and childishness and what all; and Despair says that bein' as he was mostly just a figment he'd much prefer to return to the All of Things anyway.

"So for three times three seasons Natooma shared her breast with each child born of woman and in that time no child was afeared of Death. Despair lingered a bit with the older folks but soon he disappeared altogether. When her time was past Natooma returned to Tokeminni and Jacumseh and it was as she wished it to be 'cause no one knew she was gone, and so they had a nice life of love and light right here in Council Grove.

"And Bay of Forgotten Seasons is what Two Tongue, Natooma's great-great-grandson, called this place, because it was in those seasons of Natooma's devotion that loneliness, fear and despair were forgotten, never to be again on the Earth Plane. NATOOMA!"

"I'm glad I saw her," Joan says. "She'd be hard to imagine. What's the key?"

"What?"

"To her. . . to her being like she is?"

"Guilt. Fear. Fear, more likely. That's what guilt's about, isn't it?"

"What did she do?"

"If she knows, she's not saying. At least not directly."

"What do you think she did?"

"Done 'sexual' with her brother."

"God," she says, and she looks out the window, for there is a window near to look from. Around here there always is.

I walked by Mildred's often that first lonely spring. I thought a lot about her and that mad cascade of symbol and torment that streamed from her mouth.

The second time I saw her was another wintry spring day. I had made my way over the hill not even pausing to contemplate the postcard beauty that stretched around me on all sides. I hastened along listening to the sherbet crunch of my steps in the half-frozen grass, oblivious until I reached the road that began or ended just above Tobin farm.

Fortunately, I saw the dogs before they saw me. They were hanging about by Tobin's small house and barn. One of them, drawing from that endless reserve of dog piss, splashed the pole that held the TOBIN FARM sign, a piece of polished pine carefully lettered in Old English script; then, noticing me, he signaled the others and the pack lit out in a howling din, paws tearing at the softening ground.

"A pack of dogs will chase deer," Andrew said. "Run'm down when things are froze up. Deer can't get hold when things is all ice. And when they slip, they're goners. Pack of dogs then's a killer. Nice gentle pets until they get together. Then there's somethin wild in them."

I flourished my pole, a solid branch of ash, swung it about and growled back in my throat, turning, darting at them as they stood about snarling. Their heads hung, tails stiffened. But they moved heavily about as if still watching for an opening.

"Brain them," Mildred shouted. "Hit'm."

She had on a coat of scrap materials, mixed areas of flannel and wool, and thin rubber boots, "shorties" she called them, from each of which climbed a crush of bleached white sock. The dogs left me and ran after her. I followed. The poor ark of a woman stamped and whirled about, squatted for a rock and tossed it awkwardly. One had her coat, another her ankle. She went down in a clump.

"Foul bitches!" she shouted. "Shits! Mangy rat-fuck bastards!"

I closed in on them with a scream and they scattered.

"Hi, stranger," Mildred said, smiling up broadly.

"Are you okay? I thought you'd given up walking," I said, helping her up. "It's not safe for you."

"It's those dogs is all. Get!" she screamed, stamping after them with one foot. "Get, get, ratshitskunkholes."

They watched from a distance. She held my arm and stooped to rub her ankle. "No damage," she said. "But they know what's good, what?"

I enjoyed her laugh. Like her smile and her humor, it was not mere release, it was something deep and natural that managed to shoot through to the surface, a constantly falling star. Falling. But that depends too on where you stand, doesn't it? I brushed some mud and wet from the back of her coat.

A woman was in the window now. Mildred waved to her. "That's Elsa Tobin. You know her? Course you'd know her, you got Lester's house, eh? Now ain't that somethin' about Lester. I knew Lester real well. Me and Lester was close, if ya get my meanin'." She winked mischievously. "Water is treachery," she said, "harsh destruction."

Soon we were in that cluttered room again. This time Morris was there, wrapped in a blanket, eyes and nose red above his long underwear, uneven heat shimmering in abstract patches across the room.

"Morris's sick," she said. "Too much a that evil rum," she

laughed. "Oh, he's a sneaky one, that one. Ain't ya, Morris."
I thought he tried to smile.

It was then I saw her. Across the room on a newly placed cot
sat a young woman, her hair thick and dark, a tangle of waves
and curls forming a nest for her face and eyes all darkly intense
above the patched white sheet and quilt. She seemed so out of
place here. I felt my ears and forehead rise. Was this. . . ?

"My daughter," Mildred said. "Nebula."

Nebula stared.

"She's an actress. She's been on TV. And she's a dancer. She
sings when she's a mind. I could always sing, too." She smiled
and glanced over at Morris. "Morris likes me to sing while I
hold his head in my lap. I be singin' sweet as a bird and he be
snoring. Won't you, Morris, you old scag-a-bag, you."

Morris grumbled something.

"But Nebula's more with the body," Mildred said. "She's
more what I used to be than what I am now. Ain't ya, ya little
cock-teaser."

Nebula watched quietly. I don't think her eyes left my face.
I felt them there. Prickles. Shavings at the magnet.

"I really should go," I said.

"Don't mind her," Mildred said. "She'll stay for a day or
two and then she'll leave and go off and find some yahoo or
Indian and shack up and get abused and half killed and
pregnant and crazy and then one day come a taxi in the drive
and in she'll walk like home from school, little Miss Uppity
Shits her Royal Self."

"Fuck you," Nebula said, leaping up. The old gown she
wore hooked on something and stuck for an instant above her
waist, revealing a rich, black bush of pubic hair and finely
shaped legs, impeccably taut flesh. No doubt she was a
dancer.

Morris stared angrily. Mildred smiled at me. Nebula
scraped through her purse.

"She wants a cigarette," Mildred said. "She can't do without one a her cigarettes. Now me, I never did smoke. That's one thing. I never took to the taste. I always found it leaves a mouth like mouse shit."

Nebula lit up, then climbed back into the cot, drawing her legs up under her in a sort of lotus position.

"See," Mildred said angrily, "I get some decent company and look what you do. If you were born Catholic instead of Church of England, you'd see. You wouldn't be so evil going and gettin' abused and done dirty, chasin' after destruction. No. You'd be a pride to me and poor Morris what can't hardly walk from being wet from cold."

Nebula looked at me. "Who are you?" she asked.

The voice sounded strange there in the chaos and debris. It was a husky but soft sound. Musky. Yes, hers was a musky, dusky, mosslike carpet of sound. Nebula. Shade spots in the forest and cream thick on top of milk.

"Harry Fleet," I said. "I bought Lester Pheeps' house."

"Lester's dead, then."

"Yes."

"Kill himself, did he?"

Mildred grinned.

I stared.

"No matter," she said.

"May have fallen overboard," Morris said. "May have slipped or fell and couldn't get back. Yes. May have been an accident."

"He was nice," Nebula said.

"You didn't know Lester," Mildred said menacingly. Her face was red. She turned to me. "Don't you believe a word she says, you understand?"

I stared through the wretchedness at Nebula's calm face.

"You didn't know him, you little liar," Mildred said, taking a step toward Nebula.

Nebula blew smoke at her mother.

Morris stared at the wall. "He could have tripped," he said.

"Motor was runnin'. Happens sometimes. Yes. Happens."

"Bullshit," Nebula said.

Mildred smiled again. "Now she'll go and be right brazen and tell some stories. Don't you listen to a word, Mr. Fleet. Everyone around these parts knows she's a liar. Little Nebula Nonsense. Miss Uppity Slut Her Royal High Ass."

"Stories," Nebula scoffed.

Morris, his head now deep in the pillow, went on muttering. "He wasn't well, you know. No, not well at all. No, Lester was a sick man. Yes. Lester was sick. Sick."

After I left, I passed Timothy Tobin standing in the early spring cold with a rag and a can of some waxy substance. He was polishing the TOBIN FARM sign. It was almost dark. The dogs were gone. His face was slack. Piles of gray skin and whisker peeked from beneath a soft cowboy hat, the first one I'd seen around here. Spindle legs. He stopped polishing and nodded at me. His winter coat seemed sizes too big for him. I decided it was one of Lester's.

"Jesus hot," he said.

"Well," I said, turning my head to one side. "It is warmer than it was."

"When she's fierce like she is today, he does the lighter chores." He kept polishing, his eyes averted. "Was you back on the hill?"

"Yes."

"Hot there too, is it?"

"About the same."

"He don't go back there day like this."

"Timothy Tobin, supper," Elsa's voice from behind a flutter of curtains. "Mr. Fleet, tell him it'll be right cold if he don't come soon."

"Weather ain't good or bad," Timothy said. "Just weather. But you know that, eh?" He winked, then headed for the house.

Nine

Deep in bathtub sloth, my hairy legs sticking past the faucets, I gaze absently at the steam rising. I can go anywhere, but I am still dogged by honesty. It leaves a ring around the tub.

I slip down farther and the life slips from my nose, rippling the water like spring winds. When I pull the plug to enjoy the obscene gurgle of the drain's first slurping gulp of dirty water, I look up at my toenails. Soft armor.

Next to the warm stovepipe, I rub briskly to ward off the night chill that licks about the bathroom.

Are those footsteps on the stairs?

Morris sat like a zombie. Ramrod back, gray pits for eyes, his tongue moistening the few words he'd say.

I helped him back to the house, held his muddy arm still wet from the fall he took chasing Nebula down the road. Everything he might say was in suspension. It was as yet too overwhelming. Nothing was physically more pitiful than Morris standing naked in his boots, his once hard body ever-softening, covered with liver spots, tiny dips where muscle was losing its tone, retreating from the pressure, yielding like the fatty underbelly of a fish poked by fingers, and with nothing really to say.

"She'll be back," he said. "Girl like that wants a father. She'll be back."

He gripped the warm cup I gave him tightly in his hands. Hot tea with rum and honey. His penis stood like a flagpole, pulsing farm cock two fists tall.

"Mildred don't like her," he said. "No. Mildred thinks she's too pretty. Too young." He looked into my face. "No, Mildred don't like her."

I saw Nebula gesturing in the window behind him. I couldn't understand. Her hair was black against her face, her coat tight about her naked body. I heard Mildred calling from upstairs, enticing grandma fox beneath the covers, her smother fat oozing over the vast white of my bed.

"Mr. Fleet. Mr. Fleet, dear."

"Mildred wants manners," he said. "Yes. Mildred wants manners."

He sipped at the rum, then held the warm cup on his corrugated, cardboard-colored balls.

Nebula pressed her face against the steaming window and flicked her tongue about her lips.

"Mr. Fleet, love. Mr. Fleet."

She was on the stairs, swelling soft elephant flanks dripping from above.

Morris wrapped his long fingers into a fist and pulled absently at himself. "Should be home," he said. "Should be home for a young girl. Should be. Yes. Should. You bet. Should after all."

Mildred peeked in and laughed. A hundred of her hundred seventy-five pounds was loosely stacked about her ass, thighs and breasts. Thick central zone.

"Encore," she said. "Encore." And then she saw Nebula, and Nebula saw her. Eyes meeting at the glass.

"Pig!" Mildred shouted. "Slutty pig shit fuck woman."

Morris shot out onto his knees and almost immediately his prick sagged and disappeared into his fingers, noises like breathing coming from his hanging mouth.

Nebula's face was still pressed to the glass, her nose mashed to a snout, her lips in a pucker.

Mildred took my hand and smiled her warm-honeysuckle-and-sun smile. Polka-dot-and-pudding face. She pulled me toward the door and led me up the stairs. I followed the roll of her body. Oh, great whale wash of flesh, monstrous earth mother, sound and smell of female lands.

She unbuckled my belt, her flesh and breath overrunning me, sucking me passively into the shapeless vortex of an ancient lust, stripping away everything, lifting me, placing me like a baby on the bed, and behind her Morris and Nebula holding hands and watching and everything, everywhere, going round inside out, ouside in, hovering, absorbing, smothering flesh of my flesh over my, in my, flesh saying Natooma, saying Natooma, say Natooma, Natooma, right now, right away.

"Harry," Joan calls. "Harry, where are you?"

I stand in the garden. Taller than the tallest hoe. My back is stiff.

"There you are," she says. She is barefoot. One of my shirts drapes her body. She throws her arms open wide and up. "What a gorgeous day." She is naked beneath the shirt. There is something in her hand.

"What's this?" she asks, holding Andrew's dead rose toward me.

"I bought it for Andrew."

"When he was in hospital?"

"Yes."

"Well. . . why didn't you give it to him?"

"I don't recall."

"It's been in that jacket all this time!" She holds it gingerly between thumb and forefinger, wrinkling her nose. "Well," she says and drops it in the grass. "He sure won't want it now."

"No."

"A yellow rose?"

"Yes."

She starts back toward the house, then stops. Away across the wood atop the open hills she hears the steady sound of a tractor.

"Hay already?" she asks.

"Yes."

She nods her head. "You can tell," she says. "You get to know." And she hurries back to the house.

Nebula walked out of the fog lugging a bright red suitcase, something tucked beneath one arm. The dogs obviously knew her. They stopped barking almost as soon as they started and greeted her with tails wagging. She was wearing sandals that slapped at her heels, a white ski jacket and a becoming but incongruous short black dress.

"Nebula," I said.

I took the suitcase and her free hand went immediately to her head where she moved the soft, black springs away from her face. The thing under her arm was a duck.

"I found it on the trail," she said. "It's yours."

"They all look the same to me," I said. "I don't know if it belongs here or not."

She set it down and it winged a couple of steps, then stopped.

"I need a ride."

I looked over at the car. I pictured the gauge just above empty. "Okay," I said.

"How about tea first." She poked at the corner of one eye. "That's a long walk with a suitcase and a drake."

The back of her legs and her skirt were spattered with mud. Her feet were red from the cold. Patches of snow still soiled the ground.

I opened the door and she stepped in.

"I always make two promises when I leave here," she said. "One, I won't come back. Two, if I do it'll be in the summer. So much for promises."

I set her suitcase near the woodbox. She sat and began to unbuckle her sandals. I couldn't resist glancing at her crotch, strands of pubic hair in tufts and dribbles peeking out onto her thighs, the quiet melt of black behind the thin, silk sheath. I smiled to myself. Yes, she *is* a Patch. Nebula Patch. I opened the oven door and set a chunk of wood on it.

"Put your feet up there."

"I always liked this house," she said, placing her feet up, drawing her skirt into her lap.

"It's a big house," I said.

"There are bigger," she said. "Aren't you using the furnace? It's still cold enough."

I couldn't tell her there was something in the cellar. I couldn't tell anyone. It pulsed down there in the dark and would not hide from the light. With Elsa Tobin I'd entered the cellar once but did not stay. I knew it was there waiting. Amorphous, devouring thing. It waited in the close to envelop me. I bolted that kitchen door leading to it.

"I don't need it," I said. "I'm warm enough with this."

She put her hands over her feet and squeezed. "My feet are froze. Will you warm them for me?"

I stared emptily.

"Never mind," she said.

"No, I . . . "

I knelt close to the stove, its heat striking the side of my face.

"It doesn't really matter," she said.

I braced one knee, then set her foot on it. The metallic cold of her flesh bit through my jeans.

"Cold," I said.

"Here all you get's winter and summer. The old people sit next to the heat like zombies listening to the stoves sing. I remember the cold coming at me from every direction from the time I was crawling. I'd sort of hold my hand out against it like this. Testing, or for some kind of relief. The things you remember, eh?"

She laughed. One of her teeth was missing. A dark cavity to one side, a space in the white line, compliments of a drunken sailor who hit her in the face with a bottle of rum. She often ran her tongue over it and through, soothing it for its loss, for being out of place; but for me it was always discovery, always new and exciting, I never sought it, but my tongue was always drawn to it, and I accepted it joyfully again and again.

"I'll get the tea," she said, and as she swung her legs around, the faint smell of her registered the memory of another getting up, a cot, Morris's eyes, Mildred grinning.

"You're *deadly* serious," she said, opening and shutting cabinet doors and drawers. "Aren't you?"

"Deadly," I said, smiling, "but I'm getting over it."

"Everyone figures something about you. They puzzle you out. You're an educated man. You're too young to live alone and do nothing. How old are you?"

"Forty-six."

"Being young and alone is a lot of things all grouped together that no one understands or likes. They put you in that category."

As she rinsed the cups, I stood close by watching. The wildness of her hair intrigued me, soft brush, fur tails, trails of soft snarls, dark eyes like sculpted coals beautifully set in cream-smooth caverns.

"Personally nothing matters to me," she said. "I don't see anything as *significant*. You know what I mean? Anyway, I never believe what anyone tells me." She laughed. "I lied to myself long enough to know not to trust anyone else. Besides, I'm Mildred's daughter." She laughed again.

"She seems unhappy," I said.

"Sure, she's unhappy! She had an upbringing, didn't she."

She was teasing me, tossing me the tips of icebergs.

"Did you know them?" I asked. "Her parents? Your grand-parents?"

"Molly and John Miller. Baked bread. Homemade brew. That's a sign hanging still today in their cellar. Red letters, a tavern sign for a tavern that never was. All sorts of old dreams were down there in that cellar. I looked around. I was what you'd call an inquisitive child. But to answer your question, no. I didn't *know* them. But it's there all the same anyway, isn't it. I mean, Mildred didn't *know* them either. They didn't know themselves. Do you know yourself?"

She stared at me. A simple question. I didn't answer.

She went on. "You're there before you even begin, and it's all a part of you for as long as you can remember. It's sort of where you've been before you know you've been there." She got a kick out of her words, so she was laughing as she folded the dishtowel and hung it over the back of a chair. "They give you a hell of a lot more than eyes and ears and the occasional smack on the ass," she said, smiling, "God bless them."

After her bath she returned carrying her wet dress in a crumpled roll. She was wearing my bathrobe. Her hair: wild, wet clusters, mats, strings, strands, and clumps.

"I forgot a hanger," she said, and she went to dig one out of a cupboard. She was at home in this house. She hung her dress over the stove. Drops of water sizzled as they struck the hot surface.

I poured her a cup of tea. She scrubbed at her hair with a towel. I thought of her on the cot, carrying the duck, stepping out of her dress. I couldn't see her face, the towel moved in long folds over her head.

I tried to explain, feel, sound out reactions to the long silence, the chilly dive of my winter within.

"It's not words," she said, sipping some tea. "You and Mildred, you talk too much. And talking, as far as I can see, is as close to blaming as a match to fire."

"Professor Feet," I laughed. "Someone wrote that on my office door. Professor Feet." It bombarded the senses. I doubled over, nearly hysterical with laughter. "Pro. . . fess. . . or Feeeeeet."

When I was able to see through my tears, she was smiling with her mouth closed.

"It sort of builds up," I said.

"They accept you here," Nebula said, "if that's what you want."

"Like illness or rain or drought."

"No, people here respect education," she said, "as long as it's on paper, that is, a good and proper *fact*."

Ten

Joan and I sit watching the birds in the feeder. They bob and peck and hop from level to level. The fat robin is the only one I can recognize, and he is not here today. In his place are two smaller — I decide younger — robins on the ground. Soundless walkers, these birds. Spastic hunters. No ears that I can see. Vibrations. Worm movement through the soil signaling the feet like nibbles on a fish line. Peck. Peck. Pull. Peck. Pull. And bobbing erect, listening, chancing that the worm may slip away deep into the earth — or relax and become easier to pull to the surface. More to eat, less to break.

The soil browned by the weight of the wood. Now removed, in its place is a more fertile darkness, for the absence of light first breeds decay, before a more primal order establishes itself. In this quiet life away from the killing sun, flow rises and then dies — almost.

"A pretty bird were it not so common."

I look at Joan, but she is quiet, staring out the window.

Sun on the sea. Quiet brilliance of a midsummer day. I park the car and walk to the dock. In the boats, on the pilings, gathered fish, their bellies splayed; loose, white flaps, shingles of fat; soft doors behind which their insides used to stay.

The voices of the men are but rhythmic murmurs tuned to the easy swing of two-pronged forks as they toss the bodies onto the docks. At first I thought they spoke softly because I was near, standing hard by, a stranger looking on, but that is not so; their thoughts run like the fish, instinctive and certain, in trusted depths, and my presence in no way changes anything. The words come when necessary. And watching them, choked as I am on years of voices, my mind a sea of them and me, I want to say something accurate, something precise and definite, something that comes of being between fog and water with space all around and only a compass to see.

I want to know how this life feels. I want to know what they think. The fish slap in fatty gurgles, piling up near the scale. Overhead the gulled sky moves. Is there fear? Is there something unique, something extraordinary out there in a small boat, strips of wood, felled trees floating beneath the feet? I hold a red plastic bucket full of sun and shadow.

"Look at the fucking fish," Joan says. "Yuck!"

I hadn't heard her approach.

I leave her on the wharf and walk into the gray-brown shack. The puddled boards are flecked with fish scales, oily wet splatters over my toes. Two men are inside: one is at the scale; the other hoists crates of fish to the conveyor belt that pours fish out the wall to a waiting truck. It is like walking on lard. At the end of the building, through an open wall, I see the heads of men, forks lifting, and beyond them more boats waiting to unload, and then a vast glittering expanse of sunlit sea.

"Slippery," I say.

"Yes," he says most seriously, "it is slippery."

"I'm looking for a halibut," I say.

He moves the weights along the scale arm. He looks like a railroad engineer, a stevedore, a sailor, a man from a picturesque history.

"About five pounds," I say.

"Yes," he says and writes in his book.

"Last time you only had haddock. And cod. Some mackerel."

"Two here somewhere," he says.

He begins looking through the open boxes filled with fish. There are rope handles on the boxes. Something to do with the slime? Slivers?

"Jerome, was halibut hereabouts?" the man sings out.

Jerome comes to life. His boots slop toward us. He is talking so quickly, I can't understand him. Grinning, too. Something about herring and cod with quick jerks of the head, looking around non-stop, but never at me; one thick arm forms a triangle out from his hip, the other moves a crate along the conveyor belt as he tells — the ceiling perhaps? — where the halibut have been all along.

Joan comes in. "Have they got one?"

The men look at her. Queen of the Deep Sea Smell.

A silent moment except for the fatty creases, crevices, the gurgle of fish pitched from the boat.

Finally the first man says, "Here she be." He holds the fish by one gill. "No meat on her though. I dasn't sell you that one. No." He tosses it down and looks further. "Here's the other fella. Right t'ick, it is. Some meat there, all right. Yes."

"Okay," I say, and he lays it on the scale.

The men below are finished unloading their catch. They stand smoking, waiting for the tally. When I step nearer the scale, I can see another boat, a little farther off, an old man washing it down. Joan is approaching him, stepping along the longer outside wharf that runs at a right angle to this fish store.

When I join her, she says, "This man wants to take us for a ride in his boat. We can see the islands." The man is tall and thin. The bright red-checkered shirt and green suspenders are too wonderful for words.

"Good day, sir. Good day. I suggested to the missus that I take you folks on a trip around the bay."

The boat sounds like a grown-up version of the little red metal craft that I ran in the bathtub so long ago. Soft, deep-throated gurgles bubble beneath the water. Mine was candle power. Could it have made such a noise or did I supply it with one? Don't get water on the floor, Harry!

We all stand forward in the boat beneath the overhang.

"Old Ford engine," he says, beaming.

Everything is accurate. The crates are neatly positioned; the lines, nets, buoys and other, for me, nameless parts of his life are all here, all in order. And the smell of fresh fish above the sea, even my red bucket with the halibut tail poking out, all these things seem selected for this moment.

As we'd boarded he'd introduced himself with a curious graciousness and delicacy that cast him in my mind as an archbishop, a man of soft reserve with dignity and power, a sense of himself that would make him safe and accurate in any place. He was in fact an archbishop, a Pope, a scholar who'd chosen rather to make his life at sea.

Joan is taken with Elwood's charm and his obvious delight in showing us his world. She stands close by, listening as he explains the markers he shows us on an old map: the ledge and shoals, the islands we are seeing or are about to see. Joan's eyes are dancing. I think of the endless, crushing mob of part-timers, summer people who scour these beaches and wharves, this countryside, in their hunt for authenticity, orig-inals, moments to fill their film and time and, much later, their hours. They will serve up this Maritime salad, tossing it with words like *genuine*, *real*, *quaint*, *basic* and *cute*.

Joan shakes her head and looks at me. "Can you imagine we've never done this," she says. "All this time we've been here and we've never even been out in a boat. At least, I haven't."

Elwood indicates where they'd found Clive Hampton's body early that spring. A sandy stretch of beach. Clive was one of three lobstermen lost that winter. I remember him at the garage filling a can with gas, an image that will now live with me forever. He was smiling.

"His boat was still running," Elwood says. "Gone and not a trace."

"He fell over?" Joan asks.

"Lobster trap can be pretty heavy. A bit of ice on the deck. Wind. Caught in the ropes most likely's my guess." He touches his shirt-sleeve. "Clothes get snagged." His eyes are steady now, neutral. "Fishing takes its toll," he says. And then smiling at Joan's fallen face, he shouts, "Look there!"

"What are they?"

"Seals!"

I recall Andrew looking out over the rocks at the ghosts of vanishing herds.

"That's unusual, isn't it?" I say.

"Yes and no. They're killed off mostly. From what they once was, you know what I mean. Good riddance, if you ask me."

"The fishermen?" Joan asks.

"Fishermen want to fish, isn't it? Then they gots t'kill seals."

"You can even make out their whiskers!" Joan shouts, pointing at their tiny heads and eyes. "God, they're cute!"

Elwood smiles and puts the craft about.

Clive Hampton wasn't the only fisherman lost that winter. Hewitt and Stern went down too. Hewitt they still haven't found. And of course, in my first fall, Lester Pheeps drowned. Lester Pheeps who everyone thought had retired from the sea. It happened while I was staying with the Haywards.

Andrew and Della had gone to town. I made a fire and brewed some tea. When my parents went food shopping, they always brought us Animal Crackers as a treat. Happy circus boxes with tiny carrying cords. Inside was the browny-green wax paper, and behind its crisp, crackly sound waited a circus of faintly distinguishable animals. "One at a time, now. Don't get any crumbs on the floor."

When someone knocked on the door that day, I was startled. I glanced out the window. No car. I opened the door a crack and an old lady, pouches of skin hanging from her face, stared back at me as if I were an ax murderer.

"The Haywards have gone to town. I'm Harold Fleet," I said. "I'm staying with the Haywards for a while."

"I know who you are," she said. "You've got peanut butter on your nose."

I stepped aside, rubbing my nose, and she came in.

"To town, are they?"

"Yes. I'm just making tea. Would you like some?"

"Thank you, no."

She walked to the counter where Della kept assorted useful things and picked up a pencil and paper, then she sat and, with great deliberation, wrote.

I made myself a cup of tea.

"There," she said, folding it carefully in half. "I'll leave this for Andrew. Not to tell Della." She handed the note to me. "Put it in a safe place."

I wanted desperately to read the note. I didn't know the woman, but that mattered little. When I was a child I searched through the garbage pails looking for letters, clues. There would be no secrets from me. I read of aunts, uncles, brothers, sisters, fathers, mothers, neighbors, bosses, schoolteachers, colleagues, friends. Most with names, but all strangers to me. These letters had a superficial and silly sameness, yet I clutched them from the yawning chasm, word after dismal word intriguing me. People were alive out there. Was this the proof I needed? Was my boring little life made more valid by toothaches, boils, new shoes, jobs, good and bad days?

"I'll take care of it," I said, placing her note in my shirt pocket.

She stopped and returned from the door and placed her

hand on my arm. "Not to worry," she said. Then she left.

I sat drinking tea. When the car lights broke through the fall night, I climbed anxiously to my feet and went into the kitchen.

"Elsa Tobin was here," Della said, placing a bag of groceries on the counter.

"A woman with glasses," I said, not as surprised as I once would have been at these magical deductions.

"Now what do you suppose she wanted?" Della asked herself and her eyes rolled back in wrinkled thought. "She must have seen us leave."

"She didn't say," I said. "Maybe she wanted to meet me."

"Do you suppose?" She went straight to the phone.

Andrew pushed through the door lugging a heavy box of groceries. "She's turned cold," he said. "Be a hard frost tonight."

"What's this?" he asked when I handed him the note.

I put my finger to my lips and nodded toward the kitchen where Della was roasting chicken for supper.

He cupped the paper in his large hands like a trapped insect and stared at it. I glanced through an old newspaper.

"Lester," he said, and he slipped the note in his pocket.

The rest of that evening he was even more quiet than usual. Recently he spent most evenings caning a beautiful hand-carved chair, enhancing its cat's-paw feet and hand-painted back. That night, however, he sat and stared, seeming more an old man, more in his past, swallowed up in a kind of primordial imminence. Della was her perpetual self. Talking over her dancing hands, she sewed, darned, began hooking a rug of yellow, green and brown. It'll show the dirt, my mother would say. I went up to my room early, and it wasn't long before they began to talk. Later that night, after they'd gone to bed, I heard them, her soft *ooo*s and *ahh*s accenting the deep wordless drone of his voice. Then he went downstairs and I heard the car start. In the morning when I looked out, hoarfrost lay glistening in the grass and soft rivulets dripped down the windows. The wheelbarrow was piled high with pumpkins. Andrew was backing the tractor from the barn. I waved to him and he gazed toward me, but didn't respond. For a moment I took offense. I pulled on my cold socks. The tractor stalled, then started again.

As Andrew rolled along far down the road, I walked to the garage. The chill fall air nibbled over my bare arms and neck. Early light framed the open space, the rear of the car, then fell short of darkness. I don't know what I was looking for there. The mystery of Lester Pheeps? That night, halfway between waking and sleeping, I had watched Elsa eternally folding the note, folding the note, and each time she'd hold it out to me, hang it at arm's end, her arthritic fingers around it in a bunch, press it toward me, smiling as I never knew her to smile before, or since, and I would want to unfold its contents, want to discover its truth, and I would pinch the corners apart to open it and there would be laughter that I could not define, so I would stop, stick it deep in my pocket, content that it was for the time someone else's truth.

My restlessness continued through the night. I never heard Andrew return. As I absently placed one hand on the warm hood of the car early that morning, I realized he'd only just returned to go out again on his tractor. It was too early to haul wood, too late to plow. The soil was wet with frost.

Della, large and heavily flanneled, flapped about the kitchen. She seemed to avoid looking at me.

"I guess winter's on the way," I said.

"Yes?" She paused.

"There was quite a heavy frost."

"Yes," she said firmly. "It's been simply awful this fall. One thing after another."

I'm part of this. I realized it suddenly. Staring at Della stirring porridge, steeping tea, forking fatty slabs of bacon into a pan.

"Can you mind . . . " she said, and near tears, she flew out of the room.

I poked absently at the bacon. Hebb's pork. When Hebb had carried in the cardboard box of meat I was entertained with bloodless tales of slaughter. Oh, she was some smart, that one. Him now. Scoff, scoff. There was a prize, I'd say, that one. So many things. My mind spitting and exploding like fat above flame.

Della came back red-eyed and vacant. I felt superfluous, but substantial. I recalled the shells of snails cracking beneath my feet.

Della puttered aimlessly about the kitchen. On the phone to Elsa the evening before she had stared at the bank calendar *oo*ing and *ahh*ing, but she couldn't have known then of Lester's plan, could she? No matter. "She came on business with Andrew," she had said later. "For Lester. She's Lester Pheeps' sister, Elsa."

Suddenly Della collapsed into a chair.

"Are you all right?"

"Yes. Yes," she said almost angrily. Then, "Oh, don't pay me any mind. I just didn't sleep is all."

Neither of us ate much. We sat there picking absently, sliding food around in the fat, moving it aimlessly across the hard flowers. When Andrew finally walked in, he looked haggard and worn. The crow's-feet that lined his eyes with craggy delicacy seemed strung tight like laces.

"We got her in," he said.

"It won't storm?" Della said.

I excused myself and made for the bathroom.

Andrew looked straight at me, his eyes grabbing like hands. "It's Lester Pheeps," he said. Then, "My Lord, the water's cold!"

I stopped next to my seat.

Eleven

L ester was best man when Della and me were married. He was working a coaster then, running dynamite down and rum back.

"Once when he was firmly into his sixties, a hurricane threatened his boat. Lester tied one end of a rope to a tree, the other to his waist, and eased himself along the wharf into the gale winds to firm up the lines. The boat was still lost. Just a miracle he weren't as well.

"When Lester's sister, Elsa, got married, Lester, who was forty-six, no, forty-eight — yes, he was forty-eight then — well, didn't Lester burn all her clothes and possessions and dump the ashes into the groom, Timothy Tobin's yard?

"When the Consolidated School talk began, Lester stood by Miss Prescher, who wanted to continue the one-room school. There was them what say Lester was sweet on her, but she was twelve years older than him and moved away that same year.

"Some say the starlike scar on his chin is from the heel of an angry woman.

"Two days before Christmas in '25, Lester's father and mother were killed in the county's first car fatality. Most think the driver, a close friend of the family, had a heart attack and drove them over a cliff. Still, different ones will mention liquor.

"Lester Billy always had dogs. Neighbors laughed secretly at the dogs' names. Cotton, Small, Beaver, and finally Tongue and Boss. The cats, as far as everyone knew, never had no names. He called all of 'm Cat.

"I was the only man Lester spent much time with. The only man invited to Lester's house. Lester's house was built by an old rumrunner named Last who disappeared without a trace. There are dozens of tales about him. Lester purchased the house for back taxes and he and his sister, Elsa, made a home there until Timothy Tobin took her away, or she left, depending on how you figure things stood. I dasn't ever get in twixt those two. It were too bad though, 'cause they were right close forever before."

They talked for hours. Andrew mostly. Della filled in here and there. They were unhappy but thoughtful. When the phone rang, they knew it was Elsa and they knew what she had to say.

I imagine that long last night the marriage of Lester and Andrew's voices across this round oak table. Two old men preparing for death, the floor crowded with dogs, the cat on Lester's lap. I know Lester. I saw him leaving Bones' store carrying a large bottle of Pepsi-Cola. A round-shouldered man with a ponderous heavy-booted walk, lugging himself along, his hands hanging like hams from long arms. He smiled at me and said hello, the word dividing itself into three or four rumbles as it tumbled from his tongue. I don't remember a scar on his chin, but I'm sure it was there.

How can you speak to another of assisting a friend to his death?

Timothy Tobin was building a new gate for the fence, though the fence itself lay rotted, tangled and torn. He went into the barn as I approached.

Elsa Tobin clipped batter onto the cookie sheet. She is big

with muscles gone soft. A more motherly, if homelier, version of Mildred Patch. When she whips and stirs, her arms shake like loosely packed sausage; fleshy layers of skin leap in soundless slaps and her soft face jiggles. She is a woman strange in her happiness, for even her smile seems but a thin coating for a deep despair.

"As soon as I finish this batch we can go," she said.

I sat with my jacket unzipped and watched her bake.

"Lester liked my cookies," she said. "No telling how many he'd eat. 'Lester, you'll burst,' I'd say. Yes, that one was some fond of sweets."

Lester was buried the week before. Nearby, back on Cemetery Hill, is the family plot, a square of tomb-stoned land open to the sun and not far out of the way. Early the morning after the burial, I went to the grave. The grass tromped flat around it on three sides was wet with dew. The stones told little. Dates: artificial boundaries to measureless years. I stared particularly at Elsa's own small, gray memorial, the size of a double loaf of her brown bread, complete except for the space after Died.

"Now, Timothy won't eat many cookies," she said. "Timothy's not one for sweets."

"He's one for heat," Timothy said, shaking and slapping away the cold. "Some cold, what? He gets cold outside so he comes in where's she's warm."

I gazed absently as he unlaced his high rubber boots with their pale yellow insulation, knobby and worn, creeping over the top. He dropped them near the stove, blew in his cupped hands and grinned. Suddenly I realized he must be twenty years younger than Elsa.

At home in his thick wool socks, he clapped his hands. "Ladies and Helephants," he trumpeted. "Allow me to do my stuff. Hee-honk. Hee-honk."

"Timothy," Elsa said, but she wasn't looking, just sliding the cookie sheet into the stove.

Timothy then began to make bagpipe sounds, screeches, shrieks and whining brays while dancing a comical high-stepping, arm-swinging dance that rattled the pans on top of the stove.

"Don't pay'm any mind," Elsa said, shaking her head. "It's his way, that's all."

I smiled tentatively and pressed against the chair. Everything loomed. Gigantic reflections.

The sound went on and on, interminable.

"How about some water," I said.

"You're thirsty," Elsa said, walking to the stove. "Timothy," she said, "what must Mr. Fleet think?"

Timothy laughed and slipped into silence. I was by the sink, quiet all around me. Elsa opened the tap and water rushed into the glass. I gulped at the water and my throat made a desperate little sound as I attempted to swallow, but it was that old heave in the throat, something trying to get out, or in. I drank, and breathed, trying to wash it away.

Timothy, looking right at me, laughed again, running his head back and forth in firm nods while in a strange, childish singsong tone this man's voice wailed again and again in that eerie falsetto of laughter.

"Now ain't you some foolish," Elsa said, smiling at him. "Now ain't that a burdock brain."

"Let's dance," Timothy said softly. "Only a dance in Cockney France, can give the chance. . . " His voice drifted into silence and he began to leap about again, his stocking feet paddling the floor, his head back, his eyes searching out phantom rhythms. I listened to his socks whisper across the boards. I stared at him, swallowing a glassful of screams. Elsa put out a hand toward me and only her words, sudden and unexpected, drifting away from the open stove, held me together.

"My, that man loves to dance," she said. "Give him the least opportunity and he'll dance and dance and dance."

I fastened my eyes to the steaming cookie sheet.

"They're almost ready," she said. "We can go in a minute."

The cold slap of fall sobered me. Behind us, back in that house, in a chair, Timothy sat quietly staring at the floor. The new gate hung on one hinge, a hammer with a rusty claw, some nails and screws, a screwdriver all lay in a neat row on the frosty grass.

I was thinking of my hometown. Its main street was a close place, a tart, ugly street whose buildings were no more than brick sores. But it wasn't that particular street I was recalling as much as it was him, there walking, warbling; the small man with thinning hair who greeted us kids as we passed. "Cuckoo, cuckoo," he'd call, all the while twirling a gray finger in circles near his head, his straight sparse hair in strands like splintered rubber bands. For years I saw that thin-lipped, toothless smile, that pained face in the same degree of disrepair, the words so regular, so sought after by frightened children ourselves calling back and forth "Cuckoo, cuckoo," egging each other on, twirling *our* fingers by *our* heads, laughing nervously, for inside we shared more than a game, more than the mockery with the man. We were scared. We ran. We were always ready to run.

Elsa showed no emotion as we approached Lester's house, although for her it might have been the last of hundreds of trips along that road, or if the weather was fine, walks along the paths twisting over the rolling hills from the Tobin place to this. Still nothing gathered in her face. No accumulation. She walked toward a house for which she had a key. I saw Lesters everywhere, leaping up suddenly like targets on a range.

We went in.

"Place is bright," she said. "Lester demanded windows. Light from all sides. He liked the feel of the sun."

The kitchen was clean except for the dog-hair kittens that blew across our feet in the escaping rushes of air when Elsa first opened the door. Along one wall was an overstuffed chair actively popping its springs, its color shading off into time-worn greens. A woodstove, IRON DUKE embossed on its enameled front. Stalwart singer of songs, soft crooner, belly full of heat. Stiff-back chairs around a large oak table with worn spots where resting arms had moved their way through the years.

Lester getting up and going to the woodbox, gathering a bunch of sticks for the stove; Andrew chewing on his pipe; outside, the car dripping with dew.

I was thankful the clothes were gone from the closets and drawers. Those large droopy socks on Timothy's feet, did they come from one of these bureaus?

"This chest has been to the end of the world and back. Jamaica," she said. "East Indies."

"He must have had a full life," I said.

"Lester?" She seemed to be considering. "He went to Africa," she said. "Him and Basil Ruff. Not many what's done that, I guess. He was the free one in the family."

"Were there many of you?"

"No. Leastwise not for those times. But I'm all that's left now. 'Cept maybe Carter. Lord knows what happened to that one. George died of TB. Tremont was lost at sea. The old gent's house burned down. That's when Carter went away without a word. Only Lester and I stayed on. Then there was Timothy."

"Timothy," I said.

"Lester never looked kindly onto him," she said. "He found him odd."

I took a cookie from my pocket and chewed.

"Did he like to cook?" I asked, glancing through a stack of hand-written recipes without names or proportions.

"Lester? Oh my Lord, yes. Cooked to sea for years. Cooked his way to Africa and back."

Finally she sat on a living room chair.

"Don't think you must take all this stuff," she said. "I can get Timothy to take it out to the dump, or we can store it in the barn. Actually, Lester would have just pitched it. Surprised he didn't. Lots on his mind, poor man. Most of this is only fit for the woods anyway, far as I can tell."

"No, it's fine. I love old things."

"Some is funny about that, I know. Other people's memories and such like that, but if you don't mind. . . "

"It seems right that it stay with the house. And I can use it. Thank you."

"Look around," she said. "There's a cellar and an attic. Take your time. I'll sit."

I glanced down the cellarway. I couldn't go down. I decided to try it from the outside, with the sun at my back.

LESTER PHEEPS 1952 scratched in the top step of the outside entryway.

I opened the lower, inside door. The cellar was heavy with ledge. A frame of wood slats covered the dirt floor. Dampness dripped from the beams. A spider raced by at eye level. Pump for the well. Old wires like dehydrated skin strands. As my eyes adjusted to the dim light, I made out years of wood ash mashed into a near corner. Must be a furnace back there. I thought of the beaches littered with refuse, everything tossed at the sea. Private and public clutter.

"Yes," Andrew drawled. "It's too bad."

"Cuckoo, cuckoo," I said, stepping from the cellar, and I liked the feel of sunlight on my face, and I didn't care that I hadn't seen all there was to see. I decided this was my place now, where I had to be.

Twelve

The overgrown trails be-
hind the house lift away in
smothered lines. I follow them. The nearer paths lead to
rubbish piles, the lofted refuse of early years. I rummage
through with pick, hand and shovel, uncovering old bottles,
glass crocks, bells, belts, dishes, cans, furniture, plumbing
parts, tools, wagon parts and other farm equipment.

This prospecting seems to me not an uprooting but a
discovery. I imagine someone, maybe a settler, tossing this
down the hill. "Just fire 'er into the woods, son." It is a baby
cup with a picture on one side. A large, almost mongoloid
child's head with a halo accenting his immensity. It is a head
large enough for a milk can. Beneath the dried mud is a name.
James. His cup, or head, or both. If I dig further will that large
skull be there, gold halo like a handle from ear to ear? Even
now it may be working its way past the rock and glass, the
matter mire, finally getting clear in a closing rush, earth's lips
melting back unburdened, delivering.

I wasn't aware that I was getting lost until I was lost. So it
was a shock. The sun was still high in the early evening.
Mosquitoes were feasting on my face. Blackflies in swarms
dined silently, lightly stalked beneath my clothes, leaving
behind hundreds of tiny empty platters overflowing with itch.

"Flies can drive an animal crazy. Get in his eyes and ears and nose till he's in a bloomin' rage. Cause'm t'kill himself."

I broke a branch from a fir and waved it about like a fan, but they were too many and too small and too close. Don't panic! I tucked my pants in my socks, pulled my jacket up over my head and face. Breathe deeply. Steady sweat poured from me. I thought I heard them; knew I felt them. But I couldn't see. I pulled my jacket down again and ran. It was hard to get the needed speed because of the thick brush, and when I stopped, my chest tight, burning with exertion, gasping for breath, there they'd be, or others like them, indistinguishable legions enjoying my blood.

I scraped the scum and larvae aside on a stagnating stream and reached down into the mucky bottom, raising the brownish ooze, smearing it over my face and hands. It ran, dripped, dropped, but it soothed; and with my clothes back on it would protect me from many of their bites. They still swarmed, their number seeming to increase by the minute. I stared out at them. The realization I was lost in the woods, and the fact of a rapidly falling sun, took prominence. The flies shifted into a more distant perspective. I had about an hour until sunset. By ten there would be full black.

I decided to follow the sun west, figuring that would get me to Birchtown or Queenstown. But only minutes passed before the sun was too low to see beyond the tall pines and fir and so, inside the thick forest where I moved, where everything was soft and moist and hidden from the passing sun, I accepted my fate.

The embarrassed cry I made was as deep-throated and manly as I could muster. I listened to it going way out, fading across the still forest. And I was still getting bites. I pushed ahead, or back, or around, for an hour more, calling now and then, until it was obvious I was to stay lost at least this one night. I found a fairly open ridge of pine, its soft needle rug as quiet and thick as pile carpet. I pulled up some large ferns to cover myself.

I couldn't sleep. I knew things passed. Living things. I felt them stop and stare. They sensed me or saw, did whatever they did, then moved on. I listened. I thought of wildcats and bear. Each crack of twig, each sound, whether mice or moose, caused my heart to explode.

Hours later, my eyes still pressed wide against the dark, I heard wind from a nose. Rooting. I moved closer to the tree, one I had selected because of its ladder-like branches.

It was a bear, pawing and sniffing around my fern bed. It's hard to say where the fear struck first or most fierce. Even without the moon I could climb that tree. I heard the bear fall back in a rolling lump of confusion as I whimpered up to the uppermost branches. I listened to him snorting and scratching around in my brush bed. Finally it was quiet again.

When the sun rose I was still hanging there, and from the appearance of things, I was all that there was to see.

Things are soft in the morning after night bathes nature in silent wash. I yearned for the first hot strike of sun that might burn the dampness from my bones. I ached. My face was swollen with fly poison, the caked mud split and cracked into a strange terrestrial geography above the flowing bites. Below me as far as I could see, a natural extension of color and form. My fern bed seemed undisturbed. Everything fit. Except me in the tree.

I recalled a primer picture of thick, cloddy men with heavy, stooped bodies sitting in trees. Tree dwellers. And on the page right opposite them, birds louder than thunder with great wings and beaks, and dinosaurs with long necks like weapons, great heads of teeth, whiplash anger on heavy, charging feet. And somehow those dumb grunt tree dwellers with wooden clubs and apish faces seemed to me no more real than the funny little fellows of the Sunday comics. I didn't ask why the tree dwellers weren't hiding, why they were sitting right out in the open like that. Were they chased from their caves? I didn't ask about fear, either.

Early on, Lester Pheeps' house tucked about me, my hopes if not soaring at least above the cold floor, I gave myself to discipline. Pattern. Ritual. My myopic version of the ordered life.

I know. I'll caulk the window.

I take the caulking gun and I place the can inside. I'll be free and cleanly occupied. I'll lose myself in reconstructing edges long ago established. I'll circumscribe each piece of glass, run a trail of white putty from the snout — but nothing comes. I pull and feel the tube swell. Still nothing. The trigger will go no further. I cut the tip. I peek inside. A bronze bubble. A cap. Double protection.

CAN'T YOU DO ANYTHING RIGHT.

Out to the garage again. Nail. Too short. A longer nail, still too short. A coat hanger. None. A piece of wire. This will do it. White flows freely from the tube. I place a finger over it. The mess of it sticks to my fingers. A cloth. Traces remain. I'll have to pull the trigger with my left hand.

Back to the window. It spills and dribbles, snakes, curves, falls away from the edges. Too much here. Too much.

HOW MANY TIMES DO I HAVE TO TELL YOU.

I run my finger over it, pressing it into the cracks. There. But the glass smears as it spreads around the tip of my finger. A cloth. The tip has leaked more onto the sill. The floor. It still runs. Back to the shed. Preparation. Be prepared. The Boy Scout marching song. I'll take a putty knife, too. I fail miserably. I touch and retouch. Clean up. How? Gasoline? Ammonia? Vinegar? I dab, and mar the already imperfect job by opening sealed areas, pitting them.

I must do something! I must not think. There must be work without echoes. The dishes. I'll wash the dishes. I stoop over the sink. I burn my hand in the scalding water.

WHY DON'T YOU BE CAREFUL.

Soap. I squirt some in the pan. My back aches from the too-low sink. I splash water on my pants. My head spins. I grip the stained enamel to keep from hurtling. Better. My first break. I wash. It's dark. It's early and it's dark that we might have our ultimate tryst. A climax to the lusty frustration. I feel it exploding, coursing through me, warm piss and shit, the stuff of life.

DO YOU WANT YOUR MOUTH WASHED OUT WITH SOAP.

But wait, but wait. I've forgotten to rinse the dishes. I do that now. The clatter as I shift them about is deafening. I tremble. I can feel myself oozing. I'm oozing out over the sink.

DO YOU WANT THE STRAP. WELL, DO YOU. DO YOU.

It will not be foiled. No, no telling, no emptying of it. It is like an inner skin palsied and itchy straining for the light, but it can't get out. If there's no way out for it? I reach down inside to pull it from myself and I retch. I can't even cry now. No tears.

GET TO YOUR ROOM.

I kneel here by the sink with my pants wet, smelling of gasoline and putty and I can think of the things I don't know that chew on me, knowing, chewing.

GET TO YOUR ROOM.

I can think about them and think about them. My boots. My out boots come off and my in boots go on. The laces are too tight. I have socks to go with my out boots when my feet are wet, but they make in boots too tight.

GET TO YOUR ROOM.

I think I may be able to cry. No. I don't. I take off socks. Get boots on. Phone ringing. Someone else's ring. Rings! and Rings! and Rings! I won't pick it up. No. Rings! No. Rings! I pick it up. Slam it down. There is time enough. Time. It rings again. Tremble. Clutch. Squeeze. It rings on and on. I must. I speak to the raised receiver.

"Is it you? Is it, is it you?"

No one answers. I say, "Don't hang up. Don't hang up." But they do, and I do, and the phone does not ring again. They are giving me something to cry for.

123

"Hello!" I shouted to the forest. "Hello-hello-hello."

"Helloooo."

A woman's voice came back toward me from far across that place, faint on the tail end of the wind, but definite.

"Hello," I called again, and I wondered what more I could say. I didn't need help now that I had direction, so I moved quietly toward the voice, calling every couple of minutes or so, she responding. I imagined an Indian maiden, a Micmac princess in a headband of dyed and woven porcupine needles, wearing skins, the same rainbow colors throughout, triangular kisses at the hems, skin bronze, eyes deep soft stones, hair gleaming like dark coal, foxfire lips. . .

"Hello."

I saw her at the side of a long hill, standing near a rock. Jeans gone gray tucked into black fisherman's boots, an old shirt, its stripes fading one into the other, blonde hair tied back.

As I drew nearer, she said, "I'm not alone."

Then I understood, felt myself coming at her like a great muddied sore.

"Flies," I said. "Don't be afraid. I'm lost. Or I was. I've been out all night."

She caught each phrase in reluctant silence. Hers was the look students wear on the first day of class. Defiant compliance.

"Where are we?" I asked. "What is this place?"

"Birchtown," she answered. "How did you get lost?"

I laughed. "Now there's a question," I said. And I laughed some more, stretching the dried skin of my muddy face painfully far out of place.

"Never mind," she said, picking up a plastic bag. "It's your affair. I'm gathering greens. They're a delicacy. There's so much to eat in the woods that you could live off the land right in your own neighborhood even if you live in the city."

She swung the bag over her shoulder and stepped through the towering trees. I followed.

"My name is Starsparrow," she said. "It used to be Annie. What would you like to be called?"

"How about Mudman," I said.

She nodded. "Come on. We're just over the hill."

Thirteen

Snatches and strings of mucus wrap round Joan's fork as she whips the eggs. I stir the onions and peppers. The sounds of cracking K's, the hot kisses, and Z's in the woodstove's belly warm the ears. Everything is soft in the pan.

"I never felt that," she says as she stirs the egg. "I always felt I was the one rejecting. My mother always accused me of being too independent. What did you do after she said that?"

"I just stood there."

"That's incredible," Joan says. "Funny what happens to people."

"People usually don't think. They react."

She pours the eggs over the onion and pepper. They swell yellow. Flecks of green. Soft steam rising.

"I would have run away. I did run away. Once." She laughs at the memory. "What did you do then?"

"I jerked off in the sink."

She laughs again. I join her.

"Got a grip on yourself," she says.

"For too many years it was about the only real grip I had."

"Parents. God love them. They mean well, usually. Always, in most cases. They have their own shit to deal with — not that all that many of them knew it was shit, or that it could be dealt with.

"You want to get some plates? My father always said, 'A place for everything, everything in its place.' If you put the milk on the left side of the fridge instead of the right, he'd hunt you down and demand, in his judgmental voice, 'Where does the milk go?' Being a kid, which is to say a bit of a smart ass, I'd try to keep from laughing and say, 'In the fridge. Why? Where is it?' In absolute incredulity he'd say, 'It was where the prune juice goes, and the milk is in the prune juice's place.' God forbid!"

I loved the way she did the voices of people. Me included. It wasn't our exact sound she captured, but rather our character and style.

"Is he still like that?"

"Sometimes. But now we laugh about it. Now I put his things in their 'right' places, too. Back then he'd go away angry. His day would be ruined. He made a habit of ruining other people's days, too. My mother would come into the room and say, 'It's cold out today,' you know, small talk, and he'd say, 'How do you know it's cold?' She'd stop dead in her tracks and stare and say something like, 'Huh?' And he'd repeat, 'How do you know it's cold? Have you been outside?' Mom would lose all her color and she'd be almost apologetic. 'Well, no, dear,' she'd say, 'but I heard it on the radio. Bob Steele said . . . ' Dad would shift gears then. 'Bob Steele. The radio. They don't know everything on the radio.'"

"What did that do to you, do you think?"

"At the time it just pissed me off. I thought he was being a jerk. Of course being pissed off wasn't allowed in our house, so I just sucked in all that anger and frustration and . . . and grew these big tits. No, really. It's funny now. It wasn't funny then. I packed it all away for the longest time. I put it in that little hothouse inside, you know, the one where we grow assorted pains and disorders, like your cancer that wasn't a cancer."

We sit to eat. A voice calls from beyond the screen. It is near dark. We look at each other.

"Anyone home?"

"The dogs didn't bark," Joan whispers.

I stare at him.

"Harry," he says. "Harry Fleet."

I feel my face burn, draw red with embarrassment and pain.

"Harry Fleet?"

All twisted around like a towel wringing, wrung, last drops
dripping agony not yet done, I see that child again drawing a
child's drawing. Let me see, I say, and a shy smile lifts toward
my downturned eyes. It seems a house, I say. A large one. It
seems a building. He answers that it's The Block. I study The
Block, its windows, almost-squares, evenly rowed, interrupt
the red brick. Overhead the learned sun: yellow ball, uniform
spokes.

What is this? I touch a smeared mess of gray, intersecting,
dissecting lines denying perspective. That's The Pit, he says.
Ours. And these are . . . other Pits. He takes me there, and his
hand in mine we walk around the building that I might see all
the sunken porches of concrete, wooden stairs overhead, these
"pits."

And I am him and the shade is down in the upstairs room,
a darkness at all its edges and an empty circle dangles from a
string at the bottom of the shade. I bounce a ball against the
bricks below the window until it skitters off into The Pit. I
find it near the screen door. Darkness there is cool like the
feel of mushrooms' shade. A sound! I clutch the ball and look
up through the light to the shade now slightly raised and no
face visible, but a voice. Come on in, it whispers. The door is
unlocked. I remain motionless till a strip of bony face, not
unattractive ugliness, creases the window's edge. Benny. He
smiles. An accent of familiarity. Come on. I smile back. Come
on, he encourages. I want to show you something. I've got a
surprise.

The screen pulls open without a squeak. Inside cave-cool rag carpets, colors twisting one around the other in thick pleasantness, flowing over floors, tables, hanging from walls. And ancient scents, foreign fragrances lick the air. I shove through the room enraptured until I hear feet halfway up the stairs. Benny is calling. I move toward the retreating voice, walking carefully around the rugs, still clutching the pink rubber Hi-bounce ball. I glance furtively at clay and glass figures, the plants crawling green across the windowsills and counters, and finally I feel the heat where the front door screen casts sun's half light against the stairs where again the painted whisper, smile audible there, calls me one at a narrow and dark time up the steps toward the shadows where I find him, naked, his organ throbbing, his hand around it, knuckles bone-white and artificial in the dusk. His thin body seems to gravitate about the scum and shine and slick of that red, pulsing staff. He leans back as if it is a burden, all this weight, as if he would shove it all into some emptiness just ahead of him. Do you want to touch it? Did you ever see one like this? You've got one. Isn't it nice? It won't hurt. Here. He takes my hand and the sticky smoothness is warm on my fingers. How could that hurt? and that's nice isn't it, and well, isn't it, well, isn't it, spitting on my hand and his hand, and all over everywhere more and more coming and coming.

"Who is it?" Joan asks. Her voice scrapes me up from beneath the steps where I sat again, longing for a mother's hand, another's hand to reach out to me in absolution.

"It's. . ."

"Danny," he says.

"Danny," I say. "The face at the top of the stairs."

"What?" he says.

"You remind me of someone I once knew. Benny."

"Is that good?"

"It's just a fact."

He is a young man with shoulder-length hair and a long, gaunt face. Eighteen. Twenty. Twenty-eight. On his back is a large pack and tied against that a violin case, its thin neck poking past one of his almost floppy ears.

"Hi," Joan says, stepping around me. "I'm Joan. This is Harry. Come on in; there's no need to talk through a screen."

Their exchange of smiles isolates me. I am lost in the suddenness of their meeting.

She helps him with his pack. "We're having eggs," she says. "Fresh from the farm, fertilized. Little tadpoles right in them. How about some?"

"Great," he says.

"Enough for two; some extra toast and it's enough for three!" She puts two more slices of bread in the toaster.

Relaxed, leaning over the table, he smiles at me. "Great place," he says. "I like the feel of it."

"How do you know about me?" I ask.

"The whole world knows about Mudman," he says, laughing.

"The commune," Joan says, tumbling eggs from each of our plates onto his. "Now that's something I'd like to see."

"It's there," Danny says. "Anytime you want to see it."

I sense in him a detachment that disturbs me. I see his assured manner, but know it to be a thin shell, the defensive covering of so many of his generation, a veneer of "owedness," give me, give me, give me. I am reminded of the legions of students I taught, all those kids unfairly led, unknowingly conditioned to think challenge and contradiction are all, not yet wise enough to see that they are controlled by what they challenge and contradict. Danny's posturing is as plain to me as the pedometer attached to his left leg, or the fiddle case on his back.

"I'm going to see it someday," Joan says. "Harry doesn't think it's much to see."

"It all depends on what you're looking for, eh?"

"They sent you here?" I ask.

"I suppose you could say that." He has a strange laugh. It seems a response to something tickling his neck and face.

"Do you walk?" Joan asks, nodding toward his pedometer.

"Sure. That's what feet are for, eh?"

"You don't hitch?"

"Well . . . " He grins around a mouthful of egg. "Once in a while. No one's perfect."

"Why did the commune send you here?"

"Do you really want to know?"

"I asked."

"Because they believe in balance. You came to them out of nowhere, and they thought someone should come to you out of nowhere."

"Why you?"

He laughs again. "I was headed this way."

Joan is staring at me. I am staring at Danny.

"Less talk, more eat," Joan says. "The eggs are getting cold."

Danny is gifted. He plays his fiddle for us. Sad, sweet, somehow eternal songs. I have always loved the violin. Its strings plumb inner and outer universes making every nowhere known. Night rolls over on its side and moans with quiet pleasure. Danny's interpretation is deeply personal. I wonder that such humanity makes it to those fingers, that someone with so bland a surface sounds such depths in himself, wonder even more that he can sound them in me. Joan is lying on the couch asleep, her tits spread like melting mountains.

He stops playing. "Actually," he says, "a man named Everett told me where to find you."

"And Mudman?"

"They still talk about you. It's the way legends are started, eh? A manlike creature appears from the woods, disappears down the road, and is never heard from again."

"What do you hang on that?" I ask him.

"Whatever you want, I guess. How about a hat."

"So you weren't really looking for me at all."

Joan's breathing oozes toward us in airy ripples, the sound of sleep's excess washing over the dam.

"Not really. Does that bother you?"

"No. It just seemed strange that anyone would be looking for me here."

"This isn't exactly the end of the world," he says, and he laughs while plucking the strings roughly, creating a curious harp-like sound.

Joan glances over sleepily, then sits up and stretches. "I was asleep," she says.

Danny places his violin across one knee and leans toward me. "Don't be so paranoid, Harry," he says.

"Harry's not paranoid," Joan says. "He's not scared of anything. He's got everything worked out. There isn't one single thing Harry needs."

That from a dead sleep. I feel betrayed by her recklessly laying me open at Danny's booted feet.

"I need a lot of things," I say. "We all do."

"I'm sorry," Joan says. "I couldn't resist."

"We all need things," Danny says. "That's why I'm here. I needed a place to spend the night. And of course it's always nice to meet a legend . . . and his lady." He nods to Joan.

She is quiet now. Possessed. So accurate a word for us, possessed.

"Well, I'm going to bed," Joan says. "Harry, you show Danny the room. The bed needs to be made. Where do you sleep when you're on the road?"

"Wherever. Barns mostly. Laundromats. Bus depots. Service stations. Around here there's always the beach. In the city if you see someone sleep outside in the park or somewhere it's sad and makes you a little heartsick, ya know? Here it's romantic or nostalgic or something entirely different. There's not the faintest hint of human neglect or corruption. No morning breath on the beach, if you get my meaning."

"Well, I'm folding," Joan says. "Good night."

"After" — he raises a booted foot into the air and reads his pedometer — "after I walked 9.3 miles to meet you, you're sacking out." Danny frowns conspicuously.

"Just another of life's little hardships," Joan says, stretching. "I'll see you in the morning."

We hear her footsteps on the stairs.

"I think I'll fold, too," I say.

"Suit yourself."

"It's the room with the porcelain knob. Take a right at the top of the stairs."

He tips his head forward and salutes me with two fingers.

Late into the night he plays. When he stops, I awake suddenly and sit upright in the silence. Joan puts her hand on my back.

"He's going outside," she says. "He's decided to sleep in the barn."

Fourteen

In the morning, dew heavy as rain drives you barefoot. It hangs in the sun in transparent shimmers, sits in tiny drops on plant and stem and makes a soft green mouth of the grass. The birds are in the garden. They fly up into the apple trees as I draw near and enter the edge of their widening circle. They watch. How do you smile at a bird? The soil is cool beneath its surface. I crawl along the rows of potatoes. The weeds, a wealth of green and texture, crowd up from the earth. Bees busy in cucumbers. I hear voices past. A man and a woman, hating.

She crying tears and words: "Have you ever worked the land? Did you ever get your hands dirty? Did you ever feel dirt beneath your nails? Did you? Well, did you? Did you?"

He snorting back: "You sound like a dime novel. Doesn't she sound like a dime novel? Don't sound like a crummy dime novel."

Joan is washing salt from herring. I stand next to her. Her long fingers flow back and forth across the speckled flesh, patting, pressing, caressing; transparent scales stick to her hands and clog the sink's drain.

"I had to do more than see my past to have my present," I say. "I had to go through with it. I had to step beyond it. I couldn't till I was ready. It has nothing to do with education."

She cuts away the fish's head and tail.

I want to stop talking. I can already hear myself lecturing.

"Step beyond what?" she says, slapping another bluish fish across her palm. "Tell me, or how am I going to know?"

"It's the biggest step. Reaction is just another part of the trap. Say someone spent thirty years helping you rehearse for a speech. Then suddenly you realize you don't want to deliver it because the words aren't yours. Once you know essentially why it's not for you, there's no sense spending thirty more years brooding about lost time, because then it still controls you, only from the other side."

"You're a word acrobat," she says. "Sometimes you're up so high I can't even see you."

"Or down so low." I reach around and hold her close. "All I'm saying is, what's past is past. Accept it. Isn't that what you tell me I should be doing?"

"Accept," she says, "and go chasing ghosts down the beach."

I release her. The vinegar and pickling spices gurgle on the stove. I hold my hand toward her. "Look," I say, showing her my thumbnail. "That blood blister was down here at the bottom of my nail. Now it's growing toward the top. Soon it'll be gone entirely."

"Professor Fleet," she says.

I sit at the round oak table and watch her back. She rinses her hands and turns toward me, twisting the hand towel around her fingers.

"It's not real, Harry. The Rocking Chair Lady's not real. It's something you don't want to face, isn't it? She's something you wish for; no, not even something you wish for, really. Harry, the problem was back there somewhere in your past. It's too bad it was like that, and we would all like to have had perfect lives, and we all know what we would do to make it better. Hindsight is twenty-twenty, as they say. You can dream all you want, but you'd save yourself a hell of a lot of time and pain if you'd get present."

"Oh! Now I'm not even here."

"Stop your wallowing! Don't you know when you do that? Oh, poor little me. The cruel world and the cruel people. You have a choice. Stay stuck in all that blame and accusation, wear that forlorn, long-suffering glaze over the rest of your life, or forgive — and why not start with yourself . . . "

"What are you feeling now, Harry?"

"I was thinking . . . "

"No! Listen! What . . . are . . . you . . . *feeling* right now this minute?"

"What am I feeling? I'm not sure . . . "

"Doesn't that say something to you?"

"I know I can't explain everything. I'm doing the best I can. Rome wasn't built in a day. Never mind Nova Scotia."

"Is there peace in metaphor?"

"No, but there's proximity."

"Come here," she says.

She is standing by the window where braids of onions hang. I go to her. She stands smiling, expectant.

"I love you," she says, and she kisses me long and passionately. "Go ahead, say it. It doesn't hurt. I . . . love . . . you. It's simple. Try it."

I pause just long enough to hear the silence explode. You'd have thought I was asked to choose between two unmarked doors: behind one, life; behind the other, death.

Joan hurls the onions across the room. The cat named Cat runs for its life. "Jesus," Joan says, "Jesus! Jesus! Jesus!"

"Of course I love you," I say, regretting the "of course" the minute it crosses my lips. I want to go to her where she stands with her back to me across the room, but I can't move.

She turns to me then and in a voice so calm it belies the outrage in her eyes, she says, "Of course I love you, too. Of course."

Later, as I put in poles for a new fence, Danny steps from the barn. He doesn't look toward the house. He fumbles with his fly and urinates on a stack of compost. I tromp down the dirt around the pole with my boots. When I look again, he is half immersed in the rain barrel at the edge of the barn, the ducks tilting by him pedometer high. I measure off the next pole. I'll need the pick to break through some rock.

I hear his feet on the steps, then see his shadow precede him into the shed where I kneel with a gasoline rag scrubbing rust from the pick.

"It's real nice here," he says. "Quiet, eh?"

"Yes."

"I was in the store when they were talking about some crazy bugger named Tom." He sits on a paint can. "I chatted them up a bit and before you know I heard tell of a strange young man what bought Heep's place. Sounds like the mysterious Mudman, I said to myself."

"Pheeps' place," I say. The anger I hear in my voice surprises me.

"Does it matter?"

"To me it does."

I step from the cool into the sun. Images of transition, things between birth and death, surround this place. Process is transparent here and lushly variable. My shoulders tremble as the pick strikes the rock. He stands watching. When I tire of his presence I tell him there is coffee inside. I want Joan to talk to someone else, to feel another life. No, I want her to feel her own life again, that we can better feel each other. I am worried to see her struggling against me. She was once so quick and free. The two of us harmonized. We were functionally and essentially complements, but lately I irritate her, fly into her like acid.

Danny smiles and shakes his head. "I don't drink coffee. Can I help?" he asks, pointing at the pick.

"No . . . thanks. I'm almost through." I begin to swing again. Water drips from my face and neck. I feel it soaking around the lip of my trousers. "It must be ledge," I say. "There's ledge all around this place. See the pitch and roll of the land. Rock. Under a . . . grass . . . cushion."

His eyes follow the landscape. His thumbs are tucked beneath his belt. The door slams and Joan, loving as she does the feel of wet grass between her toes, lopes out barefoot. She has a lovely animal way of moving. She looks sleepy in her sexy and sensual way. I want to make it up to her, lay her in the grass, feel her legs around me all open and soft and warm, the two of us locked close and the sound and smell of the sea . . .

"You can really hear the ocean today," she says. "Is that from Tuesday's storm?"

I grunt yes, then break the rock and wiggle it. "They're always bigger on the bottom. Like glaciers." I begin to break more sod from above.

"Don't lift that alone," Joan says.

I struggle with the boulder. I am on my knees.

"He doesn't want any help," Danny says. "I already asked."

"I got it, just . . . a . . . "

Joan stoops and reaches a hand, then Danny kneels and we all roll the rock out.

"You'll hurt yourself doing that," Joan says. "It's not worth it."

I clean the loose stones and chips from the hole. "Feel that," I tell them. "There's cold air in here. A draught. Feel it?"

They both stoop again, hanging hands into the hole.

"You should keep digging. There may be another world there," Danny says.

"A treasure," Joan says. "Do you think there could be? There used to be Indians around here. Did Indians bury treasure?"

"Pirate Indians," Danny says. "Good concept. The totem and crossbow, instead of skull and crossbones."

"Winds do blow beneath the surface," I say. "Think about it. The same winds that are . . . well, like the winds of time. Winds that touched people thousands of years ago could be lying there trapped, waiting, and now they're touching us."

"Profound," Joan says. "Profound."

"Just *cold* hard facts," Danny says, and they laugh. "Say, maybe it's dinosaur breath."

I go in the house to regain my grip.

I catch myself sometimes behaving as if it has to do with Joan, how she is, what she does. I think if I am withholding love, it is because of her. Through the years I've held back, keeping always separate enough to ensure my independence. I had always trailed friends like ragtail pieces on a kite. I fit around them, a soft mouth for their concerns, a receptacle for their varied ways, because I denied myself. Mine was the collective ego. What else for a collective ego to do but collect? Sure, I'd sit — or more often lie — next to women and be half responsive, but I'd resist all their efforts to be really close, really intimate and they, having opened themselves up so wide to me, having trusted me, allowed me to reach their special spots ever further within, would grow confused by my reluctance. That's when I would unload and hit the road.

My eye carries across the wide plank floors to the sea chest, a rustic Spanish medieval Gothic castle kind of thing with its great latch, steel tongue down, stained straps, buckles and leather edging and trim all in swamp shades, the colors of earth away from the sun. Nowhere is there another like it. I moved it to the bathroom from the bedroom, sliding it across the floors on an old blanket. The chests of time and tale. Images plummet to mind, chests filled with booty, coin, body: stowaways in lace. In this one: old socks, overalls and the loose parts of an overhead lamp I decide to fix. Nebula sitting there, mermaid song wet on her lips, her breasts soft hills for her hair, saying:

"One dream I had was of a great bird, an eagle or hawk, only bigger. It was fierce and silent. It swooped down, thrusting its feet ahead, a scream of claw and talons, and then I was in its grasp, and we flew higher and higher. I was dizzy and gasping. I was scared. I had no more breath, no more air. I remember thinking, So this is how it kills its prey, but later I awoke, and I wondered, Is that any way to tell a girl she's suffocating? I had my face stuffed into a pillow!"

Or: "I walked by the barn. The door was open. Morris had skins hanging all over the place. Rabbit and mink, squirrel. Then I saw a black pelt. Not skunk — a blacker black, a fuller coat. It was Lester Pheeps' cat tacked to the door."

Or: "A lie's not untrue. It's not even a sin. All it is, is just a waste of time."

Or: "People can rationalize all they want about Mildred and Morris, but they aren't so weird if you're really looking. They're everyone else turned inside out, is all. That dark shit inside that your precious Andrew and Della and so many of these other flakes are scared of, the Patches wear right on their sleeve. Myself, I admire their honesty."

Joan is calling. "Harry . . . Let's go clamming. Harry. Harry. Harry, you up there? Let's go clamming. Danny's never been."

Danny's never been.

Nebula and I wound hard through the countryside. The farms scattered about across the hills, gravel slapping against the fenders in a clatter that violated the silence and isolated us from the place we moved through. Nebula was driving. She drove well but seemed out of character behind the wheel. I like being the passenger, especially with a woman driving. I sat a bit sideways so I could see her along with the autumn pastures, woodlots and ponds. She seemed to belong to all this as certainly as sunshine and shadow, billowing grass and breeze.

"Where's the best place to find them?" I asked.

"Rinehardt's," she said. "Used to be, anyway."

"I wouldn't know a magic mushroom from a toadstool," I said.

"The amanita are different," she said. "You can't mistake anything else for them. It's apples and oranges. You'll see." A few minutes later she pointed out Rinehardt's farm, a small house, a barn and other such buildings sprawled along a rocky hillside. We drove past without slowing down.

"What's the matter?" I asked. "Why aren't we stopping?"

"The best spot is past his woodlot on the far side of here. This ground is too high. Too dry." When we pulled off onto the tongue connecting the road to the fenced pasture beyond the drainage ditch, she shut off the engine and the sudden quiet set off a buzzing in my ears.

"Do your ears buzz?" I asked.

She smiled. "Just when people are talking about me."

"My ears buzz. I wonder sometimes if it's normal or just me."

"I don't know," she said, and she climbed from the car. I followed her to the old rail fence where she stood quietly staring out. "We'll wait here for him."

"For who?"

"Simon. He won't mind, but I like to tell him, let him know."

"Does he know? About the mushrooms?"

"He knows they're there. He knows people pick them. He don't care. Most people see amanita as wearing the skull and crossbones on their caps. That's the difference between a European and an Indian. The European eats a mushroom and gets high, hallucinates, is thankful he didn't die. He lives through it. Endures it, let's say. He is thankful not to be dead and swears he'll never do it again. The Indian says 'Wow!' The Indian sees the gift in it. The Indian thanks God and starts picking for a rainy day. The Indian is thankful to be alive. That's quite different from being thankful not to be dead."

"Fear," I say. I hear a car approaching.

"It's attitude," she says. "All in the way you look at things. I never worry about being dead."

"Never?"

"Why would you worry about it? You're on this side, or you're on that side. Worrying about it, or anything else for that matter, is a big waste of time."

The man getting out of the long blue Lincoln was pure fisher-farmer. If he'd climbed from the cab of an old Ford pickup, or even a new one, it wouldn't have seemed so strange to me, such a rupture of my image of this place.

"How is she, La-la?" he said.

"Finest kind, Simon," she said. "Is it good for to see your old puss or what?"

They laughed and hugged warmly and I was introduced. Simon Rinehardt nodded as I told him where I was living. "Oh yes. Lester Billy's house."

"So! We thought we'd pick some mushrooms, if that's all right with you."

"Oh sure. Pick your fill. I just don't want any of those outsiders trompin' round here. Startin' to come from all over, they are. Damn nuisance." He looked at me. "You're all right. You're with her. Anyone's all right, they're with her."

"Mildred been by?"

"Not this year."

"Don't you like them?" I asked.

"Mushrooms? No. Right slimy things, they is. I eat'm on a pizza's about all."

"Eat some of them ones I showed ya, Simon, and you can *be* the pizza," Nebula said.

He smiled and pulled his vest to one side, showing a mickey of rum.

"This is enough for me," he said. "The Captain treats me good."

Nebula and I picked near one another at first, but we drifted some distance apart, pursuing our individual rhythms. The few freshly picked pieces we swallowed at the start gave me a pleasant buzz at first, then placed me inside timelessness, gave me powers of absence or selflessness that I never knew before. I loved everything. I felt so good, so connected. Grounded. I guess I was grounded! I was down on all fours, crawling around searching, when suddenly they would appear, like a tiny village of peters, waiting, calling; joyous to be beheld, beholden to be had. Into my bread bag they went; on I went.

Whenever I looked up, I smiled so broadly my cheekbones ached. Everything was perfect. Even me, I was perfect. The day was perfect. That woman, that gorgeous lady far across the field by the edge of the wood, that Nebula, she was perfect. I walked toward her, stopping occasionally to accept another batch of magical callers. Some had heads no longer than my fingernail, others had tops large as my thumb.

"La-la Nebu-la," I said.

She smiled. "My, my. What have we here? I do believe you're stoned, Mr. Fleet."

"I've never enjoyed myself more, Ms Patch." Her face was infused with a magnetism and vibrance more felt than seen. "The stone is so visceral," I said. "My whole body is alive." As soon as I said it, I laughed. She laughed too. Together there in the fields we roared and roared.

"I like you," she said.

"I like you, too," I said.

She held up her almost full bag, indicated another full one tied to her belt, then she came over, still smiling, and kissed me.

"Later I'm going to blow your mind," she said.
Later, she did.

After Nebula left, I unbolted the cellar door. There was a light switch at the top of the stairs. I flipped it on. The stairs twist sharply to the left halfway down, so you can't see a great deal even if you crouch low as I did. But I heard it. Sloshing around. And with my eyes closed, I could see it, too. I knew it was approaching. I could feel it, almost *realize* it. Then, just at the last second, I would slam the trap door shut and return to the kitchen. It couldn't have me yet. I wasn't ready. But I didn't have much time, I knew. The water was rising. It was already inches above the pine planks Lester had spread about the cellar floor. Lighter planks and bits and pieces of wood, dirt, muck, floated aimlessly about. Did I have ballast enough for this, I wondered.

"She wants some work," Andrew had said. "Yes, she wants some work. She may be all right. But then again, a good rain. . . A man just don't know about an old drain."

We were staring at the broken pipe in the cellar floor. It was barely apparent beneath the water freshly stirred up by his rough fingers as he felt in and around its depths. I stood back.

"She's seeping now," he said, shaking water from his hand. "How long she'll drain I couldn't say."

The water went on rising. It was there. I recalled that child running, leaping down dark stairs, sharp knives thudding into the door just as he made the corner, barely, and only till the next time when squeezing his little balls, hoping not to have to piss again and go alone up those unlighted stairs where always the back had finally to be turned against the dark (DON'T YOU LEAVE THE BATHROOM LIGHT ON), fighting it, holding it (KEEP YOUR HANDS AWAY FROM THERE. IF YOU HAVE TO GO, GO!), and finally, reluctantly, the child does go, again makes that trip with its final desperate dash, leap and dive to safety (I'VE TOLD YOU A THOUSAND TIMES NOT TO

JUMP DOWN THOSE STAIRS). And that's true, too.

"Could ream her out," Andrew had said. "Della's waiting supper or I'd lend you a hand. Do you have a coil?"

Then Della on the phone concerned that I might be flooded out by a coming storm. No, it's okay. Yes, it's all right. No. No. Yes. Yes.

"Harry," Joan calls. "We're going for clams. Danny and I. Want to come?"

I made out the base of the furnace, the water nearing its door. All night I sat watching, waiting. The gray wood in uneven lines trembled below the water. I stared and shivered in the stammering spring cold. I closed the door behind me and shut off the light before feeling my way down step by awful step, and in my head the scream grew louder and louder, detonating and immense until there was only that and nothing else.

By morning, I had gathered the remains in runny pools on the puddled floor. Globs. Like jellyfish. I walked around these and poked about the drain with a stick. More of it. Matter. I lifted out the slippery eel-like mass in pieces. Rubber flesh. I laughed. Elastic flesh. Nonflesh. Blobs. I hauled them out. I whistled. It was shattered. I knelt in the wet and searched out the pieces with my hands. Jellied. Consommé. Jell-O. Nothing holding. Nothing holds. I buoyed them to the surface, then cupped my hands and splashed them onto the damp boards. I heard footsteps upstairs. Andrew's voice calling me.

"I'm down here!" I shouted proudly. "I'm down here. I fixed it." I was grinning when through the open stairs I saw and heard his boots clomping brown and steady down to me, down in the cellar, down the stairs.

"Harry. What *are* you doing up here!" Joan says.

"Getting a little relief," I say. "Just getting a little relief."

Everyone is either figuring it out or ignoring it. Process. I breathe the sweet salt-sea smell. Intoxicant. I stretch myself between the poles of yesterday and tomorrow and the sun bakes my face. No one else is on the blanket, and I think of acorn squash, gourd-green, peeling ripe beneath my nail. Melon. Name. Family I knew. What we used to call a fair-sized breast. Seeds. All seeds and source. Allusion. "Hey, lady. Want some *bird* seed?"

Joan and Danny are digging clams. Joan has her skirt tied above her waist. The shirtless white of Danny's upper body with his red arms and neck, his back to me. They too are serious clammers. Stalkers. Planners. Quick diggers. Behind them the tide edges near. Tiny craters, shadow pits they've dug, bound in erratic patterns across the flats. Gulls sway across the sky, and sandpipers flit noiselessly across the smelly sand.

I am far from them in the dunes where the grass bends beneath soft sea breezes. I decide to think nothing. Above or below, I'll go where the threat of thought, impulsive as a schoolboy's erection, cannot reach me.

When I look again they are even farther away. They are like puppets. Stiff and formal. Rites and ritual. Kneeling in the swamp-brown sand, still picking clams. I think of Joan spreading her clove, the purple-brown-red petals rendered wet, her fingers long and tight, a smoothly nailed white against the dark of hair. I love her. It is one of the saddest thoughts I've ever had.

She waves now. I wave back and her wave grows wider, more frantic, a distant semaphore of emotion like a shout.

"You were high in my head," I tell her when she returns. "I was thinking about you." I'm excited and I'm talking quickly because Danny is catching up. He is lugging the bucket.

She smiles. Her hands are mucky and her lovely pubes drip like packing from the sides of her red panties. She blows aimlessly at strands of hair that fall over her eyes. I brush them aside for her.

"Were you really thinking about me," she says, staring deeply into my eyes, "or were you just *thinking*, with me along for the ride?" I avoid answering as Danny sidles up.

"What do we do with our clams?" he asks. "Should we wash them here or take them back? Joan can't remember."

"I remember we rinse them on the beach," Joan says, "but I don't remember whether we soak them in sea water or fresh."

"Sea water," I say.

She takes my hand to reassure me. "Then we feed them cornmeal," she says, "and their necks come way out like long skinny worms. It's how they eat."

"We eat the necks!" Danny says. "Blagh!"

"That just happens when they're hungry," I say. "They send their mouths out to look for food. Of course the mouth is at the end of the neck."

"That's right," Joan says to Danny. "Wait till you see it. They turn into long fingers with mouths at the end. Like snakes. Ick. It's awful."

Later they stand on the porch watching the bucket.

"See," Joan says. "Look at them."

"Now that's what I call real existential search!" Danny says. "They must be *French* feelers."

They laugh.

"I better feed them some more," Joan says, "before they die." She sprinkles the yellow meal over the grasping fingers of matter. "Some for Sartre," she says.

"Give Camus some, too."

They are like children. I feel shut out, though I know I am shut in, and there's a real difference.

Later Danny takes up his violin and begins to play quiet pastoral things, vaguely recognizable things, but things I'm sure I never head before. It is *right* in the kitchen. The mood

is right. The stove is right. The sun-struck window and door
are right. The dogs sprawled on the floor are right.

I walk out onto the porch to place a newspaper under the
bucket. I know from experience that these "French" clams
will be spitting water all over the place. The myth of Spitipus.
The paper will keep the salt from eating into the wood.

Through the open door I see that the fog is moving in. It
never just comes, it arrives. In wisps and waves it weaves a
tapestry of soft mystery, a wonderful kind of primordialness
to all things. One of the most intensely beautiful aspects of
this place is what happens to the space that joins everything
together. There is depth to the essence we see and breathe
here, a life and vitality that shifts suddenly, like our moods.

Right now, it is a great, brooding intelligence. I brood
within its brooding.

But I no longer wait for the word, or the man with the key,
the answerman bringing the answer, the ultimate definition. I
no longer wait for him or her to drive up in an old pickup, or
tow-truck, perhaps a duck under one arm, or maybe a violin
strapped to his back.

Tinker, tailor, manchild, sailor,
Two legs on which to stand
You run, you walk, you gladly talk
But you can't outsail the land.

In the attic are two old children's books ablaze with nine-
teenth-century transparent witchstick morality. Messages and
money dictated those times. Systems. So many systems, and
yet I find no *way* to think. Just *things* to think. As I bound
across this moonscape of everyday craters, I wonder at the
gravity I seem always to feel.

Suddenly I find myself staring down at the yellow meal and
clams, the paper and print, classified ads: Economy studs.
Lunenburg pudding. Pizza. The violin stops. I will go in.
Tonight I will ask Danny to leave.

Fifteen

S ure, I could see *myself* as an intrusive presence. But, goddamn it, Joan, you know, that's just me, that's not how it *is*. It's almost as if we were trained to see disjunctively, to recognize our difference, to believe that we don't fit, or that others don't fit, which is the same thing. Look at these trees and bushes and plants, the grass and rock and sky, the space around it all — well, that's a perspective too, you know! Who's to say what fits and what doesn't?"

I press down with my crayon and a thick line hangs there.

"Do you ever think of going home?" Joan asks.

"Home? This is home now."

"Your family, your friends."

"We keep in touch. They'll visit. I'll visit. I'm in the right place."

"Yeah, I think I am, too. Did you really like my parents?"

Joan's father, John James, is a tall, well-proportioned man with glasses. He looks like a gracefully aging basketball player from a time when six foot five was tall and dunkin' was still only a doughnut, or something we did for apples on Halloween, or a line from one of our refashioned nursery rhymes:

When the weather's hot and sticky

That's no time for dunkin' dickie
When the frost is on the pumpkin
That's the time for dickie dunkin'.

Mrs. James, Priscilla, has a calm self-confidence and a pleasantly sensual portliness that makes her and John together look like an exclamation point gone askew — the long and the short of it, you might say. Joan has her mother's refreshing charm, the kind that resides everywhere inside, but manifests finally in the face. The energy, too, is her mother's. And her sensuality. Her body beautifully and tenderly transformed comes from her dad.

It was plain to see that this family had come to terms, had arrived somewhere with each other, so when John and Priscilla left to drive back to Toronto after a two-day stay, I understood Joan's tears, and theirs, and if I wouldn't have appeared patronizing or stupid, I'd have stood there in the drive shouting bravo and giving them a long, loud hand.

"Do you think we, you and I, are getting anywhere?"

"What do you mean?"

"What do I mean! Why do you do that? You know what I mean."

"Sure, we're getting somewhere. Don't you think we are?"

"Sometimes. Then, sometimes I'm not so sure."

"It's hard to know anything for sure, isn't it."

"I know how much I love you. And it scares me, Harry. I'm not sure I can trust you. There's something of you that you hold back and it scares me."

"At the center is the primeval eye responding and registering and knowing, a brilliant flower in deepest shade."

"See!" She tosses her head in exasperation. "You and your bullshit equivocation."

She climbs up and brushes bits of grass off her pants. "You're scared to be serious — really serious. So you talk a crock," she says. "Life's not poetry and images and flowers in deepest shade. It's you and me. It's Lester Pheeps jumping in the ocean. It's that Burr. It's . . . it's her, Mildred Patch fucking dreams or Indians or spirits, or whoever the fuck in the world or woods. And this — " She takes my sketch pad from my hand. "Why are you always drawing me, anyway?"

The question comes from that surface of words like a fish quietly exploding from the sea.

"I don't know. Or maybe I do."

She stares at the pad a moment longer, one of her long fingers across her lips. It's as if she's reviewing all the sheets in this one, all the drawings of her I've done as I tried to capture her in this position and that — the portfolio of Joan.

"Every time I ask you something — every damn time — you don't know. You talk all around things. Everything is so damn debatable, so academic. You *fire* words at me. I feel them zinging by, flying over my head. Once I enjoyed it. I even thought I understood. Now . . . "

I glimpse a new sound in her voice, a sound beyond inquiry, beyond amorphous pond, cloud, sky and the soft rest of shrug. I put down my charcoal and take her hand. "Come here," I say.

She stands limp, breathing deeply, her breasts buoy, rise and fall in loose moon-guided waves.

"It's getting cool." She rubs at her arms, tucks her hands beneath her freshly shaven pits for a moment, then drops them to her sides.

"Come . . . " I repeat.

"I can't."

I look at our hands almost touching, my fingers reaching toward hers.

"You know I haven't any answers."

"Well, what about this?" She touches my sketch of her. "Look at it, Harry. What do you see?"

I shake my head absently.

"You know what I think you see? A mass of electricity,

good company wearing a better than average set of tits. It's all so damn obvious," she says. "Everything is so damn obvious. You are so damn scared of commitment."

"Whatever is, is."

"Whatever is, is," she says mockingly. "Mr. Enigma-man. Go ahead, hide in your thoughts. Hide behind your words. Listen to that wonderful ego. Watch out, Harry. It may be love, Harry. Pull back. We wouldn't want that now, would we? No. You bloody asshole! You're stuck. You're trapped in a dream. Or is it a nightmare?"

Blood swirls in hot patterns about my face. I don't know what to say.

"I don't mean to be — "

"The thing that really bothers me," she says, staring down at the pad, "the thing that *really* bothers me, is that it's finally so futile. What I am to you doesn't have a whole lot to do with me, does it? And it's not funny."

"I'm not laughing," I say, placing the sketchbook on the sand. "God, Joan, I'm not laughing."

"Something is happening to us."

I take her hand. "We'll just have to sort it out, okay? We'll have to try to understand."

She leans her head against my shoulder. I feel a distance that frightens me, and as we sit silently for what seems hours in the sand, I feel the stark, awful reality of having nothing to say and everything to lose, but without words to express it, I feel tiny and insignificant, a man blowing against the wind.

I still can't paint a portrait of Joan. I can't seem to get it right. All I can do is sketch impressions. Maybe that I can't paint her finally has, as she suggested, to do with my not seeing all of her. The danger with complements, I suppose, is that they can become merely adjuncts, decorations we wear because they suit the occasion or time.

The sense of Joan that I think will always linger with me

is of her soft sensuality, her unambiguous presence. That is still there, but there is also something in and around that presence, something that feeds that presence and transforms it. Whatever "it" is, is much more important to any definition of Joan than is my view of her. And it is that unique fuse that fuels the whole, that heart or soul that I miss when she is not here. It is not the wonderful beauty of her person, not even the immense pleasure of our physical sharing; it is the comfort she gives by being always right where she is: here, now, present.

Joan is newly calm. Her relaxed dynamism returns. We decide to drive by to see Andrew and Della. Again she loves everything. Praise runs from the car windows across the gardens and lawns. Della is hanging wash, Andrew is nearing the barn. Della glances toward the car, then goes inside. My stomach hitches. I have not seen them since Joan's arrival.

"Hello," I say to Andrew.

"Hello," he says. He is poking around the tractor, his thick hands cracked with grease, his white shirt sleeves rolled neatly over his forearms.

"I want you to meet Joan," I say.

"How do you do," he says, lines heavy around the eyes, half turning his head, his hands still rooted to the engine's side.

"This is a beautiful place," she bubbles. "I just love it."

Andrew seems to smile. I see one ear lift.

"Fixing the tractor?" she asks.

"Yes, changing the plugs."

I see Della behind a curtain, feel her eye growing large there, crushing the glass.

"I still have your Stillson wrench," I say.

"Yes," he says. "Well, you drop it by some time."

"This is a nice place to farm," Joan says.

"Yes," Andrew says.

I want to shake him. It isn't to be this way. So what if I live with this woman out of wedlock? Forget your cock-eyed, perverse morality. Don't do this to me, Andrew!

Della pulsing in the window, sucked tight to the glass like a waiting spider. Pour the tea, Della! Get out the china, the molasses cookies. Joan is here. Serve up the stories, the words that decorate our lives. Come out, Della. Resurge. Call her, Andrew. Call her tight ass out here now, this minute. Don't let "their" way rupture our embrace.

"Harry sure thinks a lot of you and Mrs. Hayward," Joan says.

Andrew wipes his hands on a piece of yellowed sheet. "Well, we've lived here a long while." He pauses. "We're part of the place, you could say."

I feel as I did when I flunked the big exam. I believed in answers, believed what they taught, and I memorized so much that words lay like hash in my head. I didn't know about words then. I didn't understand that they were inadequate.

"We'd better go," I say to Joan. "We have to stop for fish."

"Yes, well, I've work to do in the barn."

"Say hello to Della," I added, nodding toward the house.

"Yes," he says. "I will."

Small-mindedness clutters my thought. I back the car around.

"His barn is filthy," I say as we drive away.

Joan puts a hand on the seat between us.

"The cows are all covered with shit. It's matted in their hair. He keeps a pig under the barn. It roots around and keeps the crap leveled off. He raises a plank and shovels shit down the hole onto the poor pig's head."

Joan laughs. I feel a sudden burst of anger fly up from deep within me, then just as suddenly I am laughing with her, laughing so hard tears pour from my eyes.

"Then he feeds it milk," I gasp. "Actually" — I struggle to get the words out — "actually he has a real affection for that pig. The cows, too. And the milk is as clean and white as ever you'll taste. They double filter it."

Two boys are walking along the side of the road with fishing poles. We are calm. Joan unhooks her seatbelt and slides over next to me, placing one hand on my thigh.

"It's a shame, though," Joan says. "They sound like such great people."

"They are," I say. "You can't help but love them."

That night Joan says, "Forgive them. Let them go. It's very liberating. Say it. I forgive you, I love you, I release you. Try it."

I sit in awkwardness, like a child asked to perform. I say, "I can't do it."

"That's okay. You're just not ready."

I hear, close up, wind in the sails — strong canvas flapping in snatches, shedding surfaces in quick jerks, and I am chilled and scared at the immensity of it and the sea spray wet all over my face.

Rocking Chair Beach follows an old stagecoach road that trails the sea to distant places. A century ago, a century hence. Me sandwiched between, halfway from or to undefined points. I walk for miles. No one anywhere. The road becomes barely passable, narrowing to two awkward ruts like dried-up streams where some tractor or truck has been in a now-forgotten wet season.

It is early morning. Sweater-cool, the sun just rising. When I pass Andrew and Della's house it is fresh asleep, the old oak shading it from first sun. Their cattle standing in the pasture raise their heads to look at me. I cluck and make low cow sounds to them, but when I approach the fence they all move away. "Been warned about me, have you?" I say, smiling.

I walk along the sand and rock beaches whenever possible.

Someone has made a sandcastle. There is a moat around it with a popsicle-stick bridge across a riverbed of damp sand. Commerce's catalysts, they remind me of another popsicle stick with the word PRIZE printed on it. It was a hot, tenement-step summer. I sat beneath the lowest stair in that cement excavation, the porch of sorts called The Pit. Thick, creamy, teeth-stinging-cold ice cream on a stick. I licked absently until I saw the hump of the P in PRIZE. All five letters were there in the frozen deep. I was a winner. Of what?

Memories. Surfaces acting like pinpricks, taps to the sweet and sour below: A screen door with a squeaky spring making a hard rush against air, then springing to with a soft slam; church chimes; the old Packard crunching over gravel, lurching over the tree roots in the drive. An eternity of sound where you've been, where you are.

Last night as we lay in the dark waiting to fall asleep, I thought of Mom and Dad. The last time I saw them Mom ordered the All You Can Eat Rib Eye Special. Now you have to picture this. My mother was five foot nothing and a lean string bean of a woman. She always took servings that were equivalent to other people's leftovers. So of course there was no way that she could finish the meal she had ordered — and she didn't.

"Why didn't you get a regular order?" Dad asked. Mom shrugged. "It'd be cheaper," he said, finishing off the last of her plate. "You know how I hate waste."

"Yes, dear," she said, and she went on squeezing her tissue in her tiny fist.

At the salad bar there was a large sign saying CHICKEN NOODLE and another saying PEA. "There's chicken noodle soup here, and there's pea soup there," Mom said to me. "Help yourself."

"Thanks, Mom."

Even when he was being encouraging, Dad could be irritable. He was like a Good Man doll someone was always sticking pins into. That night when I expressed my surprise that a hot dish of zucchini was part of the salad bar, he said, "Of course it's part of the salad bar. It's always part of the salad bar. What else would it be a part of, if not the salad bar?"

"It was his tone that irritated me, the judgment in it, the real meaning coming across in and all around the words, the real toss like a wizard's pitch, a psychological beanball. The truth was he meant well, just wanted to brush me back, teach me respect. Now I see he was out of control. Anyway, in talking to Dad I was always so busy looking at all the stuff he threw, I never thought to look at him — or the ball. Put simply, he had a way of making people close to him feel like shit."

"Without meaning to, of course," Joan said.

"Oh yes! He'd be crushed to think he did the wrong thing or hurt anyone. It would destroy his image of himself. Anyway, he's like your dad. A lot like him, actually. Not what I see now — they mellow — but what you told me about the way he was then."

"It's really strange how all this stuff is passed along generation to generation."

"Am I like that?"

"Judgmental? Yes. Maybe not the same way, but it's there."

"In the outside world the stranger was always right. He wanted to be a good person. He tried to live like a movie hero," I said. "He always meant well. Once when we were in a long line-up to see the Red Sox and Yankees play we lucked in and got the last bleacher seats to the game. A guy was behind us with three kids who were wailing to beat the band when they realized they weren't going to get in. So Dad talked to the man, listened to his sad tale, then gave him our tickets."

"It must have been a very sad tale. You can just imagine."

"I was ten years old. All I knew was I was hurt and angry."

"You're not ten now."

"No."

"Then you should let it go. And really, in retrospect, was it so important?"

"I guess not. He really loved all of us. And he expressed that love. He showed us what affection looked like but . . . "

"Ah yes, the *buts* and the *should haves* and the *could haves*. Looking back from perfection."

"He could never let up on the criticism. If you forgot to put the kettle on for tea, or made the wrong turn, or said the wrong thing. I could never do anything right. You know what that's like for a kid? Pick, pick, pick."

"You seemed to turn out all right."

"Did I? Yes, I suppose. I just know it could be a lot easier."

"They did the best they could."

"Maybe. . . no, you're right. Of course they did."

"And you did the best you could."

"I was so messed up, I drove them nuts."

"I don't think so. But that's past. Now it's up to us to take it from here. We can learn from their mistakes and go on positively, or whine and grumble."

"And go on to make our own mistakes."

"They don't have to be the same ones."

"And someday a child will live happily from the start, not just ever after."

"It is possible, but it's not up to your father or mother or mine. It's up to us if the cycle's to be broken."

"My mother used to bake for us all the time. Even when she was working she found the time to bake us cookies. She cared so much. She didn't know how to say it, but she showed it. Him too. Saturday morning I remember was usually just the two of us. He'd make scrambled eggs with hot dogs sliced in and we'd be together, just us. Where was everyone else? Mom! God, how she worried. She kept me from playing football, convinced my father it would be too dangerous. She was scared to death out in the world."

The surf on this distant stretch of beach is dramatic. White-cap-clean spit of salt spray. Open sea. There is not the safety of the bay. I stroll leisurely and soon the sun is full in the sky. White-orange smear dodging the clouds. I strip away my clothes and stand naked. The minute my genitals slap free they shrink, but soon the sun licks them, drawing them back down. I rub my hands over my chest and my thighs, take the limp rushing meat in my hands, private muscles stemming and stretching, yearning and dancing. I want to mate the world. I want life beneath me between my legs. I want the pleasure of eternity. Instead, I go swimming.

The water is cold. I stay under the waves and swim slowly out to sea. Beneath me pebbles, shell-tiny life and rocks. Fingers of wet vegetation slip over me. When I come up covered with seaweed there is only open water ahead and to either side. The uneven line of the coast is behind me. My body is numb. I reach down to push my balls from my belly where they have withdrawn from the cold. Spare eyeballs tucked away beneath a hank of hair and bone.

When I turn to check on the land, I see the Indian. I almost didn't see him. He would be visible only from the water and then only for a moment. He is far away, but I can see that he wears buckskin and a feather points up from his head. There is the glint of what must be a knife at his hip. Dangling from his belly are some flaps, perhaps leatherwork. With beads in a colorful tribal design?

Somehow his movement appears frail, fretful. He kneels beneath a lone ash tree to perform what I take for an old ceremony. I tread water and watch, though there seems nothing to see. Smoke. A wisp of it.

"No. No Indians around here anymore." Andrew's face. Craggy skin in rubbed red blotches. I watch for a long time. A large trawler passes far out to my left. On some nights foreign vessels anchor in the bay and press cheery puffs of light into close skies. A large wave rolls water over my neck and head. Suddenly I realize the water is dangerously cold. I swim back to shore.

I stand dripping-wet on the sand and gaze around. The Indian — if he was even there — has gone. A cloud swallows the sun and the air chills me. Balls like corrugated leather. I rub them, rub my arms and shoulders, my chest and legs. Wet hair like cold snakes on my face. I brush it back with my hands. Then the sun is free again and I sit on a rock, warmer now and in less hurry to dry. Only one patch of cloud yet to come and that far away. It is the face of the wind, that cloud. I saw it above winter's poem in grade school, a stern white swirl with eyes and an O mouth blowing icy cold. I lean back, casually stroking myself, and thrust my pelvis forward. Could I fuck the sky? That cloud? Myself? My self. Could I fuck my self? Hadn't I managed to do that already?

"Harry," I say, "will you give it a break!"

I must be getting better.

Suddenly a high piercing heavy-voweled war cry. Chinese-sounding. I dress quickly and go to see. How do you address an Indian? So little is left of them now. The antique stores, the curiosity shops, have sold away the bits and pieces of interest — those pieces considered of any "value." The rest of their culture has been destroyed, damaged or displaced. Lives like the land used up and shuttled aside. "Done? Fire her into the woods. 'S no good. Fire it'n woods." I hadn't found even one arrowhead when I hoed through the brush of Council Grove. What did I expect to find there beneath the sweet, wet rot of unstaged life? Surely I wasn't seeking arrowheads. No matter. There were only pale, anemic worms, snails, slugs, two tobacco tins rusted through. But it was engaging. I found myself digging around the roots of the largest stump there, recalling the network of roads and turns I'd once carved around the roots of another tree. "You're kind of old for that, aren't you, boy."

The campfire is out. Scattered across the ground are some candy wrappers, wax paper, fresh bread crusts, wads of toilet paper, a paper bag, its insides all sticky with what I figure is semen. A few hundred feet down a newly beaten path, perched in a tree, I find young Burlap Billy, the red-haired Indian.

"How," I say.

"How," he says.

"Peace," I say.

"Peace," he says.

He looks as if he is about to disintegrate, peel like bark from a diseased tree.

"This white man" — I make what I consider appropriate Indian gestures — "this white man comes in peace. This land" — I face all the directions equally — "is Indian land. I ask nothing of you."

He is pale. Suffocating. His Adam's apple rolls up and down his throat. I want to tell him of my spirits and my ghosts, of haunted and hunted lands. I must reach him, haul him out, introduce him to himself, help him to see it's okay.

"No white man should ever come here," he says tearfully. "This is Indian place."

"And so it shall be," I say, turning to leave. I take three or four steps, feel the path of his eyes wired to my back, restraining me, and then the voice booming, "No white man knows Natooma!"

"Natooma," I say, turning to face him.

"No white man knows Natooma!"

"All men know Natooma."

He stares cautiously, a cushy, red-headed squirrel gripping the branch so tightly his knuckles are white. A pair of socks hangs from his belt. Hand-knit argyles. They would make a good headband. Later, I will tell him.

"Tell no one of Natooma," he says.

I nod and turn again to walk away.

"Harry!"

I stop.

"Harry." Tears wash a path down the charred wood designs that mark his face.

"It's okay, Billy," I say. "It's okay."

Sixteen

The days shorten. The sound of summer traffic thins, then vanishes. The small tourist shop closes. Chimneys scatter smoke in airy imitation of sound. Inside, the bellies of stoves crackle.

"I'm Burr."

He looks as he did that day on the hill, the same wool cap on his head, the same boots, the same pants, but a green-and-black checkered jacket covers his thick upper body.

"Yes. I saw you cutting Carleton's wood. Come in." As I turn, expecting him to follow, I notice Joan standing close by, curious.

"What would you like done?" he asks. He has not moved.

I feel a mild panic. Burr is supposed to know what needs doing. Everyone tells of Burr suggesting projects. "When he comes, let him do what he wants." What *he* wants, not what *we* want.

"If he's a mind to reshingle your roof, don't be settled into fences. Let him be."

I stare at Burr's eyes. Their apparent blackness is really a deep brown: swamp mud highlighted by fireflies. His face is the first truly sculpted face I've seen: the lines of cheek and chin are softly strong like fish line under pressure. When he speaks, his words act like a generator to his eyes. He seems immensely insightful. Disproportionately articulate. But how do I know this? He says so little.

"Well," I drawl. "I don't see what there is to do, really."

He stands silent. I can expect no help from him on this. The barn needs a new roof, but I don't have materials, and besides, that is more than I can allow him to do. There are still cabbages and some root crops remaining in the garden, so he can't dig that up. I flop about in my head for an acceptable need.

"The well has to be cleaned," Joan says, stepping more directly into our line of vision.

"That's right," I say. "When we last checked it the water tested 'poor.' We can't drink it. I forget what the cuniform — is that it? — count was. Anyway . . . "

"I'll dip it out," he says, looking at Joan, then at me. "There are buckets in the barn?"

"Yes. But wait, I have a better one, a cleaner one."

As I dig under the sink, I hear Joan talking to him. I can't make out the words. I knock over a can of lye. The new bucket is jammed behind a pipe. I tug and pull, but it's no use.

"It's stuck. You'd think what went in would come out." I smile and shrug.

They both look at me.

"Well, why don't you go to Bones' for the Javex," Joan says, "and I'll get it out. Can you wait?" she asks him.

Burr says nothing. I tell him to make himself at home, and I go to Bones' store.

Maud holds a postcard toward me. It is a 3-D shot of an unidentifiable terrace with an unidentifiable view. People sit in the foreground looking off at ever-receding depths of statuary, walls, gardens, water, boats, mountains, sun, sky.

"It appears to be flat," Maud says. "I don't know how they do it."

"It's three-dimensional," I say, touching the card.

"It's some smart, that trick photography," Mason says, looking at the cello tomatoes and lettuce. "That's what it is." Elsa stares at me. "A special camera, do you suppose?" "They can do almost anything today," Mason says."It's them Japs. Now they some smart, or what? I'll tell you! Give us a couple pound a them green tomatoes there, Maud."

"It's only what you always see but compacted," I say. "It's got a frame around it and it's compressed. They set one scene on top of another so you think it's extraordinary, but actually it's quite normal. Look." I point across the store. "Everything is receding, see. Some things are close, some are far, some in between. We see this way all the time, but we ignore it. What's near is big. What's farther, smaller. Farthest, smallest. It's an illusion. An optical illusion."

Elsa grins broadly. "There now, didn't I tell you he knows just everything," she says, and she picks up her bag and nods thoughtfully at me, then goes home.

I am almost overcome with shame.

Outside the store, I see Lester Billy Pheeps coming across the way. Heavy ham-hock walk. Lumberer with a ginger ale bottle dangling from his ax hand.

"Hello." Same mellow-husky voice. Same breaking of the word into parts.

"Hello," I say.

No. There is definitely no scar on this chin. This obviously is not the real Lester Pheeps. The Lester Pheeps who drowned is now a complete stranger to me; the spirit of the house is for me, has been for me, I now realize, this unknown and quite alive face.

Night. Joan sits in the tub, bleeding from one raised leg. I watch the blood trickle away from her ankle and disappear behind the calf.

"You know, once I shaved my entire body," she says. "My

girlfriend Sandra and I both did. I remember coming into the kitchen with my bald head gleaming. Mom and Dad were having a drink. He took one look and said, 'Priscilla,' and she looked and said, 'Joan!' It was a dumb thing to do, I suppose, but it wasn't the last time I did something dumb. They didn't punish me. Sandra's father, Rod — great name for him — spanked her, but you couldn't ever be sure what he thought. Besides, he used to take all of us across his knee and spank us every chance he got. In fun, of course. He had a checklist of small offenses. Twenty spanks for not calling him sir. We used to call him The Rod, but not when Sandra was around. She had enough to deal with. Ten spanks for forgetting to smile. He was twisted, but you know I sort of liked him and — don't tell anyone this — I really liked the feel of that hand on my bum."

"Bare."

"God, no! I was only about thirteen.

"It's okay, anyway. If there ever was a consenting kid, I was it. It makes growing up a little harder, but I'm working on it."

I am learning to smoke a pipe. I tamp at it. Poke. Prod. The bowl gets hot, or it goes out. There are ways to break in a pipe. I've tried all of them. Joan found the pipe in an old wooden ice chest in the shed. "Brand-new," she said. "Never been used."

She places the razor on the shelf near the tub.

"It's a shame, though, don't you think?" she adds.

"What's that?"

"That we have to do things to each other. Fuck each other up."

Later that night Joan says, "We can't sleep."

"No."

"He's really almost strange," she says of Burr, "almost beautiful. You feel that you know him from somewhere. It's a feeling. But not really *know*, either. I can't find the word."

I follow her search across the ceiling, swirling along the rivers of streaming cracks.

"Like reincarnation," she says. "Like maybe I knew him in another life. Does that sound crazy?"

"No."

She pauses. I feel the energy in her. She is breathing irregularly. She says, "I think he needs me. Does that sound silly?"

"No."

She stretches her toes beneath the sheet, tipping them down. I feel her body tighten like a bow.

"His eyes," she says. "They're almost not eyes at all. They seem detached and yet they're at the center too, somehow."

"What do you mean?"

"What do I mean," she laughs. It's more a snort. "That's a switch. What do *I* mean." There's a touch of exasperation in her voice, the hint of a hand forced against its will to cover — or uncover — its parts. "You don't know what I mean. Ha!" She sits up and swings her legs over the edge of the bed and walks to the window. "I'll bet you really don't. You're just that . . . that . . . " The moon falls across her face and neck in patchy strips.

Suddenly she spins around. "You're hurting me." Her voice is soft but sharp, like a rake of claws. Her words are knots of anger and fear. "You push and you push. You want to get at where it's soft, don't you? You want to squash out my life, take away what little I have of me."

"The soft belly of self."

"Fuck your soft belly of self!" she screams, and she comes and sits near me.

"I hurt," she says. "Can't you understand that? I hurt!" She starts to cry.

I put my hand on her. "I don't mean to hurt you."

She sits quietly for a moment, then gets up and returns to

the window where she arches that deliciously naked body, spreading the curtains aside, suspending the soft lace and letting it fall back over her. It is an extraordinary moment of eroticism.

"I want to tell the truth about me, about us," she says, "and I have as far as I know, but you know what I keep finding out? I keep finding out that always the telling is for me. The only person who really wants to hear is me."

"I want to hear," I say. "But it's true that you should listen, too."

The next day Burr is back. Joan meets him at the door.

"I thought I'd do that roof," he says.

"The roof?" she says. "The barn?"

"I don't have lumber," I say.

"It will come," he says. "Mason will bring it."

Mason is a potbellied, thin man with spectacles and suspenders. He chews tobacco, spits, and holds outsiders in contempt. He arrives about eleven, high on his tractor, a weathered, gray wagon piled with planks following behind. I stop pulling cabbages and walk toward him.

Burr has nearly finished constructing the staging for the job. Earlier, I'd watched as he rolled the long poles from his pickup. I wanted to help him with these awkward, knobby tree lengths, but when I reached for an end, he pulled it out of my reach. It could have been accidental. He was, as usual, expressionless. I went to work in the garden and from there continued to watch in amazement as he single-handedly built the tall structure he'd climb and walk, making his way to the lip of the roof and beyond.

"Got the staging up, has he?" Mason says thoughtfully. "Well, he's not one to waste time. Should have that garden turned under by now." He studies the house. "Lester's house. Nice house. Wasn't always his, though. Originally Last's. Where does His Worship wish the planks be?"

"By the barn, I guess. You'll have to ask him."

"I'll pile them by the barn."

"Do I pay you?" I ask.

"Nope," he says. "And don't 'spect to neither." The tractor jerks away.

Joan is in an upstairs window.

Mason looks up at Burr as he pulls close to the barn. Burr shakes his head and points to a spot near the empty pigsty. Mason begins stacking the wood there. I help him.

"Have much trouble with rabbits?" he asks.

"No, I don't think so."

"We got rabbits," he says. "Ever set snares?"

"I haven't even seen a rabbit near here," I say good-naturedly. "Dogs. Cats. Ducks. No rabbits."

"They're here," he says. "Eat the crops, make good stew."

As we stack the wood, Burr continues to tear away old shingles and rotten board; the pieces slide in rasping tracks to the edge of the steep roof and fall soundless into the tall grass below.

"I really should give you something. This wood costs money."

"Yes. Well," he says, staring down at his salt-stained boots. "Burr . . . Burr . . . "

"Burr paid you for it?"

"This is between you and him," he says, "so don't you be thanking me is all." He drives away.

Joan and I eat lunch quietly. Burr is out there putting a new roof on the barn. It is happening to us now. Insinuating himself into our lives, and yet not really insinuating himself. I decide that after lunch I'll climb up there to see him. I won't ask any questions, but I'll talk to him.

"And if he doesn't want to talk to you?" Joan says.

"We'll see."

My ladder leans against the staging, a simple network of planks and poles mounting toward the roof. I stand below, studying the log beams solidly anchored to the barn by two-by-fours. It all seems so unsteady: the heads of spikes not fully driven, the slight wobble. Or is it Burr I fear, Burr overhead prying, tearing, ripping and clawing away at the old shingles with his hammer and flat-head shovel?

I return to the garden. The temperature is falling but there is no breeze and the sun low over the trees is warm. It is a cloudless day. The two swallows who live in the rafters of the barn return. They seem anxious. Confused. It's the pressure of Burr working there near their place. They dart about, squeaking in anger or panic. They don't seem to know what to do. Finally they attack Burr, flying at him in frantic, fluttering lines. They are quick for their size, but small and vulnerable. They need to come too close. Burr bats one with the shovel and its body sails into the tops of some distant pines; the other lights in the apple tree, watching.

I wheel the last of the carrots and beets to the cellar. It was a dull sound, a thud, but with a flat ping, too. Bone or beak. Joan is in the cellar to meet me.

"Did you see that?" she asks.

"Yes."

"How awful."

"I left the stalks on the beets. Andrew says that will keep them from bleeding."

"He just smashed it."

"IIc's forty feet high, Joan. It could be dangerous."

"That poor bird! Where did the other one go?"

"In a tree."

"What will it do?"

"Meet another bird. The carrots will be in these boxes of sand. I cut their tops off, too. I don't know if it matters. I'd better get to the store before dark."

When I return, it is twilight. Burr isn't on the roof. The dogs lie near the barn. I go into the house. His truck is there as it has been. The barn roof is stripped clean of shingles, and the yellow-orange and gray of long-weathered wood like new skin catches the last of daylight. Joan is not in the house. I know she is with Burr, there in the barn.

"Come on back to the barn," she said to me. "I love barns. Barns are one of my favorite places."

I felt immensely close to her there, our hands softly locked, fingers feeding on feelings impossible to describe. She gazed up at the huge beams as if searching for something. I looked too and saw straw nests' remains and bird droppings, light's dapple dripping through the high roof.

"There," she said. "See."

"What?"

"Roman numeral VII."

I could barely make it out. Sure enough, there carved into its wooden immensity was the number VII and on the inter-locking beam that joined it, another VII.

"They cut and numbered each piece," she said. "Then when they fit them together, there could be no mistake. You wouldn't want to lift one of those twice."

The presence of Roman numerals here seemed strange, like finding a telephone in an Elizabethan play. Soon I explained to Joan, and myself, that Roman numerals are easier to carve and afford less chance of mistake. They are numbers tied to an alphabet.

"Once I was told why the number was there, that was enough for me," she said. "I guess I'm too practical."

"I just took the practical a step further," I said. "Or dug inside it a bit. It doesn't matter. The important thing is that the barn got built, not that we account for every detail. I'm sure the farmer didn't dig that deeply into it either. It's not necessary . . . unless of course you're into barns. Or like me, into digging."

"Hmmm," she said thoughtfully, undoing my belt, a hint

of humor about her eyes. "I'm a bit of a digger myself, sometimes."

"You are?"

"I are."

"How nice for us."

"Can I interest you in a roll in the hay?"

"Right about now you could interest me in just about anything."

I dream. Burr, a leering satyr with an immense erection, clomps his cloven hooves, prances and gibbers. Everyone is nude. Even me, though I cannot see myself. Grotto walls of animal flank, ceilings haunches, all soft fur and flesh. Men and women sprawl about not touching each other, but rather stroking themselves, caressing their own cheeks and throats, their own knees, their own thighs, their own feet. None seem to see Burr. None seem to see anything. They go on examining each his own.

Joan grabs my shoulder. "Are you asleep?"

"Hmmmmmmmm."

"Are you asleep?"

"Mmmmmmmmm."

Now he is kicking his legs against the wall and the flesh turns from milk-white to blue-yellow.

"I can't sleep."

"Hmmmmmmmm."

"I can't sleep, Harry."

I feel her breasts on my shoulder. Warm. Nippy little nipple taps, then her whole weight presses upon me.

"Harry, please wake up."

I roll over.

"I was dreaming an answer for you," I tell her. "In another thirty seconds or minutes or however long dreams take, I would have answered your question."

"What question?"

"About Burr."

She looks away from me. "I didn't ask any question about Burr."

"He's not a satisfied satyr."

"I'm really scared, Harry."

"I know." I put my arm around her shoulder. Her breasts spread like sponge against my chest. I feel her tears on my skin.

"You never beheld yourself."

"What's to behold?" she says. "I am what I am."

"What's that?"

"Human," she says with authority through the tears. "Human."

"It's okay," I tell her. "It's okay. Try to sleep."

Everything must die. Death! There starts the parade, the long irregular line of elders, alder-thick, still in time, reaching like fingers from evening sands. There starts meaningful life, too. Acceptance. All else is deception. Even as the unrelenting calm hollers round around and the eternal presses its gangrenous thumb down oozing green beneath a pale nail of black sun . . .

Stop this evasion!

Humanity starts at home. I am the person listening. I am the person. Even silently. Especially silently. It was I who sat in judgment, sentencing first myself then others. And I need not. I need not. They meant no harm. She means no harm. No one means any harm. The words repeat, fracture, shift, shimmy down like last light; then they are gone. But the experience will linger like sunset's afterglow, and longer if you believe in memory, which is akin to seeing in the dark. I will remember the past, but I will not be its lackey. Never again.

As I lie thinly wrapped in sheet, shrouded in thought, the Rocking Chair Lady runs her finger between her toes then

173

sniffs the cloistered warmth in deep draught; Mason presses a handful of green leaves against his wet bum; Tongue rolls over and over the chaos-eyed fish — cold sticks on the shore; Billy squints, squirting seed on a voluptuous expanse of hardwood floor; and Elsa waddles fitfully through, blowing a bulbous nose; a pack of dogs, limp tongues hanging out, go after Gorm; a flash of Nebula melting around me; Della's finger hurting-deep in Andrew's ass; Morris spreads apart Mildred's hairy crack; Timothy wipes his feet on his clothes; old Tom spits on the shore where the cow, dripping *looooo*s, watches the world's full mouth overrun, running and I . . . and I, more fearful than I have ever been, work relentlessly, my fingers tucking it all in at the corners, making it all nice and neat; but there is, I know, in the barn, something I can't — no one can — finally ignore.

Joan is finally asleep.

I hear the woodpeckers who live in the old telephone pole. Beautiful birds. You rarely see them, for they fly low, escaping *into* the trees, not over, and so leave no path across the sky.

If I could throw a switch to light this night there'd be animals all over the lawn from step to wood's edge. Animals half up or down trees, half to or from, animals in the tall, low and no grass, animals atop and beneath the wood, scrambling around the barn. Night's active quiet is, I now know, a sound you feel.

I place my fingers along Joan's thigh; strings of hair rasp against the back of my hand. That first day we made love, I felt a connection I had never felt before. I transcended function entirely. I penetrated to union. I thought, so this is what it is to *really* be here! And it was so beautiful, so completely fulfilling, I had no idea more was in store. Then, months after we'd met, my lust for Joan not only undimmed but enhanced by familiarity, I experienced a magical moment. In the midst of our lovemaking, I felt a passion so hot and white that I touched universes in each thrust, felt every cell of that contact, achieved a union so purely essential yet so physical that in one extraordinary stroke I burst through time into another dimension. I was there, deep inside her, but I was gone through her, beyond her, too, sailing into a space I'd never known, leaving my body behind. With Nebula I began to understand sex and came to know it as a happy and loving place, but I was not yet on my own, not yet free; with Joan I achieved, as Joan herself put it, "a hallowed place."

But she's not ready, uneasy and restless as a caged cat. She wants me to prod her, toss her meat through the bars. I point to the door. She doesn't understand, and I can't explain. So I'm going to be alone again, more alone than I have ever been before.

The sea is so near at night. It is high tide. When the eyes rest the ears start to see.

"Harry."

I squeeze her thigh.

"Don't you expect anything of me?" she says.

"I try not to."

"This doesn't bother you, does it?"

"Of course it bothers me. I would rather it didn't happen."

She smiles contemptuously. "You'd rather it didn't happen."

I know by the breeze I feel that the curtain is lifting away from the sill. Fall is the cleanest time. Its months are mature. It is spring at rest. Spring without the struggle and sweat.

I cover Joan's bare shoulder and kiss her neck, try to comfort her.

She shakes her head. "I consider taking a roll in the hay with some bizarre creep and you're so damn casual about it. You'd probably defend it. Don't you feel *anything*?"

I am quiet. Thoughtful.

"Harry," she says, "I love you. That's real for me. This is real for me."

"It's real for me too," I say. "But it's not the end of the world."

Joan hurls out of bed. "God, you're stubborn," she says. "This is insane. You really don't get it, do you? And you're just not . . . my God," she says. "Stupid stupid stupid. Am I crazy? Why do I bother? You still refuse to feel anything. You always refuse to feel anything."

I think her unfair, but I say nothing. Her pain fills the room. Light precedes the morning sun as feeling precedes thought.

"I'm sorry. I have no right to pick at you this way. I'm just frustrated. I think you're making a mistake and you don't even know it."

"How do you mean?" I ask, fully expecting she will mention my pushing her away, or holding her at arm's length.

"I worry about you. You're forty-six years old. Where is your family? Where are your friends? How do they fit into your life now? Don't you see you leave everyone behind? You don't know what you do, do you? You don't have a clue. You discard people, Harry. You open up to us so far and then when we're caught in your craw, you spit us aside. Not just me, not just women — all of us. You *think* you don't need anybody. I think you're scared to admit you need anyone. Harry Fleet vulnerable! God forbid! Well, love does makes you vulnerable. Commitment makes you vulnerable, too. You think I don't know about vulnerability! I'm a woman. I open myself to you totally. That spot you touch, that spot you feel inside me, no one has ever touched before. It was my gift to you. And to me . . . I don't believe you understand what I'm talking about."

"I do. I think . . . I do."

She lays her fingers on the side of my face. "You're a very sweet man," she says.

"I don't know what to say."

"There is nothing to say," she says, and she leaves the room.

I stare at the dim ceiling.

Joan sticks her head in the bedroom door. "Once I love someone, I love them forever."

While digging through the shed — a combination workshop and storage area for winter firewood — I find a fishpole. Cork handle. Telescoping metal pieces with eyelets all intact. A reel. Even the line is good. I assemble it, then go outside and cast into the fall wind, listening to the line spin off the reel as the lead weight carries toward the gate. I reel it back and cast again. The dogs chase about, half frantic trying to decipher the sound and locate its maker. The line is there beneath their noses, but they either don't see it or can't believe what they are seeing. Feet foursquare and firmly planted, tails erect, they investigate. I begin to reel again and the line slides beneath Tongue's nose, startling him; he leaps straight up into the air. Boss nips him a good one for the false alarm and chases him toward the barn.

My father took us fishing one Saturday. We got up before dawn so the apartment was strangely quiet and the outdoors black. Everything seemed larger and more open. Voices rushed up against the ear. We spoke softly. My father's cigarette cough hacked like anger through the silence. But he was happy there in his sleeveless undershirt, his muscled arms ignoring the cold as he packed our lunches. We sat in sweaters, eating toast. Upstairs Mom was getting to sleep in, her glasses and teeth waiting quietly for her on the table at the side of their bed.

I decide to dig some worms. The ground squishes under my feet and pockets of water press up through the sodden soil. These are not ideal worm-picking circumstances, but I am eager. And ideal or not, the worms are there in abundance; cold, mucky clumps of them drip from clots of earth. I free them, then deposit these whitish-blue-to-brown veins in a can of dry earth. It is difficult now to imagine that child's fear of such things.

There is only one other fisherman there when I arrive at the pond near Rocking Chair Beach. Standing almost hip-deep in the water, he waves as I approach. There is something vaguely familiar about him that I can't place. In the next few minutes as I ready my gear he gets a strike and sings out "Bull's-eye!" and then makes a strange bagpipe kind of whining sound as he reels in the fish. I know immediately then that it is Timothy Tobin.

I weave a worm onto my hook and cast. Nibbles. Then nothing. Then weeds. Nothing again.

"No luck, Buck?" Timothy shouts. "Come out here where the luck is. And the fish!" As an inducement he is waving a beautiful trout over his head.

"No boots!" I shout back.

He moves toward me through the water. I reel in. Fishtails poke from the oversized pockets of his jacket. On his head is a paper painter's cap that is inscribed LUNENBURG PAINTS. As he climbs up the bank I see *he* has no hip boots either, just shoes. And his pants are wet almost to the waist.

"She's shallow pretty near all around," he says. "If you want it to pay, meet'm halfway."

"Isn't it cold?" I ask.

"Not so cold you can't catch fish."

"I never fished much. A couple of times when I was a kid."

I cast and am pleased that the line makes it a fair way from the shore.

"It came upon the midnight clear," he says. "Here. Give me that water polo."

He reels in my line then demonstrates the proper way to cast. Almost immediately he has a strike. "Bull's-eye!" he shouts and he hands me the rod. It bends.

"He's a big brat," he says. "Give him line."

He coaches me and soon the fish swirls about near the shore. Timothy begins to bagpipe it in. I join him, but stop suddenly to shout, "It's a snake!"

"Eel," he says.

It thrashes about wildly in the tall grass.

"Do they bite?" I ask.

"They got teeth, what?"

He cuts away the line and tosses the eel onto a long ledge.

"Gull supper," he says, handing me another hook. "Different ones find eels good eating, but I won't eat something I was just watching dance in pieces in the pan. Them are real cut-ups then, though, what? Yippee cayo cayee."

I tie the hook snugly onto my line and look at Timothy Tobin. "Cowa-goopa," I say, "cowa bonga."

"This one's God's own," I say to Joan as I set my two trout down on the kitchen counter. "That one's just stocked fish, imported stuff. Probably Amurrican. Come over here."

"You're soaked!" she says, moving toward me.

"Hear that?"

"Yes. A gull sitting on the chimney."

"Not *just* a gull," I inform her. "That's the gull that ate the eel, that ate the worm, that ate the hook, that I found in the shed that Pheeps built."

"Oh," she says. "Did you fall in?"

Seventeen

Joan can't forget. I don't either. It's best that way. Forgetting is dangerous. What's forgotten lies in wait like an unexploded bomb in the cornfield. Yes, it's best to remember, but without rancor. I still see Della in the window. It was where she was, but not necessarily where she wanted to be. We are taught to walk. Taught and taught. And we learn even more. I watch the gulls, leaping up like helicopters in a straight, vertical climb, talons dropping hard-shelled life to pavement or rock, dashing it into a softened mass, bits of hard to peck around.

"You do what you do, they do what they do," I say, and not in defense.

"Why must you always defend them?" Joan says. "Take the stars out of your eyes, Harry. You're a foreigner here. Even I'm a foreigner here, and I'm Canadian. If you come from twenty miles away, they whisper and purr and pounce. That flabby-chested old snot hiding behind her faded curtains. Outhouse mentality. Manners of a prairie snake. This place is — "

"Just a place. And they're just people. We're just people, Joan. Don't make any of us more than we are."

She throws her head back in disbelief. "Let me get this straight, Harry. *You*, Mr. Fantasy-Imagination, *you* tell me not

to make more of something than what it is! Am I going mad?
Am I hallucinating?"

I've told her of my waking and other dreams, explained to
her how these dreams seem to take on a life of their own,
rooting out of, or into, past or present pain and essence.

"All these people, so much a part of this place, are so near
to me because they are part of how I define myself now," I
tell her. "They have been leading players, truth-bearers actually, in my dreams — and my nightmares."

"Sometimes you are so full of shit, Harry," she says, "that
I can hardly believe my nose."

I recall how she used to listen wide-eyed, marveling at my
"imagination."

"What do you want, Joan?" I ask.

She looks at me as if I were a strange creature, a curious
and unfamiliar entity, then she says, "I want you, you asshole."

I try reading. The words are sucked in soundlessly, comfort-
ably by my eyes, stored like fodder for a later time, but the
immediacy is gone and so I close the magazine and stare at
the cover.

I hear Joan on the stairs, see her tit, her shoulder, her nose
and the rest, as she rounds the corner post heading for the
kitchen.

I follow her. She is stooped over, lighting the Iron Duke,
the woodstove.

"Let me do that."

"I can do it."

I turn on the radio. The sound comes as if from a grinder,
words and music mangled and mashed, a country dish, elec-
tronic hash.

"Are you listening to that?" Joan asks, the words a challenge. Would I, could I, admit to listening to *that*? I shake my
head.

She sighs with relief as I turn it off. Quiet races through the blowing curtains. The iron lid clangs as she lifts it to poke at the wood. Her face is drawn and pinched somewhat at the cheeks. She is reluctant to accept what she's already decided. Her decision races ahead, dragging her by the britches.

"This fucking stove," she says, and she stabs into the smoke.

I get up to help. "It's green wood," I say.

"That fucking Mason," she says. "He'd screw his own mother."

"Here." I take the blackened steel poker from her. The acrid smoke stings my eyes. I poke blindly through the wood, looking for flame. Finally a spark. I avert my head, trying to see. The fire takes hold and I slip the lid back over the hole and readjust the damper.

Joan is outside. I hear her feet thud on the plank-board step. I open the other window to set up a crossdraft to carry the smoke out, then sit again in the chair. The dogs are excited. I imagine them leaping and bounding, expecting a ride, or at least a walk. She will sit in the barn with the old mattress and springs, the broken carriage, the wooden wheels, the large pulleys, those strangely sensual hunks of wooden flesh hanging high above the lofts. Where does she sit? On a sawhorse? On the stacked wood? On the old washtub, the storage box, the broken sill, in the hay?

I hear the planks again, then the door. She tries not to look at me as she goes back to preparing the chicken. Hebb's. Freshly killed and plucked. I stood over it this afternoon with the tweezers finishing the job. Bits of hair like wire. Did I see someone burning them off, rotating the bird over an open flame?

"Everything tastes like chicken," I say. "Ask someone about rattlesnake meat. Oh, it tastes something like chicken. Rabbit. Turtle. So many things. Would that make you happy or sad to — "

"Will you not!" She is red. Her lips tremble, her face is in motion. It is all rightly disproportioned, all beyond saying. I stare expectantly at her, lost in the crushing rush of emotion, unanchored and classically fluid, a wave miles from it all, pushing along seeking shore.

The options stand naked in my mind, stripped of meaning.

"Will you not," she repeats, her voice barely audible, and I take my view elsewhere: to the living room, the hall, the front stoop where the sun stirs the open cement with a shallow heat.

Night. I'm not sure what she will do. I function as normally as I can. Supper is talk of no consequence, small bites, and on my part a wish to kiss away the anxiety. But it's not mine to kiss away. I lie in bed waiting, hoping she will join me. I want the pressure to go like air out of a balloon.

She is feeling the strain of averted attention. The need to imagine me not present rounds her shoulders, and the tendons of her neck are taut like winch ropes hauling freight. I only want things to be . . . *normal.*

The word sits in front of me, my head on the pillow, watching. *Normal.* A burnt-out bulb hangs from a cord. Behind my head, smaller light casts a giant screen across the sloping ceiling wall.

I move my hand past the bulb and an enormous hand appears on the ceiling. I hold it there. Can I scare me? I move the fingers, stretch them, powerful snakes in unison, clutching, cosmic sign. A camel? I experiment, bring my other hand in. I make a mouth by way of nose, a horse's head.

Burr's truck hasn't left yet. I'd have heard it pass the front gate. Those sounds strike the bedroom window. On my way to the bathroom, I see lantern light in the barn. It is shimmering against the cracks and holes in the roof. In the kitchen, the teapot rattles and clatters with its escaping steam. I go down and slide the pot off the heat, then return to bed.

I hope she has the strength it takes.

I hear her on the stairs. Her slippers cushion her steps. Furry city slippers, smoked and matted with farm life. She is in the bathroom, brushing her teeth. The tooth powder is in clumps in the can. As I listen to her shake it I imagine her once again thinking of returning to paste. She will roll back her lips and stare. She will peer into her eyes. She no longer thinks how the light is poor, too far from the sink. She will bubble into the water she splashes on her face, and she will wash till the sooty soap in her hands is white for the tray.

Will she join me here? Light to a blinded but living moth?

The hollow between her shoulder blades has a sensual shadow softness to it. Her flesh is a skinscape of noncolor I always want to touch. She throws her blouse on the chair. I recall women reaching up behind themselves to unclip their bras. I have never seen Joan wear a bra. Her gaze in still averted and thoughtful. She has tried all the triggers. If you loved me . . . if you really loved me . . . if you only . . .

I do. I do.

Well, then?

Mr. System showed up with his blueprints and plans, his tools, all he needed. He made a beautiful world. A lovely world. The best world ever. Then one day, Anyone stopped by. "What in the world is *that?*" Anyone asked. "Oh that," Mr. System answered, "that's the way to live. That's my world." Anyone snorted and laughed, raised a leg and pissed on Mr. System's world, yellowing it and curling the corners. "Why did you do that?" Mr. System asked in resigned disbelief, dabbing desperately at the dripping pee. Anyone shrugged and shook out the words with the last drops. "It's just the way I do," he said certainly. "It's just the way I do."

Joan stands naked, showing me the finest female form I've ever seen. Old words don't work. They can only approximate, and in everything, every moment is new. She is elite and alone, a flashing tiny sun all energy and swell, done and doing heat. She is at the far side of the bed with the sheet over her when I move my nakedness close to hers.

"All I wanted," she says, "was to mean something to you. I feel sorry for you. I really do."

I feel my calluses against her soft skin. She is the caress. What I touch moves along me. I want to make love, but I know her ear is pressed to the door. Everything is interpreted. Evermore. Evermore.

"I want you to stay. I love you."

"I'm no different than anyone else to you."

"You're totally different from everyone else."

She is thinking hard. My genitals crawl along the soft muscle of her ass. Between her legs she is wet. Primal tears. Before and after entry. She rolls over to soft sheets' sound and props herself up on one elbow. In this light one of her breasts fills the ceiling, its nipple pointing out like a solitary pine on the side of a hill.

She stares where the words were and are no longer. A look comes over her when she turns to me again. It is as much felt as seen and it makes me uneasy, but I hardly have time to digest it before she moves close to me, straddles me and leans forward, dropping her hair over my shoulder. I kiss her, hold her. She shifts up and back until I am deep inside her and we move together wonderfully. When I look up at her face her eyes are closed, and behind her, above her, on the ceiling, I watch the vast, hulking shadow of us surging out and in.

She is on the glider. "It's not worth the agony," she says.

I ride the splintered crosspost of an old sawhorse. Clouds flirt with the sun, curl, arch, tip across its face. Fleshless, teasing eroticism.

"It's sad, though," she says, "because I know what I want, what you want."

"No."

"No! What do you mean, 'no!' I don't . . . oh, never mind. What am I doing here?" she says. "Why do I hang on? What in the mother-loving . . . " She leaps to her feet with her fists clenched against her thighs. "What are we doing here?" she asks. "We don't belong here. I don't belong here. You don't belong here. What are we doing here?"

"I'm sorry."

Suddenly her face softens, and with this shift her words become patently reflective, her tone befitting of seduction or repentance. "I came here to be with you," she says. "Or at least that's why I stayed. I wanted to be with you. It was going to be good and solid and basic and real. I thought, this will be it, I'll stop and face it all."

"You don't stop. It doesn't stop. Nothing stops."

"I didn't mean stop-stop," she says. "I mean slow down. Rearrange. I thought I'd get a new perspective. Will you stop picking?"

"Picking?"

I look at her and her face begins to tremble and her eyes rampage.

"You smug . . . " She stares and stammers in exasperation. "Oh, I give up," she says, and tripping over the ducks, she runs toward the house.

When I tried to decide if I was deliberately driving Joan away, two questions kept coming back. First: Given the joy and magnificence of Joan's and my sexual relationship, why did I make love to Nebula again? Second: Having made love to Nebula again, why did I reveal it to Joan? I worked and reworked the possibilities through the grinder of my mind. But these two only spawned an infinity of new questions, questions sprouted like spore till there was nothing but questions spread like quiet hysteria beneath my feet.

In truth, there was Love. And there was a bicycle: Mildred's Red Flyer. The ideal and the real, and they arrived together.

Eighteen

Nebula! When I next saw her it was early one fine, summer day. More than a year had passed. Immediately I filled with love for her and gratitude for all she'd given me. We joked and chatted, but I was feeling a little sheepish about telling her about Joan. I danced around to a mental hornpipe till she finally said, "So, I hear there's a new girl in your life — excuse me, I should say a new *woman*. What would my sisters think, what?" She laughed that wonderful free-spirited laugh, then asked, "How is it, this married life?"

"We're not married. It's fine. We haven't been together all that long. We're still sorting things out."

"Is this it?"

"It? I don't know if anything could ever be it."

The minute I said that, I felt I was betraying Joan, not being honest about our relationship. The truth is, I wanted to have my cake and eat it, too. The only way to do that was to see the cake as comprising many pieces. Right then, seeing Nebula again, I was up to my ears in frosting. There was something so deliciously irreverent about her that matched so well her absolutely animal deliciousness of person. Who she was was so honest and straightforwardly presented that it could barely be contained by the the way she walked, talked, looked.

I arranged to meet her that night. I told Joan I needed to be alone to commune with my Rocking Chair Lady, and in a way, I guess that was true. It *was* all part of the same search. Anyway, that's the position I took as I talked to Joan, trying all the while to ignore the flashes of guilt that meant to stop me from having my way with the world.

"For me it's all a soft trap, just people and places providing their comfort until one day there's no letting go, just as once there was no joining. Either way we lose because we don't belong on the inside and we feel left out on the outside. For people like me there is no way. We're hooked on the infinity of displacement, that sour bit of specialness."

"That is such bullshit, Harry," Joan said.

I could have struck her, such an anger swelled in me.

"Don't look so hurt. Your poor ego. You can't stand it, can you, when you're asked to talk straight? You don't know the meaning of *simplify*. We're talking about how you feel and all of a sudden we're into 'soft traps' and 'infinities of displacement.' You need a good shit, buddy."

I resisted the urge to laugh.

"Can't you just have an ordinary, brain-free, non-cosmic toothache? Can't you *simply* feel bad? *Simply* be lonely?"

She sat next to me and touched me, but I was frozen in my thoughts and didn't respond.

She lifted my chin up with her fingers. "You know, with that head of yours, I'll bet you frighten your own asshole when you think about having a shit."

I smiled.

It isn't a far distance and I've been there before, so I decide to put the fear aside and go for it. It has to be a calm and calculated decision, for once started there's no turning back. I wonder as I prepare why I'm challenging myself this way. Most men warned against the danger to themselves from a very young age would never even consider being so reckless.

But here I am chancing it. And at almost a half a century old, a time in life when most of my male counterparts would stare in shocked dismay to hear mention of such obstreperousness. Not even one woman, to my knowledge, had dared even attempt it, never mind know the relief of accomplishing the feat. More the shame.

I concentrate. There must be no thought of consequence, no consideration of failure or potential humiliation. There must be only the one quick and sure impulse, I think, as I escalate toward performance, that same impulse that drives seemingly sane and sensible men to climb mountains, or shoot white-water rapids, or smuggle, or take the innumerable other risks life presents.

Once again I check my alignment and consider my foot placement. I make one minor adjustment, take one last, deep breath and tip back my head, trying to stretch and relax. When I bring my head down again, I will go. I do. I listen. I've made it! I smile and exhale a hearty thank-God-it's-over sigh, when suddenly I catch myself. The worst is past, but too much complacency even now and I could through overconfidence miss my goal. So I stand quietly listening to the sound of my piss splashing the edge of the water in the toilet bowl, careful not to change the trajectory of the arc, adjusting for diminishing stream, moving forward a bit as the flow wanes. Every last drop must be in and not one aimless little renegade dot must remain on the seat. I am excruciatingly demanding of myself in this way. Perfection and only perfection my goal.

It's done.

"Harry!" Joan calls.

"What?"

She flips on the overhead light.

"What in the world are you doing in the dark! Why don't you put the light on when you go?"

"That would take all the fun out of it."

"Did you lift the seat? No! Look at this mess."

"That splashed up, I didn't hit it. You don't actually think
I missed, do you? I'm mortified."

"Men!"

"Sure. I'll admit I have the kind of mind that examines and
analyzes. So what? I was expressing something important to
me, *in my way*."

"And what about me? Where do I fit in around here?"

"That's just what I was wondering."

She stares at me as if I am a curiosity, some thing she's
never seen before.

"Okay," she says calmly.

And that is all she says. Something screams all around the
room, scaring me so badly my heart stops. I begin to tremble;
still I won't, can't, address it. I don't know how to say I'm
sorry. I don't know how to say what is the most basic and
simple thing of all — what I am feeling. And as I stand
watching her leave me behind in our favorite room, I do not
say a single word.

Once again I give in to the power of parts.

"That night on the beach," Joan says, but she doesn't finish
the sentence. Her voice is neutral, but the words I know do
not come from a neutrality; they come from fear. We are both
two months, two years, nine years old again, still trapped back
there, emotional children. Her fear triggers my own. I turn
myself onto automatic human and hope for the best.

"What about it?" I ask, attempting a pass-the-butter-please
tone.

"What about it," she repeats almost derisively.

All systems are go! Ready your roles! Prepare for pattern
launch! I know the scenario by heart. So does she. Yet we are
in it again as if expecting that if we go through it just one more
time, one or the other's resistance will cave in, and one of us
will speak the whole truth instead of splashing out our private,

191

egotistical and too often petty versions of it. But we are not ready, so we speak.

"I know you fucked her."

"Joan."

"I know you did. Women know. Why is it such a hard thing for you to admit? People do these things. Shit, if I were a man, I'd want to fuck her, too. It's no big deal."

"If it's no big deal, then why are you so upset about it?"

She stands up and comes toward me, then she stops and stares deeply at me, lost in some half-deranged reverie. I consider the buttons on my fly, look at her, consider my fly again.

"You *don't* know, do you? How old are you? Fifteen? Don't you see what this guilt of yours is doing? Can't you *feel* it? Can't you see what's happening to us? Don't you care?"

I'd decided that to tell her would be cruel. Decent me. In the Halloween of human emotion, that disguise has all the imagination, all the flash and pizzazz of a white sheet thrown over the head. I feel cheap and ashamed and pathetically dishonest. I felt this way when I was a kid, too. I feel this way whenever I get caught up in the Almost-Up-Front game.

"Wouldn't you be upset if the situation were reversed?" she asks. "My God, Harry, show me a little respect, will you? There's a place for all that intellectual stuff, but the place is not in the middle of your life. Why are you always idealizing everything? A momentary passion or a mistake is only that unless, you, for whatever reasons, decide to elevate it into something more.

"I think about all the things you tell me and I wonder if you really understand what simple right and wrong are all about. Let's suppose I was attracted to Danny — which I wasn't, not that way — and I screwed him. It's not so much a matter of right or wrong as it is of facing up. Otherwise a momentary fling becomes a trip to the stars on gossamer wings. That's it, really. The oyster on the half shell is suddenly Venus, so the simple urge of sex becomes something else."

I think of Danny and how coolly I'd gotten rid of him. And what for if not for jealousy, my fear that Joan might, however dimly, be interested in him and . . . Jesus! What the fuck am I doing? Surrendering all my prerogatives? I know where Danny was coming from. Most of my life I gave off that same tantalizingly seductive male scent: a connoisseur's blend of charmingly indifferent caring and concern, a marvelously sweet salve for spreading legs.

Joan comes over to the couch, sits next to me and puts her hand on top of Cat, who lies sprawled in my lap.

"Can't you see why I have to know?"

"There's nothing to know that you don't already know."

It's a cryptic eye-crosser. I look directly into her eyes, but try to stay on their surface. I don't want to fall into that silent center. On my face is that faint wisp of smile I wear at such moments. I recall my mother telling my father that this particular smile of mine is merely a reflection of my nervousness and not really the contempt, indifference and derision that he thinks he sees; no, it's just what I do when I get scared. He had already responded to the look by shoving me away angrily. "Don't you do that to me. No one's going to do that to me." Mother's words were just meant to keep him from hurling himself out of the chair and finishing what he had started. Unfortunately, my mother isn't around to bail me out of this one.

"You won't listen, will you."

"I'm listening. I always listen. It's just that you see this differently. You think that I . . . "

She puts her fingers over my mouth, stopping my words. The buzzing in my ears increases. She stays there watching me for a while as I pet Cat and wait. The quiet is enormous. When she finally leaves the room, I am relieved, but I also feel myself a cheat and, perhaps for the first time, I recognize that I don't feel this way because of my night with Nebula on the beach. No. It is more fundamental than that. I, Professor Honesty, am uncomfortable with the truth.

It was innocent enough in the doing. It was only what it was. I kissed Nebula. She kissed me back, ran her tongue over my mouth saying, "You're not sure about this, are you?"

"I'm never sure about anything."

The blouse she wore was the same one she'd had on earlier that afternoon. It was white and thin, almost gossamer in the moonlight and night wind. I reached under and felt her breasts. I trapped her large nipples between my fingers and scissored lightly, while our mouths continued their dance. She undid my belt. I slid my hand down the back of her skirt into her panties, roamed down the flow of her ass into the softening hair, the moist lips of her vulva.

"Wait," she whispered. Then she kissed me again and stood up. I sat pulsing as she slipped off her blouse and stepped from her panties. An ocean of sex swam off the head of my penis. I lay back to pull off my jeans. Before I got up, Nebula was kneeling over me kissing my eyes, my mouth. I drank in her dancer's body so slender and soft, so perfect, as she began to lick the dripping sex from me, her tongue sensually tracing up the sides, gathering seed.

I ran one hand slowly back and forth over the soft arc of her bum, ending with a deep grope inside her; my other hand strolled along the soft pearls of bone along her spine all the way up to that nest of hair where I dipped my fingers and massaged her neck and shoulders, all the while feeling her as an extension of me. Her wetness met me somewhere so deep inside that I had to fight against exploding.

I began to think of junking wood and talking with Andrew. I started to recite the alphabet to myself. I fried some fish. I drove down the river to town. As if sensing my urgency, Nebula lifted her head suddenly and stopped.

"Don't you love that sound," she said.

"Hmmm."

"I could never stay away from the ocean for very long. I have to come back here, to all of this."

As she spoke she straddled me.

I smiled at her and she shimmied forward, settling above my face, her hands behind my head. The juices I licked from her were being born there beneath my tongue. I felt them drip and collect, the fine honied sap rising all over in that delicate and delicious space.

She rocked her hips ever so slightly and I concentrated on her clitoris, strumming it and coaxing it until she came then rushed to get me inside that amazing warmth, thrusting down at me in waves hot and free. I could manage only seven, eight, nine strokes more and then — I joined the stars.

We lay quietly on our backs holding hands, listening to the waves approach the bottom of our blanket.

"Married life suits you, Professor Fleet," she said.

"I'm *not* married," I said.

"Yes you are," she said. "You just haven't recognized it yet. Isn't this beautiful! I spend a lot of time here whenever I'm home. There's something about the rocks and the waves . . . the sound. Yeah, that's it. The sound. There is no sound on earth like that of the ocean. It makes me want to die."

"What?"

"Oh, not in that sense. I mean like in the Eastern sense of going back into the All of the Everything. You know what I mean? Becoming One with the universe. Can't you feel that calm and peace? Do you believe in God?"

"God?"

"Yeah, God. You must have heard of Him."

"I believe in something. A sort of primal force. Why?"

"Just wondered. You believe in something. Now that shows commitment, what? You academic types are so cautious, so afraid to get caught with your intellects down. We must be rational. We must be reasonable. You never have time to get into matters of the Spirit, do you?"

"I do believe you sound born-again."

"Sure I'm born-again. Not in that throttled, underwater sense. I ain't no born-again Christian, but if you ever get your shit together, you're born again, aren't you? Didn't I watch you going through some kind of birth and death thing? Remember? You on the mushrooms? What was that if not being born again?"

"A miscarriage, I think."

We both laughed, sort of, but from the quiet that followed, it was obvious neither of us really considered it funny.

Nineteen

"Who is he?" Joan asks, staring out at the man treading toward the house, small-talking the dogs who leap and bark around him.

"It's Sam Whynott."

"Ooooh," she says sarcastically. "So it's Sam Whynott."

"He's my boss, the editor of the *Weekly Breeze*."

Sam is a squat man about my age but much less weathered and not at all fit. He affects a frown of wisdom but gives the impression of gastrointestinal distress.

"What do you suppose he wants?" Joan asks.

In his office, carefully stark except for a plaster planter of plastic flowers, lingered the Whynott bouquet all who knew him must become familiar with. I'd arrived unannounced, but that didn't really matter. The man, I would come to realize, was a windbag of gases over which there seemed to be no control.

"Mr. Whynott."

His face reddened in surprise, then went serious again.

"I'm Sam Whynott," he said. "Sorry about the atmosphere. Fat Marie's beans. You ever eat there?"

"Once or twice. My name is Harry Fleet. I live at Beach Gate." "Oh yes," he said. "The professor."

"You know me?" I asked.

"Yes. Well, no. No, I don't. I've heard. Small town — big ears. That sort of thing."

"Real big ears considering I don't even live in town."

"It's an honor accorded Upper Canadians and Statesiders. All outsiders, actually. No big deal. Curiosity about our fellows is all. So what can I do ya out of?"

"I'm looking for a job. Nebula Patch sent me."

Whynott's face mashed sallow by my words seemed almost to quiver. He fumbled in his jacket for a pair of thin gold-framed glasses, which he stood carefully on his nose.

"Nebula," he said. "Nebula Patch."

"Yes. She thought you might have something part-time. Maybe cleaning up at night or reading copy. Typing."

"Nebula's returned, has she?"

"Just for a visit."

"Of course. She's with her family, I suppose. That's where she'd be, I imagine. When she used to visit, she'd go there."

I sensed his awkwardness and attributed it to jealousy, his designing Nebula in the crook of my arm, while remembering her warm, so thick scent in his nostrils, her hair beneath his chin. She was not someone a man could, would want to, forget.

"She's gone," I said. "She was just back for a visit."

"What else?"

"What else?"

"What else did she say?"

"You have a cottage in Mill Cove. She used to babysit for you."

"Babysit," he laughed. "You're not from around here, are you?"

"No."

"Do you know the family?"

"I've met them."

"Well," he smiled, "Nebula never *baby*sat for me. As far as

I know she never *baby*sat for anyone. Can you picture Nebula a *baby*sitter?

I shrugged. "It didn't strike me as all that strange."

"Well it really doesn't matter anyway, does it?" he said. "Where has she gone?"

"She didn't say. I took her to the highway."

A woman stuck her head in the door. "Joe Piddle called, Mr. Whynott. Says he'll be here right fast o' four with that curling story. You're not to worry."

Whynott nodded. The woman left.

"Her mother's a hitchhiker, too. How well do you know her? You say you know the family?"

"I know them well enough to say I've great respect and fondness for them," I said.

He stared at me, then stood up, grimacing. First I thought he was upset at my defense of the Patches, then I thought something was wrong with his spine because his face contorted and his back seemed agonizingly bent and stiff, arthritic, but he let go a long noisy fart. He grinned and straightened.

"Excuse me," he said. "I don't know what it is with me and Fat Marie's beans. Unfortunately I love them beyond. I'd give my oldest male son for the recipe. She said no. Hard to believe. He's diaper-trained too. Cutest little bugger you ever seen. Whoo! Yuck! Sorry. We'd better go out in the shop."

Out front people were typing, slicing up copy, setting print. They all glanced deferentially toward us as Sam told me all the horror, the truth and conjecture, the I-figured and I-heards of the Patches. Standing in the belly of the small-town press, he illustrated quite graphically and in fantastic detail the myriad of opinion, truth and half-truth that comprised the myth. I recalled Nebula on the cot, that first group frieze of them, us, me and her, that so special first time when she floated up out of my robe.

"Well," I said, "I imagine everyone around here has their

199

Patch story. I don't think I know them all that well."

He looked at me evenly but memory was riding him hard.
I prodded at the something he wasn't saying, recognized the
something held back, the thing all of them held back when
they talked about the Patches — self. They kept out of it.
Rumor and disgust on one side, self-knowledge and longing
on the other, two hands held over complicity's parts.

"I can't say much about them," I added. "I always end up
interpreting."

"Someone has to interpret," he said. "That's part of life.
That's why we have newspapers. That's why I write editori-
als."

"Do you write about the Patches?" I laughed. "Of course
not. That'd get you readers though, wouldn't it. I bet you
could double your circulation."

I was surprised to see that he might be taking the idea
seriously but he finally said, "You don't like to cause people
pain, you know? There's enough pain in life without causing
more. The Patches have had more than their fair share."

And now Sam says something of more than passing interest.

"Nebula Patch is dead."

"Oh God, no," Joan says. She unplugs the iron.

"You knew her?" Whynott asks Joan.

Joan looks at me, but I'm no help. The shock is like the first
punch taken in a fight. After that first blow, nothing hurts
anymore. I hear their voices as if from under water while I'm
placing Nebula's suitcase on the shoulder of the road again,
and she is winking as she says goodbye and that means
something to me for it is the first time she's done that and
there are no more words, just me melting toward her melting,
and soon she stands in my rearview mirror, a long, mud-slung,
murky tractor trailer with a double van pulling to a stop near
her and an arm reaching out, hauling her up.

"Murdered," Joan says.

"Murdered! She was murdered?"

I feel ill. Sam looks as grim as I have ever seen him. Joan, feeling that grand compassion she feels for us all, and knowing my love for Nebula, stares at me in wide-eyed horror.

"Oh, Harry," she says.

I'm registering it more clearly now, and it's all newly recast and somehow different, though the molds haven't changed, they never do. Joan and Whynott are tossing their sensibilities like salad, not sure of how any of it will taste to me. Assholes.

"It sucks!" I say angrily. "You know that? It bloody God Jesus damn fucking sucks."

I head for the back door, grab my coat from the hook and storm out, hear myself saying "shit" over and over again.

I sit on the slab-wood pile. Soon my anger subsides and I don't feel anything. My ears buzz. I am filling with the memory of her, flooded with a sense of her existence. That will last. I embrace it. Nebula Patch is so very real. Dead, she is still alive to me in the only way I'd ever expected she would be again. Separate. But what in the world happened to her! I rush back into the house.

"Mildred found her tied to a tree in Council Grove."

"How awful," Joan says. "Imagine finding your own daughter . . . "

"Her throat was slit. The son of a bitch beat her up, raped her, slit her throat, and left her to die. Everyone knew he was sick. But no one had balls enough to do anything about it! '*He's* harmless,' they'd say. 'All *he* wants to do is help. *He* wouldn't hurt anyone.' No. He wouldn't hurt anyone. Jesus!"

Sam is in such a rage that tears drip down his cheeks. I wrap my arm around him and look at Joan. I know even before I ask who *he* is, but I'm still not ready for the answer.

"Burr!" he says with disgust. "That's why the fuck he was going crazy in Bones' store," Sam says. "It's no big mystery

now, is it? It was all over for him and he knew it. It was only
a matter of time. So he was doing one last little *job*. The man
was completely insane all along. Why didn't we do something
about him long ago?"

I sense a degree of personal indictment in Sam's harangue
against those of us who knew Burr and suspected just such a
depth to his darkness. But it was only that — suspicion.
  "My God, how she must have suffered," Joan says.
  "And *he* didn't suffer enough. All the bastard did was take
one slug and get gutted by a chainsaw."
  Sam is legitimately angry and hurt. That goes without
saying. But I have always felt uncomfortable with the anger
of revenge and righteous indignation, that Old Testament
fury. It is a sort of bravado with which we the living try to
soothe ourselves, but all we do is embalm the hurt.
  Joan asks Whynott if he wants tea, but she is really asking
me for direction. If there is more space opening up inside my
loss, maybe she'll be drawn back, find a vacuum to fill. Breast
seeking brassiere, not mouth. Support.
  "Yes," I say. "We'll have some tea. And some rum."

Sam Whynott and I sit alone in the kitchen. Joan is upstairs,
searching her head. Sam is trying to explain why he loves
Nebula more than his wife.
  "You don't have to compare them, Sam," I say.
  We are drinking straight rum from our teacups. It swirls
quite white as I move it about. I can't sort out my thoughts,
but it doesn't matter. Those who understand don't need to hear
them, and those who don't understand get confused and ride
out the wrong sense of things and start labeling. Cynic, they
say. Nihilist. Or dreamer. Or idealist, and they shake their
heads sadly.
  "Am I comparing? Sure I am. Good thing no one's comparing me, eh? Do you think I'm feeling sorry for myself?

Where's Joan? You got a good woman there. She know about
Nebula?" He slaps his face and grins drunkenly. "Tell me to
mind my own business, will ya."

"It's okay. She knows, but I didn't tell her. At least not
directly."

"Well, who told her, then? Nebula wouldn't say anything
to hurt someone."

"She just knows. Women are smarter than us like that."

"Women are smarter than us, period. I think all the bitches
are witches. Hey! That's not a half-bad line. The bitches are
witches. And what are we? Jerks. Assholes. Ask any sensitive
man about men and he hasn't one good thing to say about the
species. Do you?"

"I don't hate men, but I always liked women better."

"So there. What's that tell you?"

"It tells me . . . I don't know. I like pussy? What's it tell me?"

"It tells you, it tells us, that we're missing something. And
I really believe we are."

"Missing what?"

"You won't laugh."

"I won't laugh — at least not too hard."

"We are missing a very essential ingredient . . . our manhood," he says.

"Our manhood."

"Our manhood. Not our masculinity. Most of us are great
at getting it up and getting it on. And even four-eyed wimps
like me can play macho-man somewhere in this world."

We listen to the rain. First drops are among the best, like
foreplay or penetration, but God how I love a storm! Nebula
did, too. She slept on the window side of the bed. All akimbo
like a cat, her healthy mane shocking black nightwaves across
her shoulders and breasts. She shared my bed. We slept in the
bed together. We loved together. We were very separate
people.

"My car windows are open," he says, leaping to his feet.

"The hell with it." He sits again.

Joan comes in, pours some rum in her cup, then leaves us alone again.

Sam and I are eating bowls of ice cream.

"'The Emperor of Ice Cream,'" he says. "Did you read that? I love poetry."

"All I can remember is an old lady on the morgue table . . . 'her horny feet protrude,' isn't that in there? Why do I remember that?"

"Why do we remember anything?"

"Did Whynott love her?" Joan asks me later.

"Does it matter?"

"Of course it matters. Jesus, Harry, you can be a cold-blooded son of a bitch sometimes!"

I smile. "I am what I am."

She is gazing. A thoughtful, penetrating gaze. "You know what you are?" she says.

"You always seem to know what I am. Well, what am I this time?"

"You're confused."

After Joan goes to bed I discover the half-full box of ice cream melted in the sink. I pour the rest out and throw the box away. When I run the hot water on it, it diminishes the lumps, making it all of a kind, a sort of Alice in Wonderland soup shrinking toward nothingness without the last-minute stop before evaporation. At the end the cream flits here and there as if trying to avoid dissolution. People do not die, they vanish this way.

The fall flies stir in the window. At night they'll catch the last heat, follow its chaotic traces high and low around the room, crashing even against our heads.

Joan has been at me. It's a last stand, or an appeal. Whatever, I'm dug in.

"You're a selfish, mind-mongering fuck."

The words don't hurt.

"Nothing you do is real. You don't love. You don't feel. You don't hurt. I may be a bitch or a fool or whatever, but at least I'm trying."

She goes to the window and slaps at the flies with a rolled paper. It is futile. They are slow now, but the paper is fat and heavy and the sill is narrow, and the glass too close. She gives it up and comes back to sit at the table. She is going to cry.

"You can't love," she says. "You don't know how to love. You're going to be alone."

They all felt that. All told me that. Each in her way. Presenting me with images of myself. The sad projections of projections of projections spiraling toward Adam, raising Cain, raising the sad Lot of us to what we should be. Myriad magic, the faceless voices, the rules and standards, the unremembered times, the erected stockades, erected perhaps in self-defense, but erected. No one's fault. No one's fault. Absolutely no one's fault.

I hold Joan's tears against my face. Place kisses in her hair. Her words are directed at me in anger, but in them she cradles the hurt that carries her out to me, handing her to me like a babe. I keep kissing her hair.

"I love you," I say.

The words once sounded unreal to me. All words now sound unreal to me. Particularly *that* word. It was their word, a weapon of the goodness made, a goad for the pain. So what? I do love Joan. I love Nebula. I love Andrew and Della. I do love. But not their way. I can't accept their more than symbolic bonds and chains, the mystique of ownership.

"You don't love me," she says. Her voice is throaty, choked with tears. Everything loosening in her head.

205

"I do, Joan. I do."

She shakes her head. "Oh, sure, you'd miss me if I weren't here, I know that. But you'd find someone or something else. Then you'd miss *them* — if they hurt enough to leave. Like you'd miss this house if it were gone, but there'd be another."

My hand on her hair looks winter-pale, corpse-like. I am tempted toward death, wrapping myself in it. Embalmed in life. Am I. Am I.

"I don't know what to say." As if there are right things.

"I never claimed to be more than I am," I tell her. "And I care about you. I want you to stay."

She presses her hands against her eyes. The soft smooth backs of her long fingers curl slightly, reaching out from her face, brown, soft antennae impossible to gauge.

I am a fossil of myself. Must I go on shedding selves like lobster shells or snake skins?

"How," she asks, "can I stay? How? I'm only a part of your system. I'm only . . . I'm only *furniture*."

"Joan . . . "

"Well, it's true, Harry. It's true. I could start fucking farmers in the barn. I could put an ad in the *Weekly Breeze*: Beautiful babe has cunt will share . . . and you wouldn't care." Her voice drops. "You wouldn't care, not really. I'm just a bit of energy, a flashy lay you picked up on the beach." She falls silent. The flies buzz and stop. And buzz.

"I can't make your decision for you," I say. "I love you. I want you to stay."

She looks at me as if examining a strange language, some nonromantic script, mysterious but quite obviously lewd. My lap empties and I am warm everywhere she's been.

"But you already have made my decision for me," she says, her voice soft and even, her moist lips eased of the words.

Then there is a movie exit. I replay it as I walk to the storage shed. No one makes decisions for anyone else, I am thinking. It is hard enough to make them for oneself.

The clutter of the cabinet, twisted cords, ensnarled bits and pieces of the years, has me grabbing in handfuls shoving and pushing and finally I come up with the can and return to spray the flies. But they are gone. And Joan is gone. The empty window is glazed with smoke.

Twenty

The dogs are barking in the woods. A squirrel up a tree? A rabbit in a hole? Soon they charge out onto the beach again and chase sandpipers along the wet wash of shore. I come behind, noting the birds' tiny etched tracks, the dog prints bounding across the damp sand. Tom sat here tossing his toenails to the waves. For a few minutes this place was something more than it had been.

When the confusion is too intense, when I am overwhelmed with it and don't even know what it is, I have to do something. Often I masturbate, and in the spilling of the seed I gain some relief. It is not at all sexual. This connection to myself is a balancing of sorts, a corrective; maybe it is a purging, some kind of letting go. Even when I've just finished making love, I still might find myself in the bathroom, my crotch settled on the corner of the sink as I pound away my worries, my fears.

It doesn't always work. Sometimes the gray lingers long after the groin has passed its last little lustless licks. Then I walk and run it away, traveling miles along the beaches in search of exhaustion. I crisscross the grass-swept dunes, plop barefoot along oozing clam flats, finally recrossing the dunes to run along the sandy beach. I push and push myself till I collapse, as now, at the high-tide mark, my imprint fresh in the damp sand.

When I look up, the old lady in the rocker is there, smiling enigmatically. The wash of waves fills my ears. This is no Lady of Fatima, but she is a woman out of time nevertheless, a wonderfully worn and comfortable old woman in a puffy sunbonnet. She is wearing a dress that is partially covered by a long, white, clean but well-used apron.

I feel I'm in a dream. I cannot move to get up. Perhaps, I think, I am dying. Or perhaps I have passed through the veil of exhaustion to another dimension. But no. She is so real that I can see the peach fuzz of years on her chin, the strands of saliva from lip to lip as she chews on nothing, moistening her mouth. Her high, laced boots are merged with the sand as she rocks back and forth. All this time I have pursued her and now that we are face to face I cannot move, cannot think of what to say. Just as quickly as I acknowledge this, she says, "You don't need more words." Her lips are not moving; she seems to be looking right through me. "Don't you trust what you feel, dear? Are you afraid to grow up, dear? Do you enjoy your separateness, dear? Why can't you just be, dear? Do you believe the parts better than the whole, dear? Is the present just a po-pot for the past, dear?"

I watch a sand spider move past my nose. It gets stuck in a sand pocket and struggles futilely to climb a steep edge that keeps collapsing beneath its weight. I set up a tail wind and blow it out of the hole. On a nearby rubbery mat of eel grass, shards of clam shell like pearl glass glisten. Scattered across the sand lie sea urchin shells open as old lives. Clouds move so fast the shadows seem a semaphore of secret signals from the sun.

"I forgive you. I love you. I release you."

"I can't hear you, dear."

"I forgive you I love you I release you." Then I shout it. "I forgive you! I love you! I release you!"

Just then the old woman bursts like an egg, explodes into a rain of down covering the shore thick with feathers across and through which we come, my family, carrying a picnic lunch, blankets, pillows, and a box of toys. I am hugging the beach ball. Jan is in the braids I always loved. Fred is racing ahead with his stick spinning wheel, calling back to me to watch him go. Mom and Dad follow, laughing. It is sheer delight. Except for the feathers; they are a nuisance. They stick to everything. They cling to the plump edges of egg salad sandwiches, they get in our eyes, our mouths, they form a film over water, and they block the sun.

I stand up and raise my arms and say, "I don't like this, I don't want it this way," and suddenly the feathers are gone and I feel how right and wonderful it is and I am more calm and peaceful than I have ever been and I bask in it until the chill, fall waters wash over my toes.

The days are brisk, the nights cold. The wet, gray air presses against the flesh. The sharp, painless sting of winter is already gripping the sky. I move quickly around the barn. There is wood to stack. I have yet to cover the windows. I have yet to cut branches for banking the house against the coming cold. The well is to be covered. And the cesspool. I park the car in the barn to shelter it from the wind; but above, beyond beams larger than thighs, beyond suspended hoists unused for years, the icy winds blow through the open roof.

That clear, transparent cold starts or at least continues from far out in space, planets tucked within it in some mysterious nonorder, dead or burning nonlife, gigantic stones, spacial warts suspended like buoys in a cold, black sea. Immeasurable chills, unknowable motionless expanse stealing down into our atmosphere setting up waves and winds, whipping into a neutral fury, tossing matter higher than chimneys, swallowing smoke in windy drags, pounding like a fist against walls, rattling painted china and glasses; its bitter, raw breath filling the cellar, oozing from the cracks in the floors, sliding over window valances and under doors. Cold colder than death. Cold that freezes, immobilizes, hangs at the edge of fire; cold waiting without direction or end.

I sit wrapped in blankets, my feet past the open stove door, deep inside the Iron Duke's mouth. The icy wind dictates sound and scene, making its way even to the fire by sliding down the chimney pipes, occasionally driving smoke into the room. My nose signals that my shoes are beginning to scorch, and I burn my hands on the charred, still-smoking rubber when I try to get them off my feet. I pull on a second pair of heavy socks. Near me, on the floor, a paper flutters unevenly as cold air from the cellar seeps into the room. I pick up the paper, then prod and poke between the floorboards. Another floor beneath this one but still the cold manages to stream in. "The old folks used linoleum."

It is Tuesday. Worknight. Once a week I collect the box of transparencies from the *Weekly Breeze* and drive them two hundred miles across the Maritime countryside to the printers. The sun long ago disappeared behind the trees, so the car seat is cool. Will the car last the winter? I'll scrub the battery cables and connections with a wire brush. I imagine them clean beneath the whitish, gray-green froth of acid lumps. I glance into my mirror as I drive away, recalling Burr on the roof. In the barn. Burr.

"He wants to see you," Joan said.

It seemed a long way to the barn. So much space. Uneven earth, rock heaves, imagined heads and bodies pressing through the browning mantle. That day I saw the brilliant yellow-orange of fall grass growing into the sea.

"He wants to see you," she repeated, raising her voice.

"I heard you," I said.

Strips of tar paper lay in neat rolls inside the large doors; the scaffolding, an architectural skeleton of right angles loose and hard, clung lazily to the gray-shingled walls.

"You want to see me, Burr?"

I knew he was there. I could sense him. Deep in the shadows where the tomato stakes drip tattered rag ties and dry dirt, and the scrap lumber odds and ends stand or lean in easy disorder. The low sun doesn't reach that far. Standing back-lit as I was, I'd appear a faceless figure, a blind silhouette against day's last light.

My ears detected breathing. The oxen were long gone from this barn. Great hulking beasts. Brute strength for applause at the exhibition. "Day was everyone had oxen. Pair. Mason's father shoed thirteen or fourteen pair a day. Thirteen or fourteen pair, boy! Thirteen or fourteen pair!"

"Burr."

"In the winter they'd want the shoes sharpened to a point. If you didn't, why, they'd cut themselves up bad slippin' and slidin' on the ice."

"He wants to see you."

There is nothing to fear. Or there is everything to fear. When the ball is spinning, you stop it with your hand and, there beneath your fingers, while you hold it, is the ball not spinning, but hidden now by your hand.

"You want me, Burr."

High above him the old wood held off the sky, just pin-pricks of light peeping through, but because I moved farther into that darkness my eyes were adjusting. He was sitting in the corner, sprawled sideways against the wall, the side of his face clear to me, the rest a vague smear of dark and woolly cloth. Detail grew more definite with each step.

"Burr!"

He stayed turned away hard, twisted like a mannequin someone dumped here fully clothed. Frozen. Silence filled the space between, all space between. Distance, the meta-physical equivalent of air.

I stood and waited.

Awaken! Sleep! Come! Go! All easy distinctions drifted away and the barn whispered. It was quiet, and suddenly I knew we had nothing whatsoever to say to each other. Still, without moving, he said, "I still owe you," and I said, "If you feel that way, Burr, that's your problem. The way I see it, you don't owe me and I don't owe you. So why don't you just get off my land."

When I think of Burr now, I see him, heavy boots, legs firmly planted, and I hear the raucous sputter of his saw screaming in Bones' store. It is a story Maud never tires of telling.

" 'You can't run that thing in here, Burr,' I say. 'Syd's sleepin'.' But I'm just a woman so he don't pay me no mind. No, that Burr tromps right on by me as if I weren't even there and he begins a clean, deep cut severing the cash counter in two. Why, at that me eyes is wide as clean-licked saucers. Then that mental case is cutting through the window frames. Well, by now I'm through the shock of it all, so I hurls away toward the back of the store, but before I even reaches the stairs I stops, 'cause here comes Syd barefoot, his fly half buttoned, his suspenders hanging, and he races by me shoutin', 'What the Jesus!' Screams, 'That Burr's gone totally daft!'

"Now Syd ain't what you'd call a ninety-pound weaklin' but only a crazy man would go against a chainsaw, specially in the hands of a man like Burr.

"Well, boys, if Burr hasn't finished the window cases and sliced halfway through our fruit stand. Now Syd stares in disbelief and I know he's right desperate thinkin' what can we do. Say please stop? Hit him? With what? A pipe? A wrench? And what's to stop him from cuttin' us down? Is there time to get the gun?

"Can you imagine a chainsaw inside! The racket was enough to make a moose melt. And the air was right thick with dust everywhere so ya can't see nothin' and your throat is drier than a Mexican fart. The blade of one a them saws wouldn't just kill, it'd rip you raw and ragged before you had half a gulp. 'What the hell are you doin', Burr?' Syd shouts.

"But he don't pay Syd no never-mind. Burr's arms is right hard and round and shiny like hip joints of ham. By then Syd's run off to get his shotgun and I'm like a lost lamb watchin' as Burr cuts two supports and is after the center beam when — thank the Lord Jesus — that Bobby, the young Mountie what's from Alberta steps through the door. At first he's expectin' to see renovation and repair, so he comes in smilin' away, but it don't take him but a second to see it ain't no *Better Homes* thing that we're about, and anyway, the minute I see him I'm screamin' my head off, so he looks at me and at Burr and his smile falls down his throat and he's got his hand on his gun in a flash and he's callin' at Burr to stop, but Burr never gives as much as a glance his way.

"Well, while the Mountie is looking 'round for help, an answer, Syd is back with his gun and we're both gesturing and shoutin' like crazy that the main beam is 'bout cut in two. It wouldn't take but a push to bring the roof down.

"The Mountie flips up the flap of his holster, draws his gun and shouts 'Stop!' again, but still Burr goes on his merry way cutting down through the canned goods so's wet and tins are scattering and kicking, flyin' out all over the place.

"The Mountie's seein' no hope so he fires a shot into the plank floor and the Jesus water pressure tank in the cellar explodes. Well, if Burr don't ignore even that! 'Cause he never once looks over, never stops. And the poor Mountie's face by this time is pale and white as the flour mixin' with sawdust in the air. Syd's shoutin' to do somethin' and I'm screamin' my fool head off, and then Burr turns real slow like, and with that cold stare of his, he starts to walk right at us where we stand and the Mountie pleads with him to drop the saw and surrender, but he just keeps comin'.

"Well, now, didn't the Mountie fire another shot into the floor, but Burr is set and determined. 'You'd better stop right there and drop it!' the Mountie shouts. Burr smiled then, I swear. It weren't easy to see through all that dust, muck and such, but I do believe there was just the faintest hint of humor about the lips. Smile or no, he's coming right at us revvin' the saw and that's when he was shot and fell to the floor onto that saw. You could hear the blade grab and then seize, caught up, I suppose, in all the cloth. Certain the flesh didn't stop it. No. It was so quiet you think you hear the blood runnin' from Burr where he's lying humped there over that saw blade, the blood flowing around, drippin' down into the cellar below."

I stand quietly in the field just below the scrubland bordering the Patches' farm. My mind is frightfully clear despite the rum I've drunk. I am thinking about feeling things. At this moment I am feeling nervous about seeing Mildred and Morris. I am thinking how I am experiencing two deaths: the death of Nebula, and the death of Joan's and my relationship.

Fall light bathes the field, lending definition and brilliance to grass, stump, stem and bush. That's partly why fall is my favorite season here. The beauty and depth of everything is heightened as autumn introduces winter's approach, fore-shadows the reality of that long sheet of cold soon to cover us. Its time is so invigorating, such a stimulus, a wonderfully intense final glow before the shutting down and hibernation. Things more real before their end.

As I step over the broken fence, I see Mildred in the kitchen window. She is on the porch before I am half through the junk-strewn yard. She has on the same patchwork dress, but has a black cap on her head and a grayish-black towel wrapped around her neck and shoulders.

"Oh my dear," she says, "you've come just in time cause

if you'd been five minutes later I'd be gone and you wouldn't know where in the world to look for me, would you now? I mean, there are only so many places to go but we can't be everywhere at once, what? Now Morris, he has his places and I has my places and you have your places, and if you're smart like me, you don't let no one know where you go when you go there or you just end up like everyone else, if you get my meanin'.

"If you wait I'll just get my coat and we'll get goin'. If I'd know for a fact you was comin', I'd have been ready long ago, but no one ever gets my messages to me anymore. Which is why I guess they say that good help is hard to find?" She stands grinning at me for a moment and I smile back feebly as she disappears into the house.

I am alone again in this pristine, roughly elegant quiet. Tears fill my eyes and roll down my cheeks. I stand aside, listening to my self as I roar in pain. The sounds are coming through me but somehow are separate from me. No thought comes. No association. I hear myself wailing, listen to the awful craggle of sounds that pour from my throat, fly out into the still crisp air. My whole body aches from pounding the earth with a length of weathered two-by-four.

Then I am calm, more peaceful than I have ever been. It is an indescribable feeling. As if coming back from another place, as if re-entering reality, I see chunks of wood, rusted tractor parts, old tire rims with dead plants in them, and Mildred sitting on a wheel-less old hay wagon watching me.

"Natooma," she says.

"Natooma," I say.

Council Grove is a place among places. Like all places it possesses an energy all its own, but Council Grove is hallowed ground. I wonder if the more magical, more spiritual spots on this earth have been imbued with these mystical qualities by the spirits and practices of people, or is it the place that calls forth these qualities in us? In other words, did the medicine man say this is the place, or did the place say to the medicine man, this is the place?

"They like sunset best. And light rain. Everything with a shine onto her, even the bodies and animal skins. You have to take your clothes off," she says, hanging her coat from a nearby tree branch.

She begins to unbutton her dress. "They like nudity and sex and honest smells. They don't give a damn for none of that fancy, uppity, white man shit.

I hang my coat from a small burl on the side of an ash tree. It is perhaps a further sign of the sacredness of this place that this burl was not hacked off by the Indians and made into a bowl.

When we are both naked, she heaves toward me, immense and motherly, and she wraps her arms around me. Immediately I start to cry again. I feel absolutely vulnerable and helpless. Mildred rocks me in her arms and sings in a language I imagine is all her own. In time my tears stop and I sniffle a bit, then rest in her, snuggle into her embrace.

Mildred sings joyously. We shuffle and sway in slow celebration. I am singing with her, our voices raised to the sky. Like a more than human majestic beast, our two bodies melded now into one can only suggest the absolute communion we feel with each other and with this place. Natooma!

When we return, Morris is just coming into view on the hill. I stay outside to speak with him. Mildred disappears into the house.

Morris looks down and smiles sadly.

"You heard? You know?"

"Yes."

"Hmmmm." He stares out across the field. "Not right," he says. "Not right at all."

His tone is harsh. The words fly from him like spit into flame. His resistance pulses just beneath that wall of flesh I see around him, that shroud of body he wears over his pain. He's not letting anyone out, nor is he letting anyone in.

"I'm so sorry, Morris," I say. "She was a wonderful . . . a very unique person."

"Yes, well, she's dead now," and he shifts gears to drive away.

His words are so caustic they almost break in the air.

I watch as he bounces away on his tractor, running over the corner of the slab-wood pile then heading into the fields. I pray he is on his way to Council Grove.

Twenty-One

The staff of the *Weekly Breeze* is busy when I arrive. The town election has made them late. I watch as, huddled over slanting desks, they paste the final bits of news to large sheets. I haven't seen the front page yet. It will be interesting to see whether Nebula or the election will get the headline. Politics or poison.

"Okay, Harry," Whynott finally says. "She's all yours. Good luck." And I, feeling my usual flash of courier concern, a vague sense of Paul Revere wafting to mind, hoist the large, flat box and walk hurriedly to the truck. I am on the road.

Already leaves absent the trees and the hardwood shows its skin grayly beautiful and warm against the greens and blues of layered scene. In between or around the sylvan stretch, the splayed branches and limbs, core colors canvas the eye: carnival reds and oranges perk up and party the space deep into the eye.

That night ride and time is always a ribbon out of a circle. Tip it with an arrowhead. It has its meaning, yet is definite and confined, not at all like the circumscribed world of the farm. It is a waking dream. A trip into artificial light. There is the dimness of the van cab and the soft scream of fluorescent light in the gas stations. I am never really ready for any of it.

It is always a plunge away from my reality to which morning returns me when I awake heavy-eyed, only a solitary copy of the *Weekly Breeze* to remind me where I've been.

The strangest thing about the hitchhiker is an eerie drab kind of normalcy. He has no baggage and few words. But because he is here, I do not distract myself with the usual games. I do nothing with the shadowed, silent houses. I draw no shades. Raise no doubts. I am neither voyeur nor interloper. I am just here, and I find that strangely disquieting. We seem both stuck in an unvoiced interlocution of presence, locked wordless over wheels that thud in syncopated taps, snowtires sucking wind.

But silence builds. Emptiness strains. I consider him. He is young, but past being young. It happens first in the face. Always. Too, there is a chemistry of posture that signals distress, and it has nothing to do with flesh and bone.

This boy holds his years in a bushel basket. They tumble against one another like bingo cubes in a cage. He mentions only his destination. I can take him all the way. Something behind his eyes is reflected out there in the dark above the hood. I think of old cars with wing and horse ornaments racing ahead, reflecting sun or light, silence or dark.

He unfolds a comic book from his hip pocket. A splash of lurid color. What can he see in the dim light of the cab? He gazes sternly down. I watch him, the white line, our reflections above the dash. Without even seeming to have looked up, he spots the two girls on the shoulder of the road near a small car.

"Stop!" he screams. "Stop!"

"Don't you want to help them?" he says more calmly. "Don't you think we should help?"

I back along the gravel shoulder. It is about eleven. I am already two hours behind schedule.

"You're from the paper?" one of the girls asks as she climbs into the *Weekly Breeze* van. "Who won the election?"

"I don't know," I say. "I forget."

"Who ran?"

"I don't recall. If I knew, I've forgotten. At least I can't tell you now."

Their spare is flat. We watch for a service station. The sallow youth is transformed and becoming more definable by the minute. His eyebrows climb up his brow as he speaks to them; his neck twists sharply over one shoulder, his Adam's apple pumping up the words. He is clearly a sexual deviate — that is, someone who sees sex as deviation. I wonder when he'll make his move. The girls kneel behind our seats on the van floor. Ahead the printers will be waiting, drinking tea or Coke, right; hard-bodied men sitting on conveyor belts shouting friendly insults at Fat Jimmy the stacker.

"Where you girls going?" the boy asks.

"You girls from here?"

"What you girls doing?"

"You girls got a way back?"

"You girls need help getting that there tire on?"

"You girls . . . "

"You girls . . . "

I start to sing an old fishing song. I drawl and slur it, tapping the steering post with the cup of one hand.

"Geez," one girl says, pushing against the back of my seat, talking around a mouthful of bubblegum. "Man, you sure can sing. Are you an athlete?"

"What?" I laugh.

"You got one of those caps. Is it just a cap or you a real athlete?"

"I played right field once. I struck out and threw wild over the second baseman's head."

"That right?"

"That's God's truth."

"You girls ever play ball?" he asks, smirking.

The service attendant doesn't have the wrecker, but he offers to take them back in the wrecker, as soon as Terry gets back with the wrecker, and meanwhile there's some coffee.

The hitchhiker says thanks for the lift but he'll stay to help them with the tire. He winks and nudges me.

"And the night yawned like a gigantic pussy," I say as I speed along the highway. The cab smells of cheap perfume and bubblegum, so I open the window and the air whines in in cold rushes.

"Where you been?"

I explain about the election.

"Elections. You mean erections. Bet you been getting a little a that highway nooky. We better take a peek to see what you got in that van."

I smile politely.

"Girls! I'll go see," Jimmy says. Jimmy's fat is packing for his fixed leer. He lumbers to the window.

"Bullshit," he says. "The truck's bare as a cod's belly. He ain't gettin' nothin'."

I walk around the offices of the newspaper. I have two hours. All the rooms are empty and dark. I hear the sounds of the men cutting, framing, preparing the plates. From beyond a closet door comes the teletype's soft clicking punctuated by bells. I go in and stand for a while reading news as it happens. Letters, numbers. I read the copy, seeking the operator's presence, those touches of humanity that sometimes creep in. The large presses start to hum. Show time.

Just as I step from the makeshift teletype room the cylinders begin to creak and crank. Humping circular giants. The men work with muscle, foot and finger, race about pushing buttons, making adjustments with wrenches long as a man's arm, then stand quietly scanning copy as the first papers pour from the press. The smell of printer's ink wet on paper is everywhere.

"Set it," the boss says, tossing the front page to one side. Jimmy backs the counter to zero. The quality is there. They are ready to roll.

"Let her go."

I walk down the dark stairs, the first acceptable page in my hand. All around me are waist-high tables constructed of two-by-fours and planks, and pyramids of cord for tying the papers in bundles. I recall last week's indistinguishable voices, teenage faces working here on the large pre-election issue, their joyous attempts at erection wit. I thought of myself at that age booming away for all I was worth:

Shove it in your mouth, Madame Murphy,
For it weighs but a quarter of a pound,
It's got hair all around like a turkey,
And it spits when you rub it up and down.

Laugh-till-you-drop stuff. Funnier than an armpit fart. Ass-solutely hilarious. But behind the humor, in the eyes of some, I see already forgotten people staring from children's faces. My memory of it is always Dickensian, a humanly grotesque scatter of joy, injustice, and ignorance. Ghosts of words and deeds done or dared. And the perpetual re-examination. There should be an inoculation against self-abuse.

I stand perfectly still in the silence, bracing myself to read the paper, when one large rat then another appears near a table piled with old copy. They root about until a light overhead on the stairs startles them, and me. The rats look past me, and run.

I look up to see a tiny gray-haired lady in white boots and mittens. The boots are like children's. Beneath her open coat is a scarf of brown and green wool.

"Have you seen Mr. Sweeney?"

"No," I say. "I don't think there's anyone down here but me, more or less."

"Oh," she says. "Drat!" And she stares fretfully about the room.

I wait.

"I simply must find Mr. Sweeney," she says.

"They might know upstairs," I say.

"They don't know anything," she says, clearly vexed. "What's your name?"

"Harry."

"I'm Mrs. McCaffrey. Everyone around here calls me Ma." She takes off her coat and sets it on the table.

"If Sweeney doesn't . . . bring . . . the . . . cards . . . to me," she hammers on the table with her puffy white mittens, "I . . . cannot . . . I simply will not . . . be . . . responsible."

"Mrs. McCaffrey! Ma!"

"Yes. Yes. I'm down here."

Heavy feet on the stairs. Jimmy.

"Sweeney's back."

"Thank God," she says, grabbing up her coat. "Thank God."

"Thank God, thank God," Jimmy mocks.

The red headline announces "DAGLEY WINS." I am relieved. Sam ruled with his heart, not his head. "WOMAN MURDERED" is in a much less prominent place down below.

When I see Mrs. McCaffrey again she is shouting above the machines. Mr. Sweeney, a stooped man with shoulders poked forward like angel wings pulled close, has his face pressed toward hers.

"You're wrong," he says. "You're bloody damn wrong."

"I simply will . . . not . . . be . . . responsible." She looks as if about to strike him with the mittens that droop like wilted flowers over her breast-high fists.

Jimmy, unnoticed and behind her, makes obscene gestures with his sweaty face and body.

"You got to be responsible," Sweeney says. "You're a mother, for God's sake, woman!"

"You're a father," she says.

"Jesus!" he says.

The presses roll and clank, spitting out papers. Jimmy gathers them up in great armfuls and presses them on the automatic binder.

"Okay," she says. "I'm not going to argue with you." She walks toward me.

"Come on, Harry," she says to me.

I look at her, at them all smiling.

"Come with *me*," she says, and she takes my arm, almost dragging me away.

When we get to the front office she snaps on the light, shuts the door, then sits at the large oak desk. A picture of the Queen in a white gown holding her scepter and wearing her crown hangs on the wall above her head.

"What do you do?" she asks.

"I pick up the *Weekly Breeze*," I say. "I bring over the — "

"Okay. They're not ready yet, are they?"

"It'll be another hour," I say.

"You have a car."

"A van."

"You have a van. Good. Then — "

The door opens. Sweeney sticks his balding head in.

"All right," he says. "You win. But next time you pull a stunt like this, you'll get out of it yourself."

She rises, smiling, relieved, and follows Sweeney out the door.

I turn out the light. There is a Chinese restaurant a half block away and I'm hungry.

On my way back home I decide to stop at the gas station where I left my passengers. The van is filled with papers. I pull up to the pump and the hitchhiker comes over.

225

"What'll it be?" he asks.

"Got a job?" I say.

"Oh, it's you!"

He stares at me, then looks over his shoulder. When his head comes back, he is grinning broadly.

"Those girls? They're in there," he says, motioning over his shoulder. "Nick and Terry and a couple of other guys and Bob and me?" He starts to snicker. "They're doing it!" he says. "They're doing it for all of us. You too, I'll bet. If you want."

"Just give me some gas," I say.

"It's my turn to watch the pumps," he says. "How much do you want?"

"Fill it."

It is quiet. When I step into the garage area, I notice someone beyond the grease pit peek from a door near a barrel of empty oil cans. When that face disappears, another face looks out and smiles.

"It's okay!" he shouts back over his shoulder. "It's the guy what brung them here."

He comes out tugging at his belt, grinning. "Better hurry," he says. "Getting kinda sloppy, if you know what I mean."

"No, thanks. I just need a receipt for the gas."

He seems insulted or perplexed. His face stiffens. The hitchhiker hurries past us into the garage. "I put in eighteen bucks' worth!" he shouts.

"You're married, right?" the garageman says as he makes out the slip.

"No. I'm unattached." The words don't fit for me. I feel as if I am kidding myself, or lying. I feel suddenly empty and lost. Not losing it, lost.

He follows me to the van, small-talking and chatting away. There is a pause as I open the van door, then he says, "They asked for it, you know. They were begging for it."

"It's none of my business," I say.

"So you ain't going to say nothin'?"

"Who am I going to say anything to?"

"I don't know. The Mounties. My boss."

I roll out into the far lane. The newspapers, tied and bundled, swell the cab with the sweet smell of newsprint. I try to think about Nebula, about Joan, about what it is I'm doing, what it is I've done. But I can't think. I feel as if I want to cry. Suddenly I become aware of a car behind me blowing its horn, flicking its lights, riding my tail. It's not a cop, but whoever it is is signaling for me to pull over onto the gravel shoulder. Without thinking, I do, and the full van moves like a huge block, finally rocking to a halt.

It's dark, but I recognize my gloves, and I recognize Mrs. McCaffrey's mittens and coat, so I roll down the window.

"You left your gloves."

I open the door to climb out, but she is already a quick blur passing in front of my headlights. She gets in the passenger side.

"That's awfully nice of you," I say.

"I never do anything for nothing," she says, settling back into the passenger seat. "I like you."

I smile.

"Peanuts?" I ask, offering the bag.

She takes off her mitten and I pour some into her tiny hand. She picks one at a time from her palm, not saying anything. I suck the remaining nuts from the thin bag. We stare out at vanishing tail-lights and dark puffs of trailing smoke.

"I like you," Ma McCaffrey says again, her words hanging there, interrupted by her tongue slipping thoughtfully over her teeth, forcing out first an upper then a lower lip. "I like you because you're ... " She nibbles some more, seeming to search. "No," she says. "I like you because you're you." She turns to face me as she says "you." Her green-brown scarf is a soft place for her head, wisps of nicely laced gray hair drip from beneath her cap.

We sit quietly, our fingers intertwined. Perhaps we sleep like that, our hands joined across the space between the seats, for we are both startled when a long whiny snarl of truck horn and truck roar shakes past us in a fury of rumble and rush.

"After Manny left me," she says, "I spent months recuperating, sitting in Granny's rocker just rocking and staring out at the ocean. Back and forth. Back and forth. Like the waves themselves. I'm not sure if I was vegetating, or if I was preparing. Healing maybe. It's hard to know what's really going on sometimes. But at the end of it I got up from that chair and walked out of that front door and reclaimed my life. It is mine, isn't it? Yet sometimes we do have to stake claim to it. At least I did. Even after sixty-two years I did." She laughs. "I guess it's never too late."

There is more than pride in her voice; there is a sense of accomplishment as if she'd rescued herself against all odds from a stormy sea or a deep well.

"Drat," she says. "Well, I must go." She leans across and kisses me. Her lips are salty and soft. I cling to her hand for a moment. She opens the door, then stares. "Sweeney is a fool," she says. "An utter and complete fool. But my God, I love that man. *Ciao!*"

I wait until she is safely in her car, then watch as she moves past me, makes a U-turn across the dividing strip, and disappears from sight.

I sit.

Finally I turn the ignition on and push onward toward home, content, knowing there is someone ahead, rocking, far from me, away there, across this deeply human night.